Re:ZeRo
-Starting Life in Another World-
Ex

2

The Love Song
of the Sword Devil

Roswaal

Carol

Pivot

"Oh, I'm sorry."

Someone addressed him suddenly as he passed the abandoned works and arrived at the square.

It was a girl with long red hair, her profile beautiful enough to send shivers down his spine.

Re:ZERO -Starting Life in Another World-

The only ability Subaru Natsuki gets when he's summoned to another world is time travel via his own death. But to save her, he'll die as many times as it takes.

CONTENTS

Re:ZeRo
-Starting Life in Another World- EX

VOLUME 2

The Love Song of the Sword Devil

TAPPEI NAGATSUKI
ILLUSTRATION: SHINICHIROU OTSUKA

YEN
ON

NEW YORK

Re:ZERO -Starting Life in Another World- Ex, Vol. 2
Tappei Nagatsuki

Translation by Kevin Steinbach
Cover art by Shinichirou Otsuka

Re: ZERO KARA HAJIMERU ISEKAI SEIKATSU Ex2 KENKI RENKA
©Tappei Nagatsuki 2015
First published in Japan in 2015 by KADOKAWA CORPORATION, Tokyo.
English translation rights arranged with KADOKAWA CORPORATION,
Tokyo through Tuttle-Mori Agency, Inc., Tokyo.

English translation © 2018 by Yen Press, LLC

Yen On
1290 Avenue of the Americas
New York, NY 10104

Visit us at yenpress.com
facebook.com/yenpress
twitter.com/yenpress
yenpress.tumblr.com
instagram.com/yenpress

First Yen On Edition: March 2018

Yen On is an imprint of Yen Press, LLC.
The Yen On name and logo are trademarks of Yen Press, LLC.

The publisher is not responsible for websites (or their content) that are not owned by the publisher.

Library of Congress Cataloging-in-Publication Data
Names: Nagatsuki, Tappei, 1987– author. | Otsuka, Shinichirou, illustrator. |
Steinbach, Kevin, translator.
Title: Re:ZERO starting life in another world ex / Tappei Nagatsuki ; illustration by
Shinichirou Otsuka ; translation by Kevin Steinbach.
Other titles: Re:ZERO kara hajimeru isekai seikatsu ex. English
Description: First Yen On edition. | New York : Yen On, 2017.
Identifiers: LCCN 2017036833 | ISBN 9780316412902 (v. 1 : pbk.) |
ISBN 9780316479097 (v. 2 : pbk.)
Subjects: | CYAC: Science fiction. |
Time travel—Fiction. | BISAC: FICTION / Science Fiction / Adventure.
Classification: LCC PZ7.1.N34 Ref 2017 | DDC [Fic]—dc23
LC record available at https://lccn.loc.gov/2017036833

ISBNs: 978-0-316-47909-7 (paperback)
978-0-316-47910-3 (ebook)

1 3 5 7 9 10 8 6 4 2

LSC-C

Printed in the United States of America

THE LOVE SONG OF THE SWORD DEVIL

First Stanza

1

A stomach-turning bloody stench hung over the battlefield.

What had once been an open basin several hours before was now spotted with tongues of flame, the pop and crack of burning trees mingling with human cries. The odors of charred wood and flesh filled the air, along with the smell of the layer of gore on the ground that was thick enough to dirty one's boots. Together, they were enough to clog the nose and overwhelm the senses. The twilight and the flames and the blood underfoot conspired to turn the whole world red.

"Hrr...kk..."

In that crimson arena, a young man fell to his knees, no longer able to drag his quivering feet forward. Blood soaked his knees and shins, but it was much too late to be concerned about that. The boy had long since been covered in so much that he barely noticed the new additions.

This is awful. How could it possibly get any worse?

The young man had taken up the sword of his own volition. He had intended to make his name in battle, to rise from a nameless foot soldier to the heights of glory. Night after night, he had dreamed of the deeds he would do.

How naive. His thinking, his dreams—all of it.

The customs of the battlefield were these: blood, wounds, agony, hatred, violence, and corpses.

The brutality of this, his first battle, was unmatched by any other in the kingdom's history, even in these years of civil war. The commander had been a young noble who had launched himself against the enemy forces in hopes of buying a little glory, but he had been destroyed, and the battle line had fallen into disarray.

In the blink of an eye, friend and foe were crowded together, and then the young man had been hurled away by a burst of magic and lost consciousness.

After all these unhappy accidents, the young man—Grimm Fauzen—was alone on the field, dragging himself through the nearly palpable cloud of death.

"—"

He opened his mouth voicelessly. He noticed at last how heavy his body was, and the wounds on his feet were asserting themselves more and more painfully.

The explosions had come from overhead, landing just in front of Grimm and flinging him through the air.

He had been lucky to get away with only some burns and the wounds to his feet. How lucky? Everyone else in his squadron had been turned to ash. Their commander, who had been standing next to Grimm, had also been the only actual knight among them.

Their leader's exhortation before the fight started was fresh in Grimm's memory. So was the genuine respect he had felt for the man. But even he could easily be lost to the flames of war.

"Hrr…rrrgh…"

Grimm gritted his teeth, trying to forget the image seared into his mind of the knight's last moments. But that critical instant played against his closed eyelids over and over, fraying his nerves. In a trembling hand, Grimm held his sword, never once swung at a single enemy. The steel blade was so heavy he wanted to drop it. But to abandon his weapon on the field was unthinkable. Even if he knew full well he had no idea how to fight.

To give up one's sword was to give up one's life. And he was afraid of death.

"Aaah—!" A gut-wrenching cry came from not far away, and Grimm almost choked as he tried to flee. Was it an ally or an enemy he had heard? He lacked even the nerve to find out.

"Guh…haaah…" Everything he encountered now seemed like an enemy. Not just people. He couldn't escape the thought that the flames, the blood, even the howl of the wind were out for his life.

He dragged his aching feet into a cloud of smoke. He couldn't see what was on the other side, but that actually helped to calm his panic. Although he was hardly going out of his way to survive, the smoke would help hide him from any passing enemy soldiers and therefore might buy him just a little more time to live.

"I found someone! A human!"

"E-eyaaagh!"

No sooner was he through the cloud than Grimm found himself face-to-face with an enemy holding a bladed weapon resembling a hatchet. The soldier's huge body seemed to be all muscle; he was a violet-skinned demi-human who looked like a purple boulder.

The demi-human eyed the wounded Grimm, and a smile came over his horrible face. To Grimm, he seemed sadistic—a hunter who had found easy prey.

By some fluke, Grimm had avoided death the first time. But his good luck couldn't last forever. It appeared his first battle was going to be his last.

Why, then? Why had he been allowed those extra few moments?

"This is the end for you!"

His destiny was cursed. Grimm fell to his knees as the hatchet came down at his head. Vaguely, he noticed that the weapon was already dark with blood from the other lives it had cut short; his was not likely to be an easy death.

What a ridiculous waste of his last thought.

That was when it happened.

"Gyaaaah!"

There was a piercing shout, and he saw sparks of steel meeting steel. The demi-human grunted as his blow was deflected, and suddenly, a new figure had come between Grimm and his attacker.

The stranger had brown hair so dark it was almost black. Their thin leather armor showed copious amounts of blood, and their excellent blade reflected the flames. Amid the gruesome scene, the crest on the sword blazed before Grimm. It seemed impossible to him.

The moment of admiration, though, was immediately dispelled by what came next.

"Ha!"

The steel described an arc, and the silver gleamed even brighter against the fires. The sharp exhalation of breath and the dancing blade had their own unexpected kind of beauty.

"Huh?"

Did Grimm make the sound of stupefied amazement, or was it the demi-human? The flash of silver sent the enemy's head flying clean off, and the huge body collapsed to the ground in a spray of blood.

"—" The figure looked down at the corpse, then shook the sword. The blade must have been immensely sharp, because there was hardly any blood on it.

"Th— Y—"

Belatedly, Grimm realized that he had been given back his life. He tried to speak to the newcomer. He was so grateful. He had to offer his thanks.

Demi-humans were the enemy. Someone who had cut one down must be his friend. He owed his life to this person.

"Hey... Hey, you...," Grimm called out shakily, and the figure looked back at him suspiciously.

Seeing his savior's face properly for the first time, Grimm was surprised to realize the swordsman was younger than he expected. His short stature might have been because he wasn't yet done growing. He was perhaps two or three years younger than Grimm, who had only turned eighteen this year. Fifteen, then, perhaps. Still a boy.

But Grimm couldn't bring himself to call out again. It wasn't terror that struck him mute. He had stopped shaking. No, it was because he had seen the boy's eyes.

"—"

They were empty. Not just as though there was nothing inside him. His gaze held no emotion at all.

It was this realization that kept Grimm from saying thank you or anything else. The boy looked briefly at the silent Grimm, but then his interest—minimal to begin with—waned, and he began walking away.

"Wai—"

Now Grimm found his voice. More than anything, he dreaded being left alone in this empty place. He dashed after the boy, who didn't look back. He would not be abandoned. Now his sole, desperate wish was to survive.

He followed as closely as he could, through the blood and the smoke, until the boy stopped. Once they were past the smoke, Grimm saw it as the nauseating stench hit him.

"Wh-what in the…?"

A towering pile of demi-human corpses. Each had been killed with the stroke of a sword, and each of their faces was twisted with pain, or horror, or anger. With a shudder, Grimm realized who had killed them.

Then he heard the boy, head lifted toward the sky, comment absently, "…Hm. So this is what battle is like. I didn't know."

Grimm followed the boy's gaze to the sky, and a strained sound came out of his throat.

Red and blue circles floated in the sky, the signal to the whole royal army that victory had been achieved.

"The royal army…won?" Grimm said dimly. The sign of victory seemed utterly unreal to him. His squadron had been annihilated, he had wandered the battlefield barely able to think, and then his life had been saved at the very last moment—he had been pathetic. He had not been victorious.

But surely this young man could claim victory proudly…

"It was so trivial," the boy said. He paid no heed to what Grimm was feeling and only shook his head in disappointment.

2

It was not until some days later, when honors were being conferred for the battle in which Grimm had lost so much and achieved nothing, that he learned the name of Wilhelm Trias.

He was in the barracks of the royal army after the ceremony was over, when one of the other soldiers said to him, "That guy they said killed two of the enemy captains? Awful young, wasn't he?"

The speaker was a man with dull, short-cropped golden hair, Tholter Weasily. He and Grimm had become close since joining the ranks, and now they were brothers in arms who had survived their first battle together.

Tholter was blessed with an excellent physique, but he saw himself as having more aptitude for archery, and he didn't hesitate to regale Grimm with the story of how he had helped support the rearguard. In fact, he had actually carried himself admirably for his first battle.

"Was he?" someone asked. "They stuck us foot soldiers way off in the wings for the ceremony. I couldn't see a thing."

"Trust me," Tholter replied. "I'm an archer. If I didn't have good eyes, I wouldn't be able to hit anything. I saw him, and he was young—practically a kid."

In response to the jeers of his audience, Tholter tapped his own eyebrows proudly. But this only caused the people watching him to look at one another and laugh. It was a natural reaction. Tholter was nineteen, and Grimm eighteen; they were among the youngest of the soldiers. If Tholter considered someone a kid, that meant they might be fifteen or sixteen—old enough to fight for their exhausted nation in a civil war but hardly of an age to achieve great military deeds. Two enemy captains? That was ridiculous.

"What, *none* of you are gonna believe me?"

"Hey, Tholter, are you really sure you got a good look at that guy?"

"I'm telling you, I did! Don't tell me even you don't believe me, Grimm. That hurts. I saw him with my own eyes! I hate to say it, but a great fighter is a great fighter, no matter how young he is."

Tholter seemed annoyed at the reaction of the crowd. Grimm cast his eyes down and said quietly, "No, I do believe you."

In his mind's eye, Grimm was picturing the last thing he had seen on the battlefield several days before—the mountain of dead demi-humans and the boy swordsman who had most likely killed them. War was no place for normal expectations, age included. The memory was enough to send shivers down his spine even now.

The hellfire of his first night at war had consumed any dreams he may have had of doing great deeds. Now all he remembered was that boy.

If it's true heroes are forged in the flames of combat, Grimm thought, *then he must be one of them.*

Suddenly the door of the changing room flew open, and a rough voice bellowed, "Men, attention!"

Grimm had fully absorbed the habits of military life. He straightened up, clicked his heels, and turned to face the door, all practically in the blink of an eye. Everyone else in the room did the same.

A man with a well-trimmed beard entered, nodding approvingly at this display of discipline. His face was familiar to them—he was Razaac, a full knight of the royal army. He was thirty years old, give or take, with short green hair over a deeply chiseled face. He was known for his severity even among the ranks of the instructors. Grimm recognized him because he had spent his first several weeks in the army training under this man.

"Ready to react at all times. Good work, men. Never forget it."

"Yes, sir! Thank you, sir!" Grimm and Tholter chorused along with the platoon leader.

It was almost like the exchange of a promise. Their opinion of the instructors had changed completely after their first battle. During their training, worked to the point of vomiting, the new recruits felt nothing but hatred for the old hands, but now that they had survived a battle, there was only gratitude. Everyone here knew what all that punishment had been for.

"Very good. I don't suppose you want to see a knight's face while you're trying to get your chores done. Something came up that needed taking care of."

"What is it, sir? Our unit was just recently reorganized, and we're anxious to do anything we can."

"No worries, soldier. I know you've only just been thrown together, and this might not be the best time, but I want to add one more person to the squadron. All the paperwork is done; I'm just dropping him off."

"Yes, sir. If I may ask, sir, is he a decent fighter? I respectfully request we not be burdened with anyone who can't pull their own weight."

"Calm down. He's a bit young, but he's capable. That last engagement was his first battle, but he killed a couple of the enemy captains—they even singled him out for honors."

Grimm, along with the rest of the unit, gulped at this. It had to be the person they had just been talking about. Razaac, detecting the change in the mood, nodded and said, "I can see you've already got the details."

Then he turned to the door and called, "Come in. This is your new unit." The door opened.

A boy with chestnut hair and a hard countenance stood there. The standard-issue soldier's uniform somehow didn't look quite right on him, but his posture and deportment showed none of the softness of a new recruit. There was no mistake. He was the one.

"This is Wilhelm Trias," Razaac said. "He's fifteen, learned to fight on his own. But I think he's got a bright future. Everybody play nice."

Wilhelm stood at attention, silently bearing the gazes of the other soldiers. The introduction finished, Razaac surveyed the nervous locker room, then nodded in satisfaction. The troops' focus had slackened just a moment before, but they were now rapt. Perhaps that had been his goal. A new soldier was new even after his first battle. In the eyes of a full knight, they were still just chicks.

This meeting would have a more far-reaching influence on the nation than anything Razaac might have planned. But at that moment, even the two people at the heart of it had no idea.

3

Two years earlier, a civil war, the so-called Demi-human War, had broken out in the Dragonfriend Kingdom of Lugunica.

For more than four hundred years, there had been a lingering prejudice against demi-humans, inspired by a "witch" all those centuries before. Lugunica was no exception; relations between humans and demi-humans were cool, the status quo maintained by a tacit understanding that they would have little to do with each other.

That fragile peace was shattered by the collision of a demi-human merchant caravan and human border guards.

The story went that the merchant caravan, headed for the Empire of Volakia to the south, was suspected of crossing the border for the purpose of espionage, but the facts were not clear. What was clear was that when the caravan clashed with the border guards, the civilians were annihilated. These traders had been well regarded by demi-humans throughout the country, and their deaths at human hands inspired an armed revolt among their compatriots. Thus, the quagmire of the civil war began.

The fruitless conflict had dragged on for two years now, and citizens and soldiers alike were tiring of it.

"Then again, it's thanks to that war that we get to be soldiers. I'm not gonna say I love fighting or anything, but we get to eat every day." Tholter drained his glass in a single gulp and slammed it back onto the counter as he laughed with a little foam still stuck around his mouth.

Grimm sat next to the slightly drunk Tholter, taking little sips of his alcohol and nodding. "I guess we've got that in common, Tholter. If not for the civil war, I would never have thought I could be a soldier. Even if I'd wanted to, I bet they would've turned me away at the gate."

"There used to be some little skirmishes with Volakia, but things were mostly peaceful. I guess a demon beast might cause trouble every once in a while. But guys like you and me? If we ever want to be more than just peasants, war's the name of the game. A man proves himself by doing great deeds in battle."

As his companion eagerly ordered another mug of ale, Grimm murmured, "Great deeds in battle, huh?"

Tholter noticed the downcast expression of the young man beside him and gave a friendly shake of his head. "You just survived your first battle, and you still aren't happy? Isn't it about time you started enjoying yourself? What, you feel bad for our fallen comrades or something?"

"That's not it. Call me heartless, but as far as I'm concerned, that battle never happened. I'm just…sorry that I can't dream like I used to."

"Dream?"

"Like you were just talking about, Tholter. Doing great deeds, showing my bravery…becoming a hero. I used to think I could do that. Nice and easy. But now…" Grimm let go of his glass and looked down at his hand. It trembled ever so slightly. White burn scars remained on his palm and wrist. That first battle had marked him. Not only his flesh, but his heart and mind, too, and he would never escape it. "You can't survive on a dream," Grimm said. "Everything I thought was in my future is…gone."

"So…what?" Tholter asked. "You're gonna quit the army? You're going to give up just because you'll never be a hero?"

"Unfortunately, facing reality doesn't fill your stomach. If anything, when you can't dream anymore, all you have left to think about is how hungry you are. So no, I'm not quitting. I'm going to keep at it." Grimm smiled at Tholter, trying to hide the trembling of his hand holding the glass. Studying Grimm with wide eyes, Tholter started scratching vigorously at his head.

"…Hrmph. Somehow, all that sounds just like you. Okay, you do that. Leave the hero stuff to me. You just follow along—you can be the hero's assistant."

"But, Tholter, you're an archer. I'm the one who's up front with a sword."

"I know you're embarrassed, but just nod along."

Tholter took the new mug that had been brought to him and held it up to Grimm. Taking his cue, Grimm raised his mug as well, and there was a clink of pottery as they tapped their vessels together.

Grimm came from a village called Fleur, somewhere outside the capital. It was a small outpost on one of the major byways and had gained some renown as a stopover on the way to the capital. But a small town with its small ways didn't suit Grimm, and at fifteen he left his home and went to the capital.

He spent the following several years doing menial work at shops and taverns, until six months ago, when he happened to hear that the army wanted more soldiers for the ever-expanding civil war.

Grimm joined up, but not out of patriotism. He wanted to be a hero. He had fled his village out of boredom, and now he joined the army for no reason other than a wish for glory. He had learned soldiering under Razaac's stern tutelage, then survived the even harsher lesson of his first battle, and now he was here.

Tholter had a similar history, or so Grimm had heard. Born as the second son of a shopkeeper, he had joined the army seeking freedom and a future, and that was where the two had met.

"So you go through combat and decide you've found reality," Tholter said. "And I go through it and still have my heart set on being a hero. It's like night and day. What about that new guy? I wonder what he thought…"

"You mean Wilhelm?"

Tholter didn't seem to notice the jolt of anxiety that went through Grimm when he brought up the young swordsman. It was Wilhelm, above all else, who had caused Grimm to give up his dream of heroism.

"I believe he's good, even if he's just a kid," Tholter said. "I mean, they don't hand out military honors for nothing. I bet we'll see him on the parade ground as a full knight before long."

"I heard he didn't even have to do the drills they make all the new guys go through," Grimm said. "Instructor Razaac himself said it wasn't necessary. A lot of people won't believe he's fifteen."

It was the truth. So much lay ahead of a boy his age, and the thought of what he might yet become was enough to unsettle anyone. *Hero.* That was what they would call him as he cut down enemy after enemy and led his nation to victory. Grimm couldn't forget what he had seen in the boy's eyes. Were those the eyes of someone who should be hailed as a hero? The suspicion dogged Grimm that he might become something far more terrible.

"I definitely get the worry," Tholter said. "He's, like, the least-friendly fifteen-year-old you ever met."

"Wait, what?"

"No, it's true. I invite him along every time we go for a meal, every time we go for a drink, but he never comes. If he has one minute of spare time, he's doing sword practice. Morning, noon, and night. I swear, it's gonna make him sick. Or maybe he already is!"

"Huh. You might actually be right." Tholter had probably overstated the issue, but Grimm found himself agreeing with him.

"Ain't I always?" Tholter said, completely oblivious to the dark undertones in Grimm's remark.

"But do you think he might be onto something?" Grimm went on. "Using his free time to train instead of drink?"

"Aw, don't start. Anyway, whoever has the most fun is the winner at life! Even the first Sword Saint, Reid, didn't spend all his time waving his sword around. He liked his wine and his women, too! Heroes have more fun than anyone. Enjoying ourselves like this just shows that we have what it takes to be legends!"

As Tholter's logic grew louder and louder, he collected a few shouts of "Yeah! That's right!" from the surrounding drinkers. As the mood spread throughout the room, Tholter stood nimbly on a chair and raised his mug.

"My friends! My brothers in arms! Here's to all the future heroes sitting in this tavern right now! Cheers!"

"Cheers!" All the men raised their mugs together with a chorus of raucous laughter. Splashing alcohol and the sound of clinking mugs filled the air. Tholter gestured insistently at Grimm with his mug.

The young man finally raised his own cup, and they pressed the drinking vessels together, smiling and basking in the atmosphere.

All the while, Grimm was thinking that the drinks didn't seem to be going down so well today, but he didn't know why.

4

Grimm left Tholter in the tavern and headed out into the cold, breezy night. He turned toward the barracks. He felt bad leaving Tholter, who had wanted to drink the night away in honor of their day off tomorrow, but Grimm couldn't bring himself to enjoy the alcohol just then, and he wandered through the moonlit night, his ale-warmed body rapidly cooling.

"What a gorgeous crescent moon... It looks like a sword."

The military really had gotten to him. One had to have a certain lack of refinement to notice not the beauty but the sharpness of the moon. But then, in times of war, indulgence and luxury were stripped away from human hearts.

This inability to enjoy drink—that, too, had been a new problem for Grimm ever since his first battle.

"Tholter's certainly brave. Maybe he really can be a hero."

Almost every night, Tholter would make for the tavern, sharing drinks with a crowd of strangers. Grimm tried to tell him to stop this behavior, but in truth, he was envious. At least Tholter didn't freeze up every time he thought of that initial engagement.

And what about Grimm himself? Would the next experience of combat make him any happier than the last one? The question tormented him. When he closed his eyes, he saw the flames; when he fell asleep, he saw his comrades who had been reduced to ash; when it was quiet, he could hear their final, agonized screams.

"And yet I can't bring myself to quit the army. If I did, I wouldn't have anything left. Maybe that's what scares me."

He had left his family and his home behind to come to the capital. Sick of the daily routine, he had joined the army, but now that he knew the fear of death, he wanted to run away from this, too.

He hadn't changed. He was still weak. He had clung to a child-ish dream in the hope that he would find a place where he might be acknowledged, but then he had hardly been willing to work for it. That, he was sure, defined who he was now.

"—?"

But then, on his way back to the barracks, absorbed in self-hatred, Grimm stopped.

The reason was a noise. He thought he'd heard a faint sound from around the back of the soldiers' quarters.

He could hardly imagine anyone being stupid enough to try to break into the barracks of the national army, but this was a time of war. A demi-human on a secret infiltration mission, perhaps? No, that was overthinking it. But he had to be sure.

Grimm touched the scabbard of the sword he carried and, as silently as he could, made his way to the back of the building. He peeked out from the shadows, attempting to find the source of the ongoing sound.

There, late at night behind the barracks, Grimm saw a young man single-mindedly swinging his sword.

"…Wilhelm?"

The blade flashed silver as it danced through the night air. By the moonlight, Grimm could see how astonishingly clean Wilhelm's technique was. At the sound of Grimm's voice, Wilhelm looked up. Grimm caught his breath as the sharp eyes fixed on him.

"Um…"

"Oh, Grimm, it's you," Wilhelm said with disinterest. "Don't bother me."

After a while, Grimm spoke hesitatingly. "You…know my name?"

"Why shouldn't I? We're in the same squadron. You know my name, don't you? Or did you think I'm one of those idiots who can't remember a name?"

"N-no, I… I mean, I thought maybe you didn't care about anyone else…"

"I don't remember people's names because I care. I do it because it's necessary. If I don't remember the names of at least the people in my squadron, it'll cause me problems later. Have I explained myself thoroughly enough for you?"

He was right, but Grimm found himself agape at having Wilhelm tell him all this. He had never so much as had a complete conversation with him before. The boy didn't engage in small talk; he seemed to say the absolute minimum required to communicate. In fact, Grimm wondered sometimes if the boy was even really human.

"So you do think like a normal person sometimes..."

"Say what?"

"Erk, sorry! I didn't mean it the way it sounded..." He searched for a better way to explain himself but found none. Instead, he said, "Er, or maybe I did..."

Wilhelm shot Grimm a dubious look, but he quickly appeared to lose interest. He raised his sword and began swinging it again.

"Have you been doing that ever since training ended?"

"Yeah. Don't talk to me. It disrupts my concentration."

"We went out to get a drink after training. I think Tholter is still there."

"Oh yeah? I thought I smelled alcohol. Don't talk to me."

As he gave his curt answers, Wilhelm began swinging the sword faster and faster as if to lose himself in the act. Grimm found he could hardly follow the blade as it whipped high and low. So instead, he slumped against the side of the barracks and stared distantly.

"Why are you so into sword fighting? Isn't there anything you do for fun?"

"Maybe there would be, if we weren't at war. But we are. Practicing with the sword is a lot more likely to keep you alive than getting drunk or having sex."

"So you're training yourself because you want to survive?"

"No. Frankly, you guys don't make any sense to me. Why would you waste your time on booze and women instead of working on your swordsmanship? You think anything I'm saying is wrong?"

Frighteningly, Wilhelm's blade made no sound as it sliced through the night. It was as if the sword was so sharp the air itself didn't realize it had been cut. Only his short breaths and the sound of his shoes sliding across the earth indicated the movements of his sword.

"No...I don't think you're wrong. But not everyone is as gifted with the blade as you are. Not everyone can devote themselves to it like you do. Sometimes you turn to wine or sex just for a little comfort."

Wilhelm met Grimm's defeated words with a harsh reply. "I'll tell you one thing you're all better at than I am. Making excuses."

Grimm himself didn't know why he was asking these questions. Maybe he had always wanted to ask these things of Wilhelm, the boy who had looked at that mountain of corpses as though it were unremarkable.

"If you keep everyone else at a distance," Grimm said, "you'll find yourself alone on the battlefield someday. And what can you do when you're all by yourself?"

"Use my sword. One swing, one dead enemy. Two swings, two dead. That's all it takes, one slash after another. To me, you just sound like you're trying to protect yourself."

"—"

"That look in your eyes... I remember it. We saw each other on the battlefield, didn't we, Grimm?" Wilhelm let his sword rest, straightened, and stared at Grimm.

He felt his throat tightening. To think Wilhelm would have remembered him. Remembered him like *that*.

"So you weren't just full of it when you talked about being alone on the battlefield. But you should know better than anyone. I was alone, too. And yet I killed enough of the enemy to earn distinction. That's all there is to it. Ridiculous."

"I... I..." Grimm's voice was trembling.

Wilhelm grimaced, pointing at the other boy with his sword. "If you want to run away, don't try to cover your ass by pretending it's logical. You want your friends because you're scared? Then I guess I misjudged you. You weaklings should stick together. Or do you have proof that I'm wrong about you?"

Grimm understood Wilhelm was telling him to draw his blade. To take the sword at his hip and show what he was made of.

"—"

"You can't even draw your sword? Coward."

No, he couldn't draw his sword. He couldn't even stand up, much less reach for his scabbard.

Wilhelm looked almost disappointed as he turned his back to Grimm and resumed his practice. Realizing that Wilhelm was no longer paying attention to him, Grimm let out a long sigh, forced himself to his trembling feet, and left the place behind as if he were fleeing.

He entered the barracks, returned to his own room, and dived onto his narrow cot. He pulled the blanket up over his head, shivering violently as if with cold, gritting his teeth. Was he angry? Sad? He had no idea. All he knew was that he despised himself for being weak. At that moment, more than anything in the world, he wanted the strength that boy had.

5

Despite the events of the night before, when morning came, Grimm returned to his duties with an outward facade of calm. This was, perhaps, an unfortunate talent of his. He was perfectly able to look Wilhelm in the eye during chores and training. Nothing about his manner had changed. Wilhelm, for his part, also acted as though he had forgotten everything from the previous night, annoying the squadron by keeping to himself as usual.

Hence, the squadron was home to two armed bombs, one visible, one invisible. And the proof that they weren't duds came with a sudden, major clash with the demi-humans. Grimm's squadron was thrust into it, along with the rest of the royal army.

The fuse of this decisive moment was lit as the sun went down. When the battle began on the plain, the royal army appeared to have the upper hand. They leveraged their numerical superiority to smash the demi-humans' coalition forces and push back the front.

Grimm and the others, assigned to the tip of the spear, were swept up in their allies' joy at their success and pressed forward, slaying one demi-human after another.

"I don't know what the problem was last time," Tholter said giddily, shooting an enemy with his arrow and then drawing another one. "But this is easy!"

Grimm heard Tholter behind him. He kept his sword and shield up, carried along by the momentum of the attack.

Morale was high. The retreating enemy could barely resist them. The royal army had every advantage, yet Grimm couldn't bring himself to move as he desired.

"Damn it... Then why am I even here...?" In a tiny whisper, Grimm cursed the weakness of his own spirit. His only salvation was his friends' success; he himself had yet to kill a single enemy. He only used his shield, desperately fending off the foe's attacks. True, this did his forces some good, but it was cold comfort to him.

"Wh-what the hell?!"

Cries of shock rose up from the ranks. Everyone looked to see what was going on.

Someone dashed across the battlefield, cutting off demi-human heads as quick as the wind. It was like an explosion of blood and limbs, echoing with the sounds of steel cleaving flesh and dying cries.

"Ruuuuahhhhh!" The cause of all this was the dark figure of a young boy flying across the field like an arrow. He leaped into the enemy ranks, his stance low. His sword worked tirelessly, stabbing and mowing down demi-humans in an ever-increasing pile of lifeless corpses. Friend and foe alike watched him in amazement.

"Wilhelm..."

The squad leader didn't order them to advance behind this murderous dervish, as he should have done when momentum was on their side. He, like everyone else, feared that anyone who got too close to Wilhelm would be cut to ribbons, enemy or not.

As everyone else stood transfixed by Wilhelm's display, Tholter gave an excited shout. "Commander! We've crushed them here—let's get a move on!" That brought the squad leader back to himself, and he ordered everyone to advance into the breach Wilhelm had carved.

Tholter could be heard laughing wildly. "We might not show up Wilhelm, but we can do our part!"

But their clear advantage failed to excite Grimm. He only felt a chill running down his spine.

"Doesn't this feel wrong to you?" he asked.

"Huh? How can it feel wrong? We're kicking ass!"

"Think how they decimated us last time! Why is it so easy now?"

"Maybe we've learned how to handle them. Or maybe our commander last time didn't know strategy from a hole in the ground. But it got them killed, and now we've got someone who knows better." Tholter accompanied this casual disrespect with a continued hail of arrows. Grimm, still holding his shield at the ready, watched out of the corner of his eye. He still couldn't shake the anxiety.

A moment later, a cheer rose in front of him as Wilhelm cut down an especially large demi-human. Another commander, perhaps. Another commendation.

"Way to go, Wilhelm!" Although everyone continued to keep their distance, Tholter cheered with his customary enthusiasm. Wilhelm, covered in the blood of his enemies, didn't react to this acclaim but suddenly looked up and said, "...Something stinks."

"Well, yeah. You're dripping with blood!"

"That's not what I'm talking about. Squad Leader, I have a bad feeling about this. They're planning something..."

He had turned back, about to offer his advice, when the earth shook. It was so powerful it made Grimm's vision blur; he lost his balance and fell down. Several of the other soldiers collapsed, too. Only Wilhelm and a few others remained on their feet.

"What...? What just—?"

They never got to *happened*. A second after the impact, a hot wind rushed at Grimm and the others. It carried dust that got in their eyes and mouths; coughing and choking, they tried to stand, only to be met by a chorus of agitated shouting.

"Fall back! Fall back! Fall baaaaack! It's a trap! Demi-human ambush! They've got magic circles on the ground! We're going to be destroyed!"

"Valga is here! Valga Cromwell! Bring me his h— No, retreat!"

"Fire! Fire is coming! My—my feet! No, wait for meeeee!"

The awful screams came from everywhere at once. The soldiers, blinded by dust and now in a panic, started shoving one another in the scramble to retreat. Grimm found himself in danger of being trampled.

"Grimm!"

Tholter grabbed his arm, pulling him to safety in the nick of time. But the chaos was worsening by the moment. The mood of victory was shattered.

"A—a trap?! How can we be surrounded? When did that happen?!"

"I can't see anything! Damn it! Squad Leader! What do we do?!"

Out of the cacophony, Grimm's ears picked up the most dangerous words, and his teeth chattered as his terror built. Tholter looked grim, too, as they turned to their leader for their next instructions.

The terrified squad leader answered Tholter's shout with a tremulous cry. "R-retreat! We fall back, and link up with the other units…!"

"No!" Wilhelm bellowed. "Don't! Advance!"

"—?!"

Wilhelm grit his teeth and snarled at the squad leader, as well as all his subordinates attempting to withdraw. He raised his blood-soaked sword and pointed it at what had been the vanguard a moment before. "Retreating is exactly what the enemy wants us to do! Why can't you see that?! Our only hope is to move forward!"

"Are you insane?! If all you want is to kill the enemy, then shut up and leave us out of it!"

"The enemy laid a trap for us using magic circles! They only pretended to fall back so they could draw out and destroy our army! They would obviously count on a fear-crazed, ambushed enemy making a retreat!"

The squad leader shut his mouth, not expecting such a thoughtful response. Wilhelm pressed closer to the mute commander, his bloodied face twisted as a demon's.

"Go forward!" he howled. "The only way out is through! Fall back, and you'll be surrounded and die! We have to break through before the net gets any tighter—it's our only hope!"

But the squad leader lurched and exclaimed, "Th-that's impossible! Retreat! There's no help ahead! Marching into the enemy territory alone is suicide!"

Wilhelm bit his lip fiercely, and with blood pouring from the edge of his mouth, he began striding away. He readied the sword in his hand, turning his back to the squad leader.

"Stop, Wilhelm! You can't just—!"

But Wilhelm wasn't listening. "If you want to run, then run. Run and run, and when you're finished with that, just die. As for me, I'm going to fight. I'll fight and fight, and when I'm done, I'm going to live. You insufferable cowards."

This tirade left everyone in the unit speechless. Grimm alone felt differently from the others, because he was the only one not hearing it for the first time.

"Wilhelm!"

The boy didn't stop at the sound of his name but dived forward. He was going to attack the enemy alone, in defiance of the squad leader's orders—an indefensible choice, surely.

As soon as Grimm realized what was happening, he demanded his shaking feet to move, to take one step after another, and ran after Wilhelm.

"Grimm! You too?!"

"I'm bringing him back! I'm going to bring Wilhelm back! He can't die on us yet! This army still needs him!"

His feet pushed into the dirt. His body felt heavy as he struggled to stay upright and advance. A hand reached out to stop him, but the fingertips only brushed him and fell short.

"Grimm! Don't you die! You damned idiot!" Tholter's condemnation was also a bold encouragement.

"You think I'd die? I'm just a coward!" Even Grimm barely

understood what this meant, but his friend's shout gave him strength. A warm emotion filled his heart as he chased after Wilhelm.

"—"

Breathing hard, dust in his eyes, stepping over the bodies of his fallen comrades, Grimm immediately began to regret his decision. He always did. Whether he had run after Wilhelm or not, he was sure he would have regretted the choice. But now, for once, he put it aside and kept running.

He had his shield up but realized he had lost his sword somewhere. Most likely, it had been when he'd fallen after that first impact. It didn't matter. Who needed a sword when the boy ahead of him was ten times the swordsman he would ever be?

A fresh geyser of blood, a death rattle. Grimm had lost sight of Wilhelm, but he was easy enough to find—just follow the noises of battle. Grimm crested a hill, jumped over a rift in the earth, wove around corpses he couldn't even identify as friend or foe. Finally, swallowing hard, he caught sight of a faint gleam.

In front of him, the ground gave off a dull glow. The shimmering lines formed a geometric pattern.

"Is this what a magic circle looks like…?" Grimm wasn't one for the mystic arts himself, nor was he familiar with the glow of mana.

Even in the capital, magical devices like crystal lights weren't universal, and rare was the individual with the talent for such techniques. The demi-humans as a race were more magically inclined than humanity, and one result of that disparity was the trap the humans had fallen into in this battle—or anyway, so the bits and pieces he had heard suggested.

At the sight of the faint glow from the magic circle, Grimm experienced a wave of the greatest fear he had yet felt.

"Err— Gh— What…? What is this feeling? I hate it! Go away! Go away!" He rubbed the back of his own head vigorously, hoping to banish the terror. It was a habit he had developed ever since that first battle had taught him to fear. But he hated doing that, too, and began kicking at the magic circle with his feet in an attempt to erase part of it.

Almost immediately, the glow faded until the shape was just a scribble on the ground.

"Huh? Is that all it takes...?"

"Hey, Grimm."

The voice came from behind. He looked back, his heart in his throat. Wilhelm stood there. He was covered in a fresh layer of blood. He looked Grimm up and down, his mouth twisted into a frown.

"What are you doing here?" he asked. "I thought the squad made for the rear."

"Y-you just went off on your own, and I came to stop you! Come on, let's go back! We can't just stand here alone, no matter how good you are..."

"I don't need you to worry about me...but you do have the strength to survive. As only a coward does."

It was the same charge he had leveled that night. Grimm found he could say nothing. Wilhelm, however, looked at the other boy's feet with a puzzled expression.

"Grimm, what happened to that magic circle?"

"...It was glowing, and it gave me a bad feeling. So I kicked at it until it stopped. Was it supposed to be a trap?"

"Yeah, it was. Maybe it still is. You doused it while it was still in the preparation stages. Which means..."

Wilhelm's gaze hardened, and a second later, Grimm's eyes were wide, his intuition of terror back in full force. A red tracer was streaking toward them from the right, trailing a cloud of dust.

"Get down!"

Grimm was shoved to the ground and landed on his backside. Wilhelm was in front of him, his sword at the ready. He deflected the bullet and dived in the direction the light had come from. He swung his sword in a sidelong motion, cutting into the dust cloud.

A green-skinned demi-human emerged from the haze. Covered from head to toe in a robe, he had a long tongue and a reptilian appearance.

The small demi-human jumped backward, targeting Wilhelm with more tracer rounds from three-fingered hands. But if they hadn't worked with the element of surprise, they certainly wouldn't be any use in a frontal assault. Wilhelm wove from side to side, dodging each round by a hair. In the space of a breath, he had closed distance with the demi-human, and with a swipe of his sword, he sent its head flying.

"Wilhelm! That demi-human was—!"

"He was probably the one controlling this circle. With him dead, the trap is disarmed. Now we have a marker to judge by—let's push through to the other side!"

Wilhelm kicked away the enemy's body, shook the blood off his sword, and faced forward once again—away from the retreating squad. Grimm grabbed his shoulder.

"Just wait, will you?! If we've disarmed it, then let's go call everyone up!"

"Don't be an idiot! If we backtrack, we'll just get caught up in another trap. They *planned* on the royal army retreating. That's how this is set up. We can't save them. You and I would just be two more useless corpses. Do you understand?!"

He tore Grimm's hand away and turned the point of his sword to the withdrawing boy's throat. Grimm was seized with fear as Wilhelm's unparalleled swordsmanship turned on him.

"If you want to die, then go back alone! If you want to live, you have to struggle and fight for every breath!"

With that, Wilhelm set off running again.

Watching him disappear into the distance for the second time, Grimm had only a moment to make one of the most important decisions of his life. If he went back, it might be possible to link up with his squadron. But he might also fall into a demi-human trap, as Wilhelm had said. But his squadron would have rejoined with the bulk of the army; they would certainly have the advantage of numbers. There was also the chance that Wilhelm was wrong, and the enemy was waiting up ahead. Splitting up could only make it harder to survive. He had tried his best to persuade Wilhelm to come back. If he didn't listen, whatever happened to him now was his own fault.

Then the choice was between life and death. Did he want to live? Or did he want to not die?

"Ahhhhhhhhhh!"

Bellowing inarticulately, Grimm dashed forward. Away from where Tholter and his other friends had fallen back. Toward where Wilhelm inexorably advanced.

He didn't know what had led him to his decision. He had simply followed his instinct. At that moment, Grimm was not thinking of friendship or orders or patriotism or loyalty. All he knew was that when he considered going back and of going forward, pressing onward held less fear for him.

He ran through the faded magic circle, ran wild and shouting across the battlefield. It was foolish and made him conspicuous, but luckily, he was just one sound in a cacophonous roar.

Finally, he emerged from the cloud of dust, miraculously not having encountered any enemies. He crested a hill.

"Shhaaaaaaa!"

He heard a terrible screech and saw a demi-human sliced in two. Wilhelm met one attacker after another, cutting them down in a fountain of blood that covered him; he raised his strained voice as the dead piled up.

Grimm could see Wilhelm's face as he howled, bathed in the blood of his enemies. He appeared to be smiling. It gave Grimm his worst chill yet. He thought he knew an appropriate word.

"Devil…"

A devil. That was what he was. A devil with a sword. A demon who laughed as he cut down his enemies. A death-dealing monster who loved the blade.

A sword devil.

"Come! Face me, all of you! Come and be destroyed that I may live!" With each shout, the sword devil's weapon flashed and took the life of another demi-human.

The awful scene inspired Grimm to turn slowly around and

survey the hill he'd come up. Smoke rose over the battlefield, pierced only by the faint light of magic circles. He couldn't have counted them all if he had used both hands and all his toes. The field was brimming with power beyond human understanding, and it would soon destroy a royal army that had foolishly let itself be enveloped.

A scorching wind, the rumbling of the earth, and the dying voices that rose up into the red sky—

"Is this…what came of my choice?"

Behind him, the sword devil was creating mountains of corpses and rivers of blood. In front of him, the screams and wails of the friends he had abandoned sounded like curses. Grimm found that he had fallen to his knees with both hands over his face and was weeping piteously.

"I'm s-sor— Sorry, I'm sorry, I'm sorry…!"

The battle ended, the royal army well and truly shattered. Until a friendly force came to collect them. Grimm sobbed and apologized, and the sword devil fought and howled with joy.

Grimm's squadron, including Tholter Weasily, didn't come back.

6

At the Battle of Castour Field, the royal forces began with the advantage, but their vanguard was undone by a nefarious demi-human trap. When they attempted to retreat, their foes besieged them using magic circles, and the army was routed. It was a notable defeat even in the lengthy annals of this civil war.

Unconfirmed reports stated that the great demi-human strategist Valga Cromwell was present at the battle, and that his canny use of personnel contributed to the human defeat.

Casualties were immense; it was not possible to retrieve the bodies of most of those who were killed in action. It was suggested that these heroes should immediately be granted distinction for their loyalty and patriotism.

Further, one name was mentioned on both the human and

demi-human sides for its owner's tremendous record in this battle: a fifteen-year-old boy called Wilhelm Trias, the Sword Devil.

This battle marked something else as well. It was the very beginning of the end of the Demi-human War, the civil conflict the kingdom had been fighting for so long.

THE LOVE SONG OF THE SWORD DEVIL

Second Stanza

1

Wilhelm Trias saw the world as a very simple place. It could be broadly divided into the things he liked and the things he didn't. And right now, what he saw in front of him was the very epitome of the latter.

"He broke through the demi-human encirclement at the Battle of Castour Field. He confronted and destroyed an entire squadron of demi-humans all by himself. The total number of heads he took was eighty-eight, including their captain's. I'd say it's a good thing he quit while he was...ahead! Ha-ha!"

"Personally, I wish he'd kept going. Nice try, though."

"Oh, come on, ya traitor, do you always have to interrupt?"

"It's my job."

Wilhelm stood at attention as two men bantered in front of him. One was well built and tall, the picture of gallantry, while the other looked kind but tightly wound. Both wore the uniform indicating they were full members of the knights' unit.

Wilhelm had been released from the medical center that morning and returned to the barracks before these two stopped him from heading to his daily duties.

He was suspicious. What could two knights want with him? The two of them seemed more and more interested in him, though he couldn't hide his mistrust of his superiors.

"Sounds like he caused the enemy quite a headache. He just kept slicing them up until our army came and stopped him… They said when they found him, there was a mountain of corpses."

"Everyone who saw him was scared out of their wits. They claimed a Sword Devil walks among us!"

"A Sword Devil!" the thin man said. "I like that! That has a good ring to it. Keep up the nasty work, boy, and make sure plenty of people learn that name. Though I've got to say, he's awfully small for it!"

The tall man laughed and placing his hands to Wilhelm's temple, but they were so large, his palm practically covered the boy's entire head.

"What is this, a zoo?! What do you want with me?" Wilhelm swept the man's hand aside and jumped back, fixing them both with a withering stare.

The well-built man flexed the arm Wilhelm had pushed away. "I like your spirit, talking to knights that way. Youth is the best time to be reckless."

"The young and young at heart aren't so different. The face may grow old, but it's only when you age on the inside that you really regret what you've lost."

"Anyone would be old compared to this kid. According to the records, he's fifteen! How about that, Pivot? Half your age! Half your age and twice as many kills! He's making you look bad!"

"I'm the brains of this operation. I handle everything the children can't." The delicate man took out a white handkerchief and dabbed at his face where some of the big man's spittle had landed on him. Once again, the conversation had left Wilhelm behind, and this time he wasn't feeling generous about it.

"If you don't need me for anything, then leave me alone. I've got things to do, you know."

"Oh you do, do you? We're just holding station. What could you possibly have to do?"

"Practice with my sword. They say if you miss a day, it takes three days of effort to make it up. I'm not going to take three swings when I can kill with one. I can only take so much inefficiency," he spat.

He was about to make for the training ground behind the barracks, when the big man burst out laughing at Wilhelm's answer.

"You hear that, Pivot? He worked that battlefield until he collapsed, but he's not even gonna sleep in—just go do drills with his sword!"

"Yes, I heard. I know people so young are always impetuous, but this is foolish even for a boy his age."

Knights or not, Wilhelm couldn't stand this ridicule. "Do you two want to see my skills firsthand?" He had two days of practice to make up.

But the big man answered Wilhelm's glare with a roaring laugh. "Ah, just what I wanted to hear. You know, there are some stories around the knights' unit of a kid with a sword who took some of our most embarrassing knights to school!"

The delicate man shook his head; the monocle over his eye glinted strangely. "Young or not, you share the blame. You may be exceptionally capable for your age, but you get carried away easily."

They radiated a readiness for battle, a confidence in their abilities. It contrasted sharply with how they had been acting just a moment before. Wilhelm licked his lips.

"Was this what you wanted all along?"

"Sorry, kid," the big man said. "Sometimes you have to do what you have to do. But don't worry. We may rank higher than you, but we're gonna fight fair. If there's one thing Bordeaux Zergev never does, it's disgrace a place of combat."

"He's a man of his word, so I wouldn't be concerned. Oh, I haven't introduced myself, have I? I'm Master Bordeaux's minder, Pivot Anansi. *Enchantée.*"

Wilhelm looked at the hulking Bordeaux and the delicate Pivot in puzzlement as they introduced themselves. They were hard to read; he didn't know what exactly they wanted, but their immediate goal was clear. It was the same thing Wilhelm wanted at that moment.

"I'll finish you two off in a hurry and get back to my practice."

"That depends. You might find yourself on another round of bed rest!"

Wilhelm set off down the stone path toward the training ground, and Bordeaux loped along beside him. There were practically sparks flying between them. Pivot exhaled softly and then followed behind.

2

Steel met steel with a piercing screech; he felt metal scraping against metal and saw the brief red glow of sparks in his peripheral vision. The sound came again as Wilhelm lowered himself nearly to the ground and moved forward, deflecting the battle-ax that descended over him and stepping on the haft to prevent his opponent's next move.

There was an instant's pause, and then a flash of silver stopped just short of a thick neck.

"I win."

"...I wasn't ready for that," Bordeaux said softly.

Wilhelm, sweating profusely but wearing a warrior's triumphant smile, lowered his sword as his hot breath escaped him in heaving gasps.

He was using a dull training blade. Bordeaux's weapon, the long halberd currently trapped under Wilhelm's foot, was similarly neutered. They couldn't take a life, but both combatants were capable enough to protect themselves from the other's blows, anyway. The battle had been intense, but neither of them had so much as a bruise. Any report on the battle would have said both fighters merited distinction.

"This means I've won seven and lost three. I think we've settled this. You were hardly worth my time."

"I can't even be angry! Wah-ha-ha, that's what I get for challenging you. I give! I haven't been beat this thoroughly in a long time. It feels good!"

"I don't know what you mean." Wilhelm had intended to sound

spiteful, but instead he had elicited some kind of merriment. He frowned.

Bordeaux dislodged his ax from the ground and rested it on his shoulder. He ran a hand through his short pale-blue hair and said, "How about a smile? You fought me—*me!*—and won. I can go toe-to-toe with anyone but the royal guard. I guess those other guys you beat weren't just slacking off."

"I suppose not," Pivot said, "and neither was this young man. It's…rather terrifying to see one so skilled at fifteen." He had been watching their duel from the sidelines.

Wilhelm had heard people say this about him many times. But Pivot's voice lacked the awe or fear that normally accompanied this judgment. Not that Wilhelm cared either way.

"My apologies that you weren't able to teach your lesson to such an ill-tempered child," he said. "What will you do now? Go crying to your own superiors and get them to send better swordsmen after me?"

"I guess I could, but when you're built like me, it would look weird to go crying to anyone except maybe the Holy Dragon Volcanica. And if I went running to the Dragon for something as minor as this, I'd probably get turned into a pile of ash!"

"Before that happens," Pivot said, "let us tell you why we're really here, Wilhelm Trias. We didn't seek you out just to carry out a personal vendetta under the pretext of a contest of strength. Although, given how you acquitted yourself, I suppose our attempt at serving justice would have been moot, anyway."

"Ouch!" Bordeaux exclaimed. "My friend isn't very subtle, is he? Ha-ha-ha!"

Wilhelm raised an eyebrow at this inability to grasp irony. "If you didn't come here to fight…"

"I assure you we didn't. That was just a way of cheering you up. But, regardless, to business. Wilhelm Trias, we have a message for you. From now on, you'll be exercising your skills in the service of Zergev Squadron, led by Bordeaux Zergev here."

Wilhelm stared at Bordeaux with narrowed eyes. The man was

the picture of a powerful knight, his barrel chest puffed out and the halberd leaning on his shoulder.

Since Wilhelm's last unit had been destroyed, he had no objection to being assigned to a new one. "Are you sure about this, though? I've been in two battles so far, and in each one, everyone in my unit was killed. Do you plan on being next?" he asked, closing one eye. It was disrespectful to those who had died bravely in battle, but Bordeaux gave a solemn shake of his head.

"There were too many casualties in those last two battles—Redonas Plateau and Castour Field. Redonas was a strategic victory, at least, but Castour was inexcusable. Those kinds of losses were unprecedented. The royal army was forced to do a large-scale reorganization."

"And I don't believe it's strictly accurate to say *everyone* in your units was killed. I'm given to understand one other young man survived. To come through all that—you two must have excellent luck. Or perhaps excellent judgment."

The outcome of the battle was well-known, as was the state of the army afterward. Drawn in by the vanguard, the majority of the units caught in the area of effect of the demi-human magic circles had been destroyed. The only survivors were those who, like Wilhelm, had had the presence of mind to drive forward, as well as those who had been able to escape the enchantments in the chaos. A handful of immensely lucky souls had survived despite being in the thick of it.

"Meanwhile, Zergev Squadron was right up front, but every one of us came back alive," Bordeaux said proudly.

"Your intuition saved you," Pivot said to Wilhelm. "You may not look it, but you're a man who can be counted on in battle. That's why we're not worried about you."

It was only then that Wilhelm realized all this had been a roundabout response to his own sarcastic comment.

Apparently taking Wilhelm's silence for doubt, Bordeaux hefted his halberd and started to expound the unit's military exploits. "You know, it wasn't luck that kept us alive. We broke through the enemy encirclement, cut them down even as they gloated over us—"

But Wilhelm cut him off. "Yeah, yeah, I believe you. Is that all you wanted to talk about?" Wilhelm wasn't going to bother pretending he thought Bordeaux was making any of this up. Although the boy had ultimately been victorious in their duel, Bordeaux was the first person he had met in the capital to win even a single match against him. And he was well aware that the large man had proven himself in his share of real battles. But then, so had Wilhelm.

"If that's all you want, then let me go back to my practice. I just have to show up at this Zergev Squadron or whatever at the barracks, right?"

"He wants to be rid of us," Pivot said. "Yes, that's all you have to do. Zergev Squadron is taking on you and one other new member as part of the reorganization, for a total of twenty people. You have a meeting with the captain tomorrow night. Try not to skip out."

"Who's the other new guy?"

"The only other survivor of your unit—Grimm Fauzen. We thought having a familiar face might help you settle in...although, having met you, I suspect we were wrong."

Wilhelm had turned away with an expression of disinterest, already raising his sword, and Pivot gave a sigh that was half annoyance and half resignation.

Wilhelm knew the name, of course. But he hardly felt any more reaction than that. The boy, Grimm, was not someone Wilhelm was much interested in. He was a useless coward—another thing he didn't like.

Rather rudely concluding his conversation with the two superior officers, Wilhelm threw himself into his practice. Bordeaux and Pivot watched him for a moment and exchanged a glance.

"He loves his sword every bit as much as I heard—maybe even more! He's seven years younger than me, and he's gonna make me look bad! I guess I need to get back to my ax training."

"To think we would meet someone so young who would sacrifice his sleep in order to practice the sword. The world is a stranger place than I realized. All kinds come to the capital, I guess. I hope Grimm Fauzen turns out to be normal when we meet him."

So there was Bordeaux, who had chosen a somewhat strange thing to be impressed by; Pivot, who could always find something to be anxious about; and Wilhelm, who paid no attention to either of them but single-mindedly performed his drills. It would be enough to make a bystander wonder if any member of Zergev Squadron was, in fact, sane.

3

It was several days after Wilhelm had been assigned to Zergev Squadron. On the first day, Wilhelm met the other members of his unit with his usual cold indifference. It was mostly made up of soldiers Bordeaux had recruited himself. This ensured a frosty reception for Wilhelm, who showed little respect for the squad leader. But all thoughts of personally teaching him some manners were put on hold when they heard Bordeaux's report.

"Wilhelm is even better than me! And I'm better than all of you, so how are any of you going to give him a taste of his own medicine? Damn shame! How about a little early-morning practice?"

Indeed, starting the next day, the squadron could be found at the training ground at dawn. The talk of each day was the mock battles between Wilhelm and Bordeaux, which were so intense that someone could nearly have gotten killed.

As for Grimm, who joined the squadron at the same time as Wilhelm, he continued to get by as he had before, trying not to be notably incompetent. He was soon attached to Pivot like a shadow.

People began avoiding Wilhelm even more studiously than they had before, sometimes eyeing him as if they thought he was crazy, but the boy wasn't interested in any of that. His previous unit had treated him like a hideous curiosity, and this one meddled with him far too much; Wilhelm found them both equally troublesome.

At heart, Wilhelm liked to do everything alone, including training. As the mock battles with Bordeaux continued, he started to see how the man breathed, what his tells were, until nearly every victory went to Wilhelm. The boy failed to see the point of training so hard against a single opponent. If they met on the battlefield, they would fight only once; there would be no second chance.

If at any time during training a soft spot developed in his heart, it would become nearly impossible to focus his entire spirit on the task at hand. More than once, he had felt the urge to cut down opponents who trained less than wholeheartedly. It was so much easier to stay utterly focused on training by himself.

"I want...to go into battle."

It wasn't that he wanted to kill. He didn't seek to take life. He just wanted to use his sword. True swordsmanship could only be found in combat, in a contest where either person could lose their life at any moment.

Wilhelm spent weeks in the capital with this gloomy thought—until he was given a chance to go back to the place of that terrible defeat, and the Sword Devil crossed paths with a new enemy.

4

It was about eight hours by dragon carriage from the capital to Castour Field. Zergev Squadron split into two groups, ten people to a carriage. Between them was a third vehicle, carrying a VIP.

Bordeaux had sounded suitably excited when he described the mission to them. "You should be happy! Our valor is so valiant that we've been given a special assignment. We're escorting someone important to Castour Field. This is an honor!"

Pivot, fiddling with his monocle, was left to fill in the details. "We will be escorting a specialist who is exceptionally adept at magic. Until now, our nation has had few prominent figures with much magical capability, which has been a fatal disadvantage against the mana-wielding talents of the demi-humans. We learned that the very hard way during the recent battle at Castour Field."

"I guess they want to inspect the magic circles the enemy used to trap us," Bordeaux said. "The circles probably aren't active anymore, but they want to take a look for themselves. And here I thought spell casters always stayed locked up in their rooms!"

Bordeaux had chosen a somewhat odd way to express his admiration—but the even stranger thing was that Wilhelm somehow agreed with him. He had always thought those who relied on mana instead of steel were missing something from life.

The foremost carriage included Bordeaux and Pivot along with eight other squad members; the rearmost one carried ten more people, including Wilhelm and Grimm. The carriage in the middle, carrying the VIP, also had a contingent of knights from a different squadron to help keep guard.

It seemed excessive, sending this many men to look after a single person, but that only emphasized how crucial this mission was. To Wilhelm, though, neither the identity of their guest nor the details of the mission mattered much. The only thing he cared about was whether there would be anyone left on that field worth fighting. He judged that, unfortunately, it didn't seem likely.

All this left Wilhelm on edge.

"Hey, Grimm. You don't look so good. You all right?"

The voice brought Wilhelm back to reality, shocking him out of his mental sword practice. Across from him in the narrow carriage, he could see the pale-faced boy. Another squad member was rubbing his shoulders.

Grimm was all but white. The dragon carriage was using a wind repel blessing, which meant this was more than simple motion sickness. It was probably psychological—a personal reaction to their destination.

"I'm—I'm okay. Just…feeling a little sick. I'll get it under control soon…"

"You sure? I don't think doctors have discovered a cure for cowardice yet. It's a serious illness—you think you can fix it on your own? I know it's chronic with you." Wilhelm broke in, angered by this attempt at false bravado.

"—" Grimm didn't say anything at first, but an expression of pain and regret crossed his face. Then anger twisted his usually calm—which was to say, weak—features, and he glared at Wilhelm.

"You seem awfully merry. Even though you ought to know full well where we're going."

"What makes you think I would act anything like you? You can hardly go to the bathroom without someone there to hold your hand."

"Our entire squad was wiped out there! Is it wrong to be upset about that?!"

"You aren't upset about their deaths. You're just feeling sorry for yourself. You're happy you didn't end up like them yesterday and scared you might end up like them tomorrow. I shouldn't have to remind you we've both lost a lot of comrades. Usually the same ones."

Their argument continued unresolved, and neither young man gave any ground.

Everyone was on edge, leaving Grimm in a worse mood than usual. As Wilhelm sat there with his beloved sword pulled close, Grimm looked nearly ready to jump on him.

"Come off it already! This time you've gone too far, Wilhelm!"

Their comrades' shouts interrupted them, and the staring contest ended without coming to blows. Grimm moved so he wasn't sitting across from Wilhelm, and Wilhelm sank back into his private world. This time, there were no more disturbances.

Thanks to the suffocating tension in the carriage, the squad members could hardly wait to arrive at their destination.

When they had set out, it was barely dawn; when the three dragon carriages finally arrived at Castour Field, the sun was at its peak.

"I know that ride was long enough to put blisters on your ass," Bordeaux said, "but you guys are in even worse shape than I expected."

The two groups had disembarked from their carriages and were now lined up under the inquiring glance of their commander. The difference between them was night and day. The two young men responsible for the obvious fatigue of the rear carriage were standing side by side—as the newest recruits, they had to—but they weren't looking at each other.

"I don't know what happened, but our work starts now. Don't let the enemy see you tired. Straighten up!" Bordeaux barked. "We'll be receiving our guest in a moment. Show them your best behavior!" At this, the entire troop stood up straighter, the concerns of a moment before forgotten. There was the sound of shuffling feet as the unit organized itself into two neat rows. Bordeaux gave a half nod in satisfaction, then looked at Pivot, who stood beside him.

Pivot took this cue to open the door of the middle carriage and usher the visitor onto Castour Field.

"There's no need to make such a fuss over me. A woman can't help but be intimidated with so *maaany* fierce-looking faces staring at her." The speaker's tone was light, and she shrugged as if making a joke.

She had indigo hair that reached to her neck and skin as fair as porcelain. The hem of her long robe hung just above the ground, the front open to reveal a generous bust barely contained within a male military uniform. In deference to the occasion, she wore minimal makeup—but this hardly kept the men from noticing her beauty. Most striking of all were her eyes, one of which was blue and one yellow.

Surprise ran through the unit; they hadn't been told the person they were escorting was a woman. This brought a smile to her face, like a child who had pulled a prank.

"I am Roswaal J. Mathers. One of the few wizards serving at the royal court—and, as you can see, a poor, defenseless maiden. I'll be counting on you today, boys."

She gave an alluring smile. In that moment, Wilhelm decided that she fell into the category of things he did not like.

"Ahem," Pivot said to the men of the unit, some of whom were still murmuring among themselves. "Now that you've been introduced to Miss Mathers, please remember that she is a lady. I remind all the uncouth barbarians in our unit, young *and* old, to mind their manners."

"Weeell," Roswaal interjected, "it wouldn't do for you to be so formal that you couldn't do your work. I was having a little fun with you by concealing my gender, but please carry on as usual. My name is the one that each head of the household inherits—it just happens to be male. Our family is raaather unique, you see."

"You heard Lady Mathers. About your business, everyone."

Of course, *business* in this case meant "taking utmost care."

As everyone set about attending to duties, Wilhelm sensed someone in the dragon carriage. This person had been waiting for the conversation to conclude, and now slipped out and stood by Roswaal.

It was another woman. She wore light armor and had a sword at her hip. She appeared to be in her late teens; she had a pretty face, but the dangerous glint in her eye would make one hesitate to approach. Her gorgeous golden hair was cut short, and she seemed prickly. A swordswoman.

"Oh, leeet me add," Roswaal said, "this is my personal bodyguard, Carol Remendes. She's quite skilled, so I'm sure you'll all get along."

"Thank you, Lady Mathers," the girl said, "but I wouldn't concern myself. I doubt we'll see them again after today. There's no reason to get close to them—and they don't seem like the types to get friendly."

In complete contrast to Roswaal, Carol seemed totally humorless. Was she arrogant, or just nervous? Either way, she looked on edge.

"…What, *both* women?"

"You! You there!" Carol immediately singled out the source of the disbelieving whisper: Wilhelm. She looked ready to draw her sword right then and there. "Are you looking down on me because I'm a woman? That sort of prejudice carries a high price around me."

"Oh, stop whining. You're obviously more worried about it than anyone else here. Anyway, my job is to guard your friend there, not to make sure you feel all warm and fuzzy."

"Th-that's enough, Wilhelm!" As the boy and the girl glared at each other, Grimm tried with a trembling voice to control his squad mate. Wilhelm raised an eyebrow at him, but Grimm, his eyes burning with anger, said, "I don't know what your problem is—not in the carriage, and not here. But you need to put a lid on it. Picking a fight with the people we're supposed to be working with? Do you know how much trouble you'll cause for our squad leader?"

The other members of the squadron fixed Wilhelm with angry stares, siding with Grimm. Between his typical behavior and the way he'd been acting that day, Wilhelm had few allies.

"…I'm sorry," he said at length, although his face suggested it was only because he knew further argument would be useless. That seemed to placate Grimm, who turned to Carol and bowed his head.

"I'm very sorry about that. We'll make sure he's dealt with…"

"You do that," Carol said. "I have no more desire to spill the kingdom's blood unnecessarily than you do."

She withdrew, and the tension in the air relaxed. Bordeaux, who had been watching the entire episode with a smirk, called the unit to attention.

"Right! We're going to split up into three groups. One will accompany Lady Mathers and make sure she's safe while she inspects the magic circle. The remaining two groups will set up a security perimeter. Watch out for looters and any demi-human stragglers. There ain't much glory in dying here, boys, so look sharp!"

Bordeaux was just about to start assigning groups when Roswaal raised her hand. "Excuse me, Squad Leader. May I ask one thing? One small, selfish request in the assignments?"

"If I can do it, ma'am, certainly."

"I want that little boy from earlier to be in my group." With a smile, she pointed at none other than Wilhelm. She winked, so that only her yellow eye was watching him. "I think the outcome will be much better that way, for me and for everyone."

All present were mystified by her request.

5

Wilhelm reflected bitterly that when Roswaal had spoken of things being better for "everyone," this apparently had not included him.

The squadron could hardly fail to oblige a personal request from someone so important. And so Wilhelm was among those who accompanied Roswaal, as was Grimm, one of his least favorite people in the world. Two other squad members were also chosen to go with them to investigate the magic circles, which made for a unit of six if you included Roswaal and her bodyguard. The remaining two squadrons, headed up by Bordeaux and Pivot respectively, busied themselves with setting up a perimeter.

"You look like someone who looost a bet," Roswaal said.

After minimal argument, Wilhelm had found himself at the vanguard of his group, but his perpetual pout didn't inspire much confidence. And his job was only made more frustrating when Roswaal kept cheerily striking up a conversation with him as he tried to focus.

"Are you as eeeager as all that to cut people down?"

"Don't talk about people like monsters. It's not that I want to kill anyone. I want to find a worthwhile opponent to fight. And if I hadn't had to babysit you all day, I might have actually stood a chance of doing that."

"Some might say that answer sounds monstrous enough. Either way, the best you could've hoped for on security detail is a little defensive action... Somehow I doubt that would be enough for you."

"Well, don't you have it all figured out. You don't know what you're talking about."

"You're quite direct, aaaren't you? Well, I don't have a problem with that."

Roswaal put her hand to her mouth and laughed. Wilhelm could only frown.

They didn't see anything unusual, but neither did they have anything to show for their efforts yet. The battle had reshaped the topography; trees had been felled, the green earth burned black. Broken weapons and empty armor littered the area. The war had well and truly left its mark.

"Does it hurt to look at?" Roswaal said.

"Not especially," Wilhelm replied.

"I suppooose I'm not surprised. You don't seem the type."

"...Well, neither do you."

"Goodness graaacious, you might just be one step aheeead of me."

Maybe Roswaal disliked silence, because she seemed to interject at every opportunity. Wilhelm had already decided he would have to watch her closely. He could tell from the way Carol carried herself that she was a capable fighter, but it was Roswaal, with her unknown depths, who demanded the most caution. He had been told she was a specialist in magic, but he didn't believe for a second that that was all there was to her.

One might have expected Carol to take more exception than anyone to Wilhelm's curt attitude, but Grimm had been keeping her busy the entire time. Realizing that she and Wilhelm would only argue if left to their own devices, he had decided to engage her in a constant stream of conversation. The talk seemed to be going fairly smoothly, which made things easier for Wilhelm.

"So you're saying you weren't originally going to be on guard duty today?" Grimm was asking.

"That's right," Carol said. "Originally, the person I serve was going to come along as a bodyguard. But something came up, so I had to come instead. I'm afraid it's most inconvenient for Lady Mathers." She sounded distraught.

Grimm wasn't quite sure how to respond. "Oh, um, but I'm sure if your master had come, someone like me would only be underfoot. I'm sure that would have been even worse…"

It didn't matter to Wilhelm. As long as Grimm kept Carol talking, that was enough. If the conversation didn't come around to him, he had no intention of getting involved.

Only the hint of someone even more powerful than Carol caught his attention. Granted, there was a distinct possibility that Carol was speaking humbly of herself while exaggerating the abilities of her master, but still…

"I believe I heard you were called Wilhelm, isn't that riiight?" Roswaal said.

"…Yeah, that's right."

"Quite a mouth you have. May I suppose you have skills to maaatch?"

"__"

"Not given to bragging? Weeell, the squad leader and his assistant didn't hesitate to give you the most important job. It's a sign of how much you're truuusted. It gives me high hopes for you."

Ignoring the silent swordsman, Roswaal nearly skipped along, fingers interlaced behind her head; she seemed ready to start humming at any moment.

Looking around, she said, "It looks like we'll be there soon."

As she spoke, she and her escorts arrived at the top of a hill. Below, they could see the faint outline of a geometric shape. The earth had been torn up in places, and parts of the sigil were buried, but it was the magic circle Wilhelm had seen on the day of the battle.

"Weeell now, I wonder what we'll find?" Roswaal immediately slid down the hill to get a closer look. Carol hurried after her, and Grimm, in turn, stuck close to Carol. Wilhelm shrugged and, along with the other two squad members, kept watch from the top of the hill.

Wilhelm hadn't sensed another living thing all day, and that didn't change now. He didn't know where Bordeaux and the others were, but it was nowhere nearby. So far the day had brought only boredom.

"...Now I see," Roswaal said. "I thought this might be what was going on when I first heard about it. They took their time setting this up. It wouldn't have been possible if both the strategist and the person who carried it out weren't very, veeery accomplished with magic. This could be a threat to the whole kingdom."

"Is—is it really? Are these magic circles as powerful as all that?" Grimm asked.

"The circles themselves are dangerous, of course, but what's more threatening is the implication that the enemy has more than one highly capable maaagic user. You'd have to be a little crazy even to think of covering an entire battlefield with magic circles. But it means they could do the saaame thing elsewhere."

"H-how...?!"

Grimm seemed more intimidated than Roswaal's assessment

warranted. He stood there quivering at a hypothetical situation. He was definitely not made for soldiering.

He kept rubbing the back of his neck and glancing around, as though he had a bad feeling he couldn't shake. Finally, he turned and called to Wilhelm. "Wilhelm! Aren't you getting a weird feeling?"

"No," Wilhelm replied indifferently to the desperate boy. "Your mind is just playing tricks on y—"

As he spoke, Wilhelm let his gaze drift to the bottom of the hill—where he saw an arrow flying through the air, heading straight for where Roswaal was crouched on the ground.

"—!"

Wilhelm's judgment was instantaneous, his action only slightly slower. He drew the sword at his hip faster than the eye could see and threw it so that it planted itself in the ground just beside Roswaal, and the blade took the arrow instead of her. The clink as the arrow bounced off the steel alerted everyone to the ambush.

But why hadn't Wilhelm noticed anything?

He dashed down the hill, shouting, "Ambush! Everyone, at the ready!" He retrieved his sword from the earth and brought it up; in his peripheral vision, he could see Carol and Grimm readying their weapons as well. The other two squad members belatedly started making their way down the hill, but Wilhelm motioned for them to stay at the crest. Then he started scanning the area.

He saw something. "...Look there."

Directly across from the hill, a figure with a bow was down on one knee. Unhurried, it drew another arrow and pulled back the bowstring. Then, without hesitation, it fired.

"—" Wilhelm swept away the incoming projectile with his sword, then fixed his gaze on the opponent. Beside him, Grimm apparently couldn't believe what he was seeing.

"Th-Tholter...?"

The attacker was, or was once, his friend—the archer Tholter Weasily.

Now, Tholter hardly bore looking at. He was barely human. Half the flesh of his face was missing, revealing bone and one round eyeball. Pus flowed from his wounds, the raw flesh crawling with maggots. The rotting specter was covered only with bits of cloth and some broken armor. The hand gripping the bow was missing several fingers.

"Is that corpse...moving...?" Carol, her sword in front of her, had gone pale at the sight of the dead Tholter. The grotesque spectacle was only made worse by the seeming impossibility of it. Still, Carol looked to be doing better than Grimm, who was beyond pale and seemingly ready to faint clean away at any moment.

"Hey, magician," Wilhelm said, "...is that something you can do with magic?"

"You're awfully cooold for a man who just saw a living corpse. I gather it's someone you know?"

"The dead don't mean anything to me. So no, I don't know him."

"A laudable view. To answer your question...yes and no. This isn't strictly the domain of maaagic. It's a curse," Roswaal answered with an air of self-importance.

Wilhelm raised an eyebrow at this. But there was no time to pursue the subject further. Tholter was not their only enemy.

"—"

There was a rustling sound as corpses began clawing their way up out of the earth one after another, all around them. Some were the dead of the royal army, others former demi-humans. Apparently the curse was not picky.

None of the undead warriors were in perfect condition, but they were nearly a hundred strong, which gave them the advantage. Wilhelm clicked his tongue, then had Roswaal stand in the center of their formation, with him, Carol, and Grimm surrounding her.

"Weeell, now," she said, "this is an unexpected development. I thought you might just run off to fight them all yourself."

"Don't think I wouldn't like to. But I can't have you dying on us, either. I won't be watching your back. Just pray those other two are useful."

"What was that?! How dare you—!"

Grimm's shout interrupted her. "Carol, here they come!"

The zombies leaped at them from every direction at once. A huge corpse with an enormous sword was advancing on Wilhelm, along with another body that had its arms outstretched, despite having no hands and no head. How much damage would they have to do to these corpses in order to keep them at bay?

"Whatever, it's obvious just cutting off their heads won't stop them."

Wilhelm struck out with his sword, slicing the hands off the creature with the massive blade. As he brought his arm back, he cut through its belly, then swept across the groin again as the body toppled. It had been carved up into six pieces, including the two detached arms. When the pieces reached the ground, they stopped moving. Wilhelm made two diagonal cuts at the handless zombie, cutting it into four pieces; these, too, laid still.

"You just have to kill them one extra time," he said.

"What a remaaarkable calculation," Roswaal said behind him. He could almost hear the grin in her voice.

Wilhelm glanced over his shoulder. Carol was slicing up three undead in front of her, and Grimm was supporting her with his shield, shoring up the battle line. The two men left on top of the hill were taking care of themselves, like the members of Zergev Squadron they were, and making short work of the undead warriors around them.

The zombies were not stout fighters. However capable they might have been as soldiers in life, as corpses, none of them had much martial ability to speak of. They were simply no match for the living warriors.

"I'm only getting my blade dirty. Where's the wizard controlling them?"

"I appreciate your trust, but I'm afraid even I'm haaaving a little trouble tracking them. But with this many zombies to handle, they can't be far."

"No? All right, then."

If they kept to this battleground, soon there would be no more corpses around them. And no more corpses meant no more zombies. But Wilhelm found that deeply dissatisfying.

"—"

Fending off the attacks of the encroaching undead, he struck with his blade and returned them to the dust. The undead warriors stank of rot and shuffled with disgusting audible sloshes, but Wilhelm took careful note of their behavior.

He cut his way to the center of the horde, where two zombies stood, unmoving. The undead pressed against him, as if they were trying to protect something. But an overhead chop and two swift kicks delivered a second death. He brought his sword back and was about to stab, when—

"Hrk!"

A gout of flame spouted in front of him, forcing him to jump back. Wilhelm slashed wildly at the approaching fire until the air in front of him shimmered, and the empty space suddenly filled with a small humanoid figure.

Wilhelm's blood ran cold as he took this in.

It was a small girl in a white robe. "…Not going the way I'd planned," she muttered. She looked to be around ten years old—a little younger or a little older, perhaps. She had long light-pink hair and a charming face. Other than her bare feet, and the robe that was her only clothing, she looked like a perfectly ordinary, if remarkably calm, young girl.

That made it all the more unsettling to know that a horrible fiend was lurking under the girlish guise. She radiated an overwhelming heinous aura, so strong she couldn't hide it, so strong one could detect it almost instantly.

"What—what monster is this?" Wilhelm said, almost to himself.

"Monster…? So I am indeed incomplete. I have a long way to go before I'm like my mother," the girl whispered sadly, frowning.

This elicited an amazed reaction from someone nearby.

"Mother? Surely you jest. To think that hideous damaged goods like you share anything at all with my honored teacher. I won't heeear of it." Roswaal stepped forward. Her easygoing amusement was gone, replaced by a furious glare that she fixed on the little girl.

The girl, for her part, appeared puzzled by Roswaal's anger. "I'm sorry. Who are you?"

"Your doom. I will destroy you, utterly and entirely."

"Then I'm very sorry. Especially as you seem serious."

The girl appeared practically emotionless, in stark contrast to the building rage and increasingly dangerous glint in Roswaal's eye. The girl took this in stride, scanning her environment and gesturing at the undead warriors.

"Happily, I was able to obtain what I came here for," she said, "and I need not trouble myself with you any further. I'll be going now. You have given me much to think about." The girl bowed her head, and her body began rising up off the ground.

"Stop right there, you—!" Wilhelm dived at her, meaning to prevent her escape, but the undead warriors closed in to stop him.

"Out of my way!" He seemed caught off guard by a zombie that dodged his attack and moved to counter. It was so fast, like a different creature from the puppets of before.

He could see that all the zombies around him were moving more readily, too. Even Wilhelm couldn't cut these things down in a single blow, and yet they still were no match for him...

"Y-yaaaarrrgh!"

"All of a sudden...there's so many of them... I can't hold them all...!"

He heard Grimm scream and saw that Carol, too, was wounded and moving slowly. Eventually, everyone but Wilhelm would be overwhelmed.

"We've reduced their numbers, but that's probably made the rest of them more powerful. There must be one 'core' zombie that's acting as a control point for all the others. If we destroy it, we might be able to turn this around."

"How can we tell which one it is?"

"It'll move differently. That's the key...if you can tell."

Thanks to Roswaal, they had a plan, but finding the core zombie in the chaos of the battlefield would not be easy. Wilhelm looked to the hill, hoping to get help from his squad mates atop it, but he found that an arrow fired with incredible force had pierced one of them at the hip and torn out a chunk of flesh.

Tholter was the culprit, as sharp with supporting fire as he had been in life. With a large body that belied his quick-wittedness, Tholter had been exceptionally distinguished as an archer in their unit, and his huge bow was capable of immense power and accuracy.

It came to Wilhelm in a flash.

The zombie whose abilities were unchanged from life—Tholter Weasily—was the control point.

"I believe we've chosen someone you will find difficult to kill. We've been watching you." This dispassionate remark came from the girl, getting farther and farther away. But it lent credence to Wilhelm's guess.

Grinding his teeth, Wilhelm counted how many enemies there were between him and Tholter, and then, practically afire with rage, he cut the undead warrior in front of him into four pieces.

It wouldn't be enough. Wilhelm could reach Tholter and kill him. But while he was busy doing that, his three companions would become zombie food. There was only one way to keep the battle line intact and still stop Tholter...

"Grimm!" Wilhelm shouted. "You have to get Tholter! He's the core!"

They were trapped at the bottom of a bowl. Out of all of them, Grimm was the least useful in battle. The deeper they went, the more enemies there would be, and losing him would have the least impact on their overall strength.

Grimm, his shield still up, looked at Tholter, then at the undead creature that had stolen his friend's body. He shook his head again and again.

"I—I can't do that! I can't!"

"You go! I'll take your place helping the girl! Get up that hill and chop off his head! He's an archer with no one to guard him. If you can get close, you can kill him!"

"It's not about whether I can beat him or not! You're telling me to kill my friend!" Grimm was practically on the verge of tears even as he desperately fended off the enemy's attacks.

Wilhelm knew Grimm and Tholter had been close. He was also aware that Grimm had been incapable of using his sword ever since the annihilation of their unit. And yet...

"Yes, I am! So what?!"

"So what? So everything! I can't murder my friend! I... I'm not like you! I can't do it!"

"What part of that thing is your friend? Can't you see through your tears? Your friend is dead and gone! That thing is a corpse. It just got a little lost—it shouldn't be here!"

Wilhelm saw Carol slip. She took a sideswipe at the zombie that was about to attack her. The pieces bounced off Grimm's rounded back. Wilhelm gave him a shove and shouted, "'*Oh, I can't, I can't!*' That's how it always is with you! You spend all your time looking for excuses! Well, if you have the energy to argue, you have the energy to go over there and kill that thing! Stop blubbering and go put an end to it!"

"—"

Wilhelm shouted his philosophy relentlessly as he felled zombie after zombie.

He sensed Grimm straightening up behind him. The boy looked at his feet and muttered, "It might be Tholter."

"So what?! Tell me!"

"I just can't use my sword anymore. I'm so scared."

"So what?!"

"Everyone else died, and I lived, and I can't stand it!"

"So *what*?!"

"I don't want to die!!"

Back to back, they shouted at each other.

And then Grimm rushed forward, shield raised. Carol hurried after him to support him while Wilhelm set himself to the bloody work of protecting Roswaal.

Grimm raced up the hill, deflecting the undead warriors' blows with his shield, reaching Tholter in one mad dash.

The massive bow let loose another arrow. Grimm blocked it with his shield, as easily as if he had seen such an attack a million times, and raising his pristine sword, he shouted.

"I'm going to live!"

And he dealt Tholter a blow that, although full of fear, nonetheless cut off his head.

So the battle ended.

6

"This's the last oooonnne!" Bordeaux slammed his battle-ax into the undead warrior with fantastic force, reducing it to a collection of fleshy bits that in no way resembled a human body. The huge warrior heaved a sigh, resting his halberd on his shoulder and brushing off the bits of gore stuck to his armor.

"Right! Battle's over! If you're dead, gimme a yell!"

"That's not possible," Pivot replied. "Because, as I'm pleased to report, everyone is alive."

The various groups of Zergev Squadron had managed to break through the crowd of undead and link up shortly after Grimm had destroyed Tholter. Both Wilhelm, with his incredible sword work, and Carol, who was wounded, returned safely. Even the squad member who had taken Tholter's arrow survived. By some miracle, the squadron hadn't lost a single person in the battle.

"My, my, myyy, what a fine display. You all saved me!"

It was sometime after the fighting ended. The squad sat on the ground as Roswaal showered praise on them.

Pivot turned to her and, adjusting his monocle, asked, "Tell us, Miss Mathers. What were those undead creatures?"

"That's an eeexcellent question. They're a sign that there's more to this situation than meets the eye. I have to report back to the castle as soon as possible. We'll have to exercise the uuutmost caution."

"The utmost caution…?" This sounded grim. Pivot raised an eyebrow. Roswaal nodded, sending waves through her indigo hair.

"Not sure I agree," Bordeaux said, crossing his arms. "It's just some walking dead. What's the danger?"

"The zombies are just a start," Roswaal said. "The question is who's controlling them, and who set up the magic circles. I suspect they're the same person."

Bordeaux, along with everyone else who didn't know the situation, looked at her in puzzlement. Wilhelm, still holding his precious sword, frowned at Roswaal. She was wearing a smile that suggested she had an idea of who this person was, and it rubbed him the wrong way.

Roswaal either didn't notice or ignored him. She pointed to what was left of the magic circle and said, "It was the same person who brought this kind of unusual magical ability to the Demi-human Alliance and used the curse to control the zombies. She calls herself...Sphinx. She belongs to the Witch's legacy, you might say. That's probably the clearest way of communicating how dangerous she is."

Everyone, including Wilhelm, swallowed heavily at this. It confirmed that the monster—Sphinx, the remnant of the Witch—was real. The long shadow she cast over the war bogging down the royal forces and the Demi-human Alliance was no illusion.

What was more, the connection to the Witch formed there would lead the kingdom of Lugunica, Zergev Squadron, and above all Wilhelm himself to an unavoidable fate.

Wilhelm Trias, the Sword Devil, had not yet encountered his destiny. It would all start three years later, when he turned eighteen.

THE LOVE SONG OF THE SWORD DEVIL

Third Stanza

1

The encounter with the witch on Castour Field, as well as the knowledge that she was working with the Demi-human Alliance, shocked the administrators of Lugunica.

"The situation is alaaarming. The person known as Sphinx can control the dead and use great magics long thought lost. We may face other losses like the one at Castour."

Now the noblewoman Roswaal J. Mathers spoke in the assembly hall before a gathering of the country's top military officials, eminent officers and Knights of the Royal Guard, as well as several of the nation's most prominent nobles.

Even though she spoke fluently, Roswaal's tendency to draw out her syllables in odd places remained. But nobody pointed this out; the officials listening to her never lost the somber looks on their faces.

"Sphinx?" someone said. "I've heard some people think she's part of the Witch Cult."

"Personally, I doubt it," someone else replied. "They only follow their own desires. It's hard to picture them working with the demi-humans to overthrow the kingdom."

"Maybe, but I think only they really understand what they're after."

At the mention of the Witch Cult, the mood in the chamber turned darker still. The Witch Cult was a group that revered the Witch of Jealousy—who had nearly destroyed the world centuries ago—and sought to revive her, according to the stories, at least. Many thought, however, that this was very difficult to believe, and that the members of this cult were simply garden-variety lunatics.

Wilhelm agreed with this latter view—or more accurately, he didn't care either way. He didn't even really know why he was in the council chamber at that moment. Bordeaux and Pivot sat beside him, but this he could understand; they were accomplished knights and could hold their heads high in this company.

Frankly, he wished some of that confidence would rub off on Grimm.

"...Hrk..."

Where Wilhelm sat looking annoyed, Grimm was going to be sick, by all appearances. His face was colorless, his breathing uneven; it seemed that if he wasn't careful, he might soon revisit his breakfast.

Just as Wilhelm started wondering if his face was ever a normal color, Roswaal said, "Now we'll hear from Zergev Squadron, who were in the actual battle. If you don't miiind, gentlemen."

Bordeaux jumped to his feet, barking out "Yes, ma'am!" in an absurdly loud voice. An instant later, Wilhelm and the others stood, too, and all four of them were led to the center of the assembly hall.

"Bordeaux Zergev, commander of Zergev Squadron, reporting! It's an honor to be summoned by headquarters!"

"I think your greeting was a little overdone, young sir," Pivot said. "Ahem. Vice Commander of Zergev Squadron Pivot Anansi, reporting." He glanced at Wilhelm. "You two, introduce yourselves."

"G-Grimm Fauzen of Zergev Squadron, reporting!"

"...Wilhelm Trias, the same."

Grimm's voice squeaked, while Wilhelm's sounded disinterested. Pivot raised an eyebrow, but the assembled officials paid this no mind. They were more interested in the soldiers' report than their names.

"According to Lady Mathers, your unit has actual combat experience against Sphinx. She controlled the undead, used levitation magic, and inscribed the magic circles on Castour Field. What is your opinion of her?"

"Sir! I fought the moving corpses but did not personally observe the alleged witch!"

"Young sir, quiet. My apologies, sirs and madams. These two are the only members of our unit to have had direct contact with the person in question. Wilhelm, Grimm, make your report."

"Y-yes...sir...!"

Grimm, somehow even pastier than before, stepped forward. Wilhelm had no choice but to follow him. Then the members of headquarters began bombarding them with questions. They weren't after anything much different from what had already been said. They wanted the young soldiers to back up Roswaal's report, as well as provide some of their own impressions.

Then came a question that was unusual in both content and the tone in which it was delivered.

"Let's say, for the sake of argument, that this was the Witch. What did you think of her?"

The speaker, his hand still raised, was a man with delicate features set in a narrow face. Somewhere around thirty years old, perhaps, he had a pleasing appearance and well-groomed brown hair. He very much looked the part of the scholar; he seemed conspicuously out of place in the room full of grizzled military types.

"Th-think, sir?! W-well, uh... She was unsettling, and frightening... I mean—no! As a member of the royal army, I was certainly not afraid...!"

As Grimm blathered on, the questioner gave a half nod and looked at Wilhelm. Under the man's penetrating gaze, Wilhelm's expression hardened into seriousness for the first time since he had come to this conference hall. The expression was hardly the limp gaze of a civil official. It had turned the point of a sword on him, the aura of a devastating warrior who had decided this battlefield belonged to him.

"...Who're *you*?" Wilhelm said.

Muttering burst out all over the hall. Beside him, Grimm practically stopped breathing. But it was the questioner himself who silenced this wave of discontent.

"Mm. Yes, pardon me. I am Miklotov MacMahon. I don't ordinarily attend these meetings, but as it was I who suggested Lady Mathers should be the one to investigate the magic circles, I made sure I was invited to hear her report."

Then the man who called himself Miklotov glanced at Roswaal. She took his cue, offering a theatrical bow. So they were friends of a sort.

Now grasping the situation, Wilhelm sighed, and answered, "That witch or whatever—she didn't look human to me. More like a monster wearing a human skin. Can you reason with a hungry demon beast that wants you for its next meal? With her, it's kill or be killed. Nothing else."

Wilhelm's blunt, uncompromising answer left the room silent for a moment. Only Miklotov, whom Wilhelm was still watching with laser-like intensity, had presence enough to nod. With an air of authority, he replied, "I see. This discussion has been most enlightening. You may all sit down."

2

Grimm exploded the moment they got back to the barracks. "I swear! How, *how* can you always be this way?! You just took years off my life!"

They had been called to the assembly the moment they returned from Castour Field without so much as a moment to rest. Now they were finally free of their duties, and Wilhelm was changing out of his stiff, uncomfortable uniform, wiping the sweat and grime off his skin.

Grimm, who had also changed out of his uniform, laid into him. "How could you act like that with so many important people there?! And after Vice Captain Pivot warned us to behave so many times! You've broken so many—"

"How many times are you going to say 'so many'? And don't act so familiar with me." Wilhelm met his spitting, shouting companion with a frosty reply. His opinion of Grimm hadn't changed. He was a coward, and he was useless. Even if he had eventually mustered the nerve to behead his old friend.

"Aw, don't get so worked up, Grimm! T'be honest, I think it's reassuring. If Wilhelm were enough of an idiot to watch his tongue in that room, what would people think of me, letting him talk to me the way I do?"

"Setting aside the question of whether courtesy is due to you, young sir, surely you, Wilhelm, do have at least some idea of what constitutes propriety—don't you?"

Bordeaux and Pivot were changing out of their uniforms, too, and joined the conversation.

"What're you talking about?" Bordeaux asked his second-in-command.

"One can see evidence of genuine education on the fringes of Wilhelm's conduct. It may have been piecemeal, but the ultimate result is enough to aid him in his daily life."

"Tch." Wilhelm gave a disgusted click of his tongue at Pivot's unexpectedly sharp powers of observation. Grimm and Bordeaux shared a look, realizing that the sound meant the assessment was right.

"You've been educated, Wilhelm?" Grimm asked. "So you didn't come from the peasantry?"

"I've heard the merchant class has been big on educating their children lately, giving them a leg up in life. Is that it?" Bordeaux said. "It wouldn't be very grateful of you to waste the things you learned."

"I recall you received formal education in manners, young sir," Pivot retorted, "yet somehow I see no evidence of it in your daily life. I've always thought it rather strange."

Wilhelm seemed to be ignoring Grimm's surprise and Bordeaux's self-important reply; he showed no sign of answering either of their questions. He appeared intent on avoiding any discussion of his background.

"Why so unsociable? You ought to at leeeast let your brothers in arms know about yourself. Such as the fact that you are the son of the Trias family, a regional noble house, and that your beloved sword bears the national crest of Lugunica."

"—"

Wilhelm spun around, his eyes full of a murderous rage to hear his past disclosed so casually. He found Roswaal standing in the open door of the changing room, a smile on her face. She gave a friendly wave, coolly meeting Wilhelm's gaze.

"It was eeeasy enough to find out… The House of Trias may be destitute, but it's still on the noble rolls of Lugunica. Surely you diiidn't think you were going to hide it forever?"

"If you have time to go digging up people's pasts, you should be spending it doing your own work. I think the court is missing its jester."

"The court jester… Ha-ha! I like it. I knew you were an iiinteresting one." Brushing off Wilhelm's angry outburst, Roswaal looked around the changing room. "Headquarters is treating Sphinx's presence as a matter of the greatest possible concern. She maaay end up handled the same way as Libre Fermi and Valga Cromwell, the representatives of the Demi-human Alliance. I appreciate Lord Miklotov's backing…although I'm not thrilled to hear her called 'the witch.'"

Roswaal shrugged, but she couldn't fully conceal her discontent as she finished speaking. Given the obvious displeasure in her eyes, Wilhelm was reminded of the events of Castour Field.

"Come to think of it, you seemed to know that monster," he said. "It was like you two wanted to kill each other."

"What's this? Interested in me?" Roswaal said. "Well, you're a bit young…but what does love care for such trivial things? Luckily for you, you're quite pretty, and I'm not opposed to—kidding!"

Roswaal raised the white flag in midsentence. Wilhelm looked like he was about to leap at her with his sword.

"Sorry, but I can't tell you how I'm connected to—you know. But I can assure you that we're not…working together, so don't fret about that. If you simply *must* know—well, maybe once we're a liiittle closer."

"This is as close to you as I ever want to get."

"Oh, don't be shy. Anyway, you're out of luck. Given what's happened, the person in charge of magical countermeasures for the royal army is now me. Unless the war and Sphinx come to an end much sooner than I expect, I think we are all going to be seeing an awful looot of each other."

Roswaal seemed to enjoy delivering this unwelcome news to the frowning Wilhelm. He turned around to find Bordeaux and Pivot nodding at him, as though they had known all along.

"Zergev Squadron really showed what they were made of out there," Roswaal said. "I assume you'll be in high demand on the front lines from now on, turning the tide in all the most vicious battles."

"Oh-ho! What an honor! I'll bet our 'Sword Devil' Wilhelm will like that!"

Where Grimm and Pivot both sighed to hear that they would be thrown headlong into the most brutal fighting, Bordeaux seemed positively elated. He gave Wilhelm a hearty slap on the back.

Roswaal, however, looked askance at the strange nickname. "Sword Devil…?"

"Some of the jokers in the army have taken to calling him that," Bordeaux said. "Because everyone's heard about all the killing he did in his first couple of battles. I tried to get a nickname of my own going, you know—the Steel Ax—but somehow it's never caught on!"

"People do have a nickname for you, young sir—they call you the Mad Dog… Er, I know you don't like that name, so I don't use it. Things can't always go the way we wish."

"Sword Devil," Roswaal said reflectively. "Sword Devil, yeees. Indeed, I think it fits you very well."

Wilhelm snorted and looked away from Roswaal and her coy smile. What did he care what other people called him? "Sword Devil" was a conveniently intimidating nickname.

"Don't imaaagine we're making fun of you," Roswaal said. "People most wish for a hero when the tragedies of war come to them, be it a Sword Saint or a Sage…especially given that Lord Freibel, the most recent Sword Saint, died in this civil waaar."

Wilhelm, still feigning indifference, said nothing, but Bordeaux nodded and said with pain in his eyes, "I heard he was killed fighting a defensive action against impossible odds so his forces could get away. Truly a warrior's death."

"Sword Saint" was the title given to the greatest swordsman to serve the kingdom of Lugunica. But if the bearer of that title had been killed, maybe his talents had not been so great after all.

"I'm going to the training ground. You can all stay here and chat as long as you like."

"You're going out to train?!" Grimm exclaimed. "After all we've—?! Ah, arrgh—! Wait, Wilhelm! I'm going, too!"

"Don't."

Grimm grabbed his sword and shield in a hurry to follow Wilhelm out of the changing room. Of the two of them, only Grimm executed a quick salute on his way out—a perfect summary of the difference in their personalities.

"There's less distance between those two than there was yesterday," Pivot commented.

"That's because Grimm's come out of his shell whole," Bordeaux said. "He's got a good look on his face now. He ain't much for the sword, but I like the way he handles that shield. He's going to get better and better, Grimm is."

"You're too quick to believe the best of everyone. People who don't grow don't last long in our profession."

"Bwa-ha-ha! People are just big bunches of problems. If you can find one good thing about them, that's enough."

Still laughing, Bordeaux changed into a light training outfit. Pivot could only sigh. The commander grabbed the halberd he'd left leaning against the wall, then turned to Roswaal.

"Sorry we can't show you a little more hospitality, Lady Mathers, after all you've done. But Zergev Squadron's headed for the training ground. Got another busy day tomorrow."

"I don't miiind at all. It's encouraging for me to see that you don't bend for anyone. And as I said, I think we're going to be spending a lot of time together. I certainly hope we'll get along."

"…As do I," Pivot said. "I wouldn't want to get on your bad side, Lady Mathers."

Then he and the grinning Bordeaux left the changing room and waved good-bye to Roswaal in the hallway. Once she was out of sight, Bordeaux turned to his second-in-command.

"Wow, Pivot. A straight arrow like you, about to turn thirty… I wouldn't have pegged Lady Mathers as your type. You dog, you!"

"Young sir," Pivot replied, "be careful not to let Lady Mathers too much into your confidence, or your heart."

"Hm?"

Bordeaux had only been teasing, but Pivot's quiet reply was accompanied by a significant look.

The commander stroked his beard lazily. "I will, if you say so. But why? You think there's something going on?"

"The woman is not easy to read. I wouldn't be at all surprised if she were up to something we know nothing about. In any event, it seems we'll be working with her at least for the duration of the war. Watch yourself."

"Poison with our meal, huh? That should keep things interesting. And I've got the Sword Devil to send into battle—a captain's life is never boring!"

Although aware that Bordeaux's bellowing laughter was attracting strange looks in the barracks, Pivot raised his own voice to match as he said, "My goodness… We always do draw the shortest straws, don't we?"

3

Shamrock Valley, in the southeast of Lugunica, was foggy day and night.

Fog was considered a bad omen in every part of the world, and the craggy ravine had become a wasteland bereft of life.

That made it the perfect place for those who worked in the shadows to hide. The little hovel tucked beneath the cliff, cloaked by the mist, was one home to such lurkers.

"All right, Valga, explain to me what exactly is going on!" The demand echoed through the ravine. It was only *almost* shrill enough to shatter glass—but the tremendous anger in the voice would have made anyone hesitate to point that out.

"Not so loud," said another. "The fog outside may be an ill mist that absorbs sound, but at that volume there's no telling who might hear you." This voice was hoarse, quiet. Its owner had his hands over his ears, obviously annoyed. But the first voice would not be placated.

"I don't care how right you think you are! I don't care! If you want to criticize me, first you'd better explain what exactly you think you're doing!"

"Explain? Why should I explain anything? Have I done something wrong? Well, Libre? You haven't done anything—so who are you to speak to me like that?!"

"Don't push it, whelp! You're awfully impertinent for one so young!"

Their anger had reached the boiling point. The two large participants in this argument were practically forehead to forehead, shouting. They seemed nearly ready to murder each other. An explosion appeared inevitable. But then…

"Both of you are so noisy. I need a quiet environment to conduct my experiments. And I've brought you both to my safe house primarily to help me with those same experiments."

The dispassionate voice sounded like it belonged to a young girl—her words were chiding, but there was no emotion to speak of in her tone. Yet the other two ceased their argument immediately.

"I suppose we won't solve anything with our fists. Very well, I'll let the boy off. But you understand, there's more to be said on this matter." The speaker snorted. He was so tall his head nearly reached the ceiling. His preternaturally skinny body was covered in a robe, and his yellow eyes flashed weirdly. The patches of visible skin on his limbs and head were green and covered in scales, and a long, thick reptilian tail dragged along on the floor behind him. Combined with his long tongue, it left no doubt that he was a demi-human.

He was known by the name Libre Fermi, and he was one of the mainstays of the Demi-human Alliance.

"Valga, explain. The magic circles at Castour, and your little game with those corpses."

"Just look at what it gained us. Must you question every last thing, you tiresome snake?"

The crude response to Libre's question came from an old giant of a man trying to squeeze into a chair that was much too small for him. Standing, he probably would have been close to six and a half feet tall.

The giants were a race of demi-humans who, apart from their size, looked basically human. This man was one of the small handful still alive, and was in fact the youngest among them. Even so, he had contributed a great deal to the Demi-human Alliance, perhaps more than anyone else. It was he who had organized the demi-humans, turned them from an aimless mob into a coalition that could oppose the kingdom. His name was Valga Cromwell.

"What complaint could you possibly have about that outcome? Wait, let me guess—you think we didn't end up with enough human corpses for all the work that went into it. I agree—I wanted to kill more of them!"

"Don't throw your little tantrums here! I'm saying we killed too many of them! This war has already dragged on for so many years. But how do you expect the humans to even consider coming to terms after losses like that? You'll doom us all!"

Valga's chair clattered as he stood up. "*I'll* doom us? Libre, this is a fight to extinction and always has been! I have no intention of leaving even a single human alive. I'll pull that rotten, immoral filth up by the roots. And when they're all dead, I'll burn the bodies!"

"Can you stop being childish for one minute?! There are more of them than there are of us! Think about it. Even if every plan of yours works from now on, even if we inflict ten times as many losses on them as they do on us at every battle—we'll still be destroyed first. That's the way this fight is!"

"So, what? I should swallow my pride and give in? Here's a question for *you* to think about: Can you hear them? Can you hear the wails of all our comrades who have been trodden underfoot? The cries of all our friends who have been struck down? I can hear them. *Answer us*, they say to me. That is the pride of a demi-human!"

"And that pride will be the death of us all! Ooh, I could just swallow you whole, you impertinent brat! Go have your glorious suicide and leave the rest of us out of it!"

"Both of you." The cold voice came again, along with an earsplitting roar and a beam of bright light that lanced between the enraged pair, an inch from their noses as they glared daggers at each other. The light cut through the air in a way that was distinctly threatening. "I have asked you for quiet. If you refuse to accept this second warning, the third will be accompanied by a display of my power. I will happily add you both to my collection of undead warriors."

The girl wore a white robe and had long pink hair—she was the witch Sphinx.

She held up a finger and asked them with a probing look, "Which will it be? I don't mind either way. You both require observation."

"I don't like arguing with this whelp enough to become a corpse over it," Libre muttered.

"Took the words right out of my mouth," Valga growled.

This time they both tried to keep their distance from each other. Seeing the two of them thus subdued, Sphinx dropped her hand with a murmur of "Ah." In a normal voice, she continued, "To your point, I believe my undead warriors can redress the disparity in our numbers."

"That's right," Valga said. "That's why the zombies are here, and that's why Sphinx is here. I'm more worried about cowards like this snake. You think the zombies are some game? I assume this answers your complaints."

"Hardly. It's against all logic. Do you feel no shame at all putting the bodies of the dead to your own uses? I don't expect sanity from a witch, but you're different." Libre's long forked tongue slid out of his mouth. Arms crossed, he glared at Sphinx.

Valga only snorted. "I disgrace the corpses of immoral filth. Why should I feel shame? The spirits of our dead allies beg it of me. And as you say, we are the weaker race. We have to rely on our wits. There's no law that says the weak always have to lose."

"I will act as I see fit," Libre said, heading for the door of the hut. Framed in the doorway, he turned, his yellow eyes narrowing at Valga. "But I say this to you, Valga. If you continue down this path, one day it will lead you to hell."

"One day?" Valga said. "This world is already hell."

Instead of saying good-bye, Libre merely sighed.

The reptilian demi-human left, and the tension went out of Valga's shoulders. Suddenly Sphinx said, "If he is going to be a problem in the future, shall I eliminate him?"

"We shouldn't do it if it's not necessary. Libre may not think the same way I do, but the alliance needs him. The alliance looks to me as its leader, but the only way I can help anyone is with my brain. To lead the charge into the enemy ranks, cut them to pieces, and raise our troops' morale to the utmost—for that, we need a hero like him."

"A difficult thing. This requires careful consideration." Sphinx paused, then said, "And what will you do next? More magic circles like the ones you used at Castour?"

Any animosity she may have felt toward Libre seemed to vanish, replaced by interest in the site of the next experiment. Ignoring the abrupt change in subject, Valga unrolled a map with his beefy hands.

"That might work if we could do it before word of the defeat at Castour spreads among the humans, but the alliance isn't well organized enough to move that quickly. The longer we wait until the next battle, the more likely they'll be to have developed countermeasures. I doubt the magic entrapment strategy will work again."

"What, then?"

"Obviously. We let them destroy a magic circle," Valga said with an evil, blood-red smile.

Sphinx had no visible reaction to this. But she glanced at the ground and murmured, "This will require observation," so quietly that no one could hear.

4

Time passed in the blink of an eye.

Frantic activity blunted their awareness of the passing days, and the Sword Devil, Wilhelm, was no exception.

Just as Roswaal had told them after the assembly, he and the rest of Zergev Squadron were thrown again and again into the most brutal battles the royal army faced. During this time, the kingdom's forces and the Demi-human Alliance traded successes—the royal army would triumph on a huge scale, only for the demi-humans to destroy their battle lines and take a strategic victory. On and on it went. The three people who formed the core of the Demi-human Alliance continually evaded the royal forces, and so there could be no conclusion.

Before they knew it, Wilhelm and Grimm had been in the royal army—and in Zergev Squadron—for one year. Then two.

Zergev Squadron, too, looked different now than it had when those first twenty had joined. Only about half of the original members remained, but for each one who died, several new ones came aboard, until the unit had expanded fully to one hundred members. It made them even more of a force on the battlefield than they had been before.

It mystified Wilhelm that through all these changes, Grimm somehow remained with the squadron. When they had met two years earlier, Wilhelm had been confident that he would soon see no more of Grimm, but somehow he, too, was one of the old hands of their crew, well regarded for his martial valor.

He was still all but hopeless with the sword, but even Wilhelm had to acknowledge his skill with the shield, as well as his ability to detect danger. The only people in the squadron with the reflexes to defend against one of Wilhelm's attacks were Grimm and Bordeaux.

Grimm was also still trying to get Wilhelm to notice him, and as he persevered despite the withering remarks of the Sword Devil, some whispered that perhaps Grimm was the bravest person in the squadron.

"Well, weeell. I hear you contiiinued to gild your legend today."

"…Keep away from me."

"Such a very chiiilly reception. Can't you at least pretend to be happy when a beautiful woman wants to get close to you?"

Ever since their excursion to Castour Field, the squadron had not been short on opportunities to see Roswaal. Since it was impossible to say when the demi-humans might attempt another magical strategy, it was only natural that she should be present at each battle. So it was equally natural that she frequently encountered Zergev Squadron, which was so often on the front lines.

"Lady Mathers, what a way to act. And *you*, aren't you ashamed of yourself?"

"N-now, now, Carol. That's just the way Wilhelm is. You can scold him all you like; he won't change."

Just as often as they saw Roswaal, they saw her bodyguard, Carol, glaring at them. At moments like this, Grimm was a lifesaver; he would appear out of nowhere to occupy Carol in conversation. Wilhelm would make sure the two of them were safely chatting, then lose himself once more in his own world.

"That Wilhelm ain't changed a bit, has he?" Bordeaux said. "Then again, that's one of his strengths!"

"Every time we go somewhere new," Pivot replied, "I hear fresh rumors of the Sword Devil, and I swear it shortens my life. If I die young, I'm going to assume it's his fault."

Bordeaux and Pivot also continued observing and considering Wilhelm from a distance, just as they had before. There was, perhaps, one difference—Bordeaux's halberd could no longer reach Wilhelm. The young swordsman remembered more clearly than he wanted to the day the difference in their abilities became unmistakable. Bordeaux had wept and laughed in equal measure, sounds that still seemed to echo in Wilhelm's memory.

He could hardly believe that was three years ago already. Three years, and now Wilhelm was turning eighteen. Three years full of things and places and people that remained in his memory.

He wouldn't realize until later how precious that time had been.

5

In the morning quiet, Wilhelm opened his eyes. He lay on his bed in his personal room at the barracks.

Normally, an ordinary soldier like him would have no right to individual accommodations. But he was an exception; this was one of the liberties afforded him by the kingdom in light of his astonishing record in battle. It had also been something of a desperate measure; the Sword Devil was not especially interested in awards or honors, leaving the kingdom at something of a loss as to how to compensate him.

"—"

Wilhelm yawned once, then washed his face with cold water. Chasing away the last vestiges of sleep, he quickly changed into his uniform. It wasn't until he had everything on that he realized today was a day off for him. He didn't need to put on his uniform.

"...Overworking, my ass."

This "day off" was something Bordeaux and Pivot had forced upon him. He rarely took his ordinary days off, preferring to continue his training—and then, of course, there were the days they were in battle. The commanders had alleged that when the Sword Devil, one of the longest-standing members of the squadron, refused to rest, no one else could take a break, either.

With a sigh of annoyance, Wilhelm left his room still in his uniform. It would be too much trouble to change back.

He thought about heading to the training ground, then realized he couldn't. The whole point of this day off had been to keep him away from there. But even if he stayed in his room, it was no guarantee that the increasingly bothersome Grimm wouldn't come and find him.

So Wilhelm left the barracks, a morning chill still in the air as he headed for the castle town. He returned the guards' salutes with a curt nod, then walked alone into the capital, where signs of human habitation had grown sparse.

The capital had gradually grown less bustling over the past three years. That suited Wilhelm well enough, but it was a sign that the civil war was becoming more of a bog every day. Battles were occurring in more places, and the effects of the kingdom's losses were being felt more widely. Lugunica was entering a dark time.

The dragon that might have been expected to take their part in the case of an epidemic or an invasion by another country had apparently decided this was a problem for Lugunica to deal with by itself and refused to lend an ear to the entreaties of the nation's rulers.

As the war dragged on with no sign of improving fortunes, the people grew more and more fatigued.

The area Wilhelm had come to was one of those affected by the civil war. As he left the peasant town in the middle district of the capital, he could see abandoned development projects. Supposedly, work would be resumed when the war was over, but that only meant no one knew when.

Now the area was home to jobless drifters and unemployed day laborers; even Wilhelm understood that it was a slum. That was exactly why it called to him when he was alone.

"Get lost," he said to a group that had set themselves up in one of the abandoned buildings. They looked like trouble, but they clearly recognized that Wilhelm would be even more trouble and made themselves scarce. Wilhelm snorted, then headed for the plaza he normally used.

This public square in the farthest reaches of the poor district was large and quiet enough to be perfect for his personal training. Everyone at the military training ground was so far behind him that these days he preferred to use this place almost exclusively.

Wilhelm had never needed others for his practice. He found the idea of crossing swords with the same opponent over and over practically disgraceful in the face of a real battle, where any fight would be settled once and once only.

Therefore, for Wilhelm, training with the sword was a battle against himself. This was not code for self-denial but a literal fight to the death with his own self. It was in this kind of training that the Sword Devil, Wilhelm, was most at peace.

"Oh, I'm sorry."

Someone addressed him suddenly as he passed the abandoned works and arrived at the square. This was supposed to be the time when he was settling into his own world, losing himself in the sword—to have an alien presence there disrupted the process. Wilhelm clicked his tongue with regret and turned in annoyance to the source of the voice.

It was a girl with long red hair, her profile beautiful enough to send shivers down his spine.

Her hair looked like licking flames, and her eyes were the blue of a clear sky. Her neat features gave her sweetness and grace; Wilhelm doubted if she were even human.

But an instant later, she was only a village girl with a noticeable but not stunning beauty.

She sat in some abandoned building project in one corner of the plaza, looking at him.

"I didn't realize anyone else came here so early in the day," she said with a smile.

"—"

Wilhelm's response was simple—he immediately turned the full force of his warrior's glare on her. It was the same thing he had done to drive off the drifters earlier. It would send an amateur running for the hills and was enough to give even an experienced opponent pause.

But it was the wrong move against this girl.

"What's wrong...? You're making such a scary face," she asked, as if all the force of his spirit were nothing more than a passing breeze.

Wilhelm realized his attempt to drive the girl away hadn't worked, and he looked away awkwardly. If his display of spirit as a soldier didn't affect her, that meant she was entirely unfamiliar with the arts of war, such that she didn't even sense what he was doing.

For those who never lived in the world of violence, Wilhelm's behavior would seem like nothing more than intimidation. Some might even take it for a simple dirty look. This girl, it seemed, was one such person.

"What's a girl doing in a place like this so early in the morning, anyway?" Wilhelm asked.

By this, he meant her to understand that she was in his way, but she only replied "Hmm," and gave a great stretch. "I'd sort of like to ask you the same question, but maybe it wouldn't be very polite. You don't look like you're much for jokes."

"There's a lot of dangerous people around here. It's not somewhere a woman should be walking alone."

"Goodness, are you worried about me?"

"I might be one of those dangerous people."

"You're not. I know that uniform—you're one of the castle soldiers, aren't you? You wouldn't do anything wrong."

This was what he got for thoughtlessly putting on his uniform and then not bothering to change again before he went out. His usual approach wasn't working. Seeing that he was disoriented, the girl giggled.

"To be honest, I am a little surprised. I thought this was my private place. It's nice, isn't it? It's a bit of a walk, but you can be alone."

"Until someone shows up and intrudes on you."

"I guess we're both intruding on each other, so it's all right. Sneaking off duty, Mr. Bad Soldier?"

"I'm sure not," Wilhelm said.

"Of course you're not. I'll keep your secret," the girl said, ignoring his excuse. "Oh, that's right." She pointed to something across from where she was sitting in the abandoned building. "Look here."

Wilhelm frowned, unable to see anything from where he was. This caused the girl to smile and beckon to him with a gesture like a small animal.

"I'm not that eager to see it," he growled.

"Now, now, just come over here."

Wilhelm grimaced at her tone—she sounded like she was talking to a child—but he duly went over to her. He came up onto the steps of the abandoned building and looked where she was pointing.

He caught his breath. A field of yellow flowers spread out before him, lit by the blaze of the morning sun.

She spoke to the speechless Wilhelm as if she were confessing a secret. "They stopped working here, right? I didn't think anyone else would come, so I planted some seeds. I came back today to see how they were coming along."

It was not appreciation for beautiful flowers that caused the unexpected sights to strike Wilhelm dumb. He simply couldn't believe his own obliviousness. He had been here so many times, yet he had completely failed to notice this unique feature. It was a world he could have noticed, if he had only stretched out, widened his perspective a little bit...

"Do you like flowers?" the girl asked the still-silent Wilhelm.

He turned to consider her gentle smile, saying...

"No. I can't stand them."

And he watched as the happiness drained from her face entirely.

6

"Looks like you're keeping busy on your days off, Wilhelm. You're never in your room when I stop by. Off killing people somewhere?"

"I'm not busy... And I'm not killing people, either."

"Sure. You look unhappy enough about it that I think you're telling the truth. Sounds like you're having some nice, quiet days off," Grimm quipped easily, dressed in his soldier's uniform as he climbed out of the dragon carriage. Wilhelm turned up his nose in an attempt to make his annoyance apparent, but Grimm hardly noticed, still all smiles. Somehow that irritated Wilhelm even more.

The ranks of Zergev Squadron had grown, but Wilhelm was treated with just as much awe as ever. Bordeaux and Grimm had known him for so long now, though, that these episodes of personal chatter were growing more frequent.

Remaining studiously silent, Wilhelm thought about the "days off" that Grimm had mentioned. It had been several weeks since Bordeaux and Pivot had foisted a vacation on him and he had first met the girl. He still didn't know her name—he thought of her as Flower Girl—but they had run into each other several more times since then.

Wilhelm was surprised to find that, although he didn't go to the plaza on any kind of regular schedule, whenever he did go there, Flower Girl would be sitting in front of her flowers as if it were the most natural thing in the world. She would continue to sit there, watching idly as Wilhelm practiced his sword. It was frustrating to have her staring at him, but far better than if she were to chase him away.

When she had first asked him what he thought of her flower garden, and he had given her a cruel reply, she had driven him away with enough anger to rival a storm. Even now, Wilhelm couldn't believe he had lost that encounter.

But there was something else he found even more perplexing. Every time, when he was finished with his practice, she would smilingly ask him, "Do you like flowers?"

She knew the answer wouldn't change, yet she asked him every time.

"No. I can't stand them," he would reply with a look of utter distaste. It had practically become a ritual.

"All right, we're heading south! That's where the battle is most intense right now! Libre Fermi and Valga Cromwell are both there. It's the perfect opportunity for us to make major gains!"

This enthusiastic shouting brought him back from his thoughts.

Up front stood Bordeaux, battle-ax raised, drumming up the morale of his troops just like a real commander. As the size of his unit increased, he had become less and less able to do things by the seat of his pants the way he used to, but it also revealed in him an unexpected talent for leadership. Zergev Squadron had only become more and more effective in battle.

Then again, more success meant more anxiety for Vice Commander Pivot. "However, our role today is not to assault the main enemy encampment. We'll be a floating unit—keeping an eye on the situation and moving in to help where necessary. Be careful not to get too excited and end up acting alone somewhere."

The field of battle this time was to be Aihiya Swamp in the south of Lugunica. The civil war had gripped the entire kingdom, but demi-human resistance was said to be strongest in the south. Reports were that the leading figures of the Demi-human Alliance had gone there to support the resistance effort, and so the kingdom's forces conceived a large-scale strategy, of which Zergev Squadron was to be a part.

"We've got a huge attacking force," Grimm said. "Maybe we can finally end this war..."

"Always the optimist, aren't you?" Wilhelm said dismissively. "I think committing a major force when we know the enemy leaders are there is begging for trouble."

Grimm looked somewhat annoyed, but he soon grasped what Wilhelm was saying. He scratched the back of his own head.

"You're...thinking of Castour Field?"

"Valga Cromwell was there that day, too. And given the presence of the magic circles, I would assume the witch was as well. They're waiting for us, and we're going to throw more men at them here then we did at Castour. What do you think's going to happen?"

Grimm swallowed, and he thought it sounded very loud. None of the soldiers around them seemed the least bit anxious as they awaited the order to move out. Maybe they were right to keep up their confidence, their lust for battle.

But if they died in vain, it would be...well, meaningless.

"I have to assume our commanders have at least thought of that possibility," Wilhelm said.

"Wha...?"

"I should certainly thiiink so. Your face just now, Grimm, it was a maaasterpiece."

A familiar female voice answered Grimm's dumb half question. The two men turned and saw Roswaal, a woman whose breezy disposition never changed, even on the battlefield. She flung back the cape she wore over her military uniform and stretched as if to show off her shapely chest.

"The VIPs are just as confident as you that Sphinx is likely to be operating here. We've taken as many of theirs with the sword as they have ours with magic. We think they'll have to reach their limit sooner or later."

"Y-you always seem so calm, Lady Mathers," Grimm said.

"Oh, you're making me blush. And if I'm here, that meeeans your little princess is, too."

She gave him a meaningful smile. Roswaal's bodyguard, Carol, came walking up behind her. As ever, she was wearing knight's armor and a sword at her hip, neither of which flattered her as a woman. Her golden hair had only grown a little over the last three years. But there were some noticeable changes in her and in the smiling Grimm.

"Grimm," Carol said, "I'm glad I got a chance to talk to you before the battle starts. I was worried that Lady Roswaal might be threatened if the fighting got too intense..."

"I—I'm glad, too!" Grimm replied. "With you behind me, uh—right! I know I won't have to worry about the enemy getting at my back!"

"I'm stronger than you, you know. I don't take kindly to people who look down on me..."

"I—I—I—I d-d-didn't mean to—!"

"I'm kidding. I'm glad that you're glad."

Grimm and Carol gradually became lost in their own world, completely ignoring the other two. When she tired of watching them, Roswaal jabbed Wilhelm with her elbow.

"How do you feel? Hooow do you feel right now? Your friend getting all cozy with a girl, a love forged in the heat of battle..."

"I think it's stupid. And don't act like he and I are so close. I don't need friends."

"I see. Whaaat a very lonely thought. Interested in flirting with me, then?"

"I'll cut you in half."

Practically before Wilhelm was finished speaking, Roswaal had taken a big step back to a safe distance.

They were waiting to go into battle, but he couldn't even get everyone to leave him alone long enough for him to concentrate and prepare. He didn't even manage a sigh when Carol gave Grimm some kind of protective charm.

"Regardless, let us worry about Sphinx," Roswaal said. "You just have fun chopping up every bad guy you can see."

"That's my plan. Try not to screw up your part."

"Aww, are you wooorried about me?"

"I'm worried about you getting in my way."

Roswaal looked like she might pout at the chilly reply, but Wilhelm rattled the scabbard of his sword and sent her scurrying back.

At a pause in the conversation, a voice called, "Is Lady Mathers here? The commander wants to speak with her."

"C-Commander! The, uh, the lady is over there, sir."

The wall of soldiers parted, and Bordeaux's hulking form could be seen. Grimm quickly broke off whatever he was saying to Carol and pointed at Roswaal, who waved affably. Bordeaux nodded.

"Lord Lyp, sir!" the captain exclaimed. "Lady Mathers is over here! If you'll come this way, sir!"

A gloomy-sounding man replied, "...You don't have to shout, I can hear you. If you insist on saying everything at the top of your lungs, people are going to think you don't have any other talents." He made his way over—Bordeaux was hard to miss. The newcomer was a knight of around thirty years old, though he looked haggard.

The knight stood before Roswaal and offered a flowing bow. "Lyp Bariel, at your service. Viscount of the south and commander of the battle line on this occasion."

"Oh? From what I'd heard, Lord Crumère was going to command."

"Lord Crumère was hit by a stray arrow in a recent battle. The wound festered, and he died. I apologize that we weren't able to notify you sooner. I am commander now by virtue of my rank and my military achievements."

His voice was even, and there was no change in his expression. Yet something in his voice indicated there was more below the surface.

Lyp Bariel was his superior's superior, but Wilhelm didn't like the feeling he got from him. Wilhelm looked away from Lyp and toward the enemy lines.

"You there, soldier, straighten up."

"…Who, me?" Wilhelm asked.

"I won't say it again." Lyp walked up to Wilhelm and began shaking his fist in his face. The instant he made the gesture, Wilhelm began to reach for his sword—but stopped.

At the same moment, he felt an impact on his cheek; his upper body turned with the force.

"It is your duty to be at attention and *paying* attention when your commander is present—to say nothing of a general. Maybe all the accolades this unit has received have gone to your head, but you won't get any special treatment from me. I don't care if you're the Sword Devil himself."

"—"

"You've got a rebellious look in your eye, boy. Maybe I'd better impose a little discipline before this battle starts."

Wilhelm spat out the blood that had pooled in his mouth and glared at Lyp, who only smiled sadistically.

That meant more corporal punishment, and as the highest-ranking person there, no one could stop him.

"Don't you think thaaat's about enough? This is no time to be plaaaying with children."

No one except Roswaal J. Mathers, who stood outside the system of military ranks and rules.

Roswaal smiled at Lyp, gently pushing down his fist, which he had raised to strike again. Lyp gave a quiet snort, turning away from Wilhelm.

"Bordeaux, teach your men a little respect, or I might have to take their impertinence out on you. The southern front isn't a playground for children."

"…Yes, sir. My apologies, sir."

"Lady Mathers! I wish to consult with you before the battle starts. If you'd come with me?"

After he had reprimanded Bordeaux, Lyp seemed to lose interest in the unit. Roswaal responded to his summons with an obedient "Coming." Carol kept shooting worried glances over her shoulder as they left.

As Lyp vanished from view, the soldiers relaxed.

"A-are you all right, Wilhelm?" Grimm asked, coming over and examining Wilhelm's cheek where he'd been struck.

"It's not a big deal. He just hit me. Don't look so worried."

"I'm not worried about him hitting you. I'm just surprised you didn't chop his head off when he did. Are you feeling okay? Maybe you ought to take today—yikes! I'm sorry!" Grimm's lighthearted tone changed quickly when he found Wilhelm's sword at his neck.

As Wilhelm sheathed his blade, Bordeaux nodded to him with a look of pity. "Sorry 'bout that, Wilhelm. You were just unlucky."

"Don't all crowd around. I keep telling you, it's not a big deal." Wilhelm waved away his encroaching fellow soldiers with one hand while wiping vigorously with his sleeve at the bruise on his cheek.

"Are we sure this guy should be leading us?" Grimm said. "He's like a soldier's nightmare of a bad commander."

"Believe it or not, Lyp Bariel actually has a fair amount of military success to his name," Bordeaux said. "He may not be the easiest guy to get along with, but… Well, who doesn't want to follow a winner?"

Grimm looked doubtful about this, and Wilhelm decided his initial judgment of Lyp had been correct. The way the commander had moved when he struck Wilhelm—he was clearly a powerful man of war. He had the distinctive strength of someone who had trained himself thoroughly and supplemented this with repeated survival on the battlefield. He might just rival Bordeaux in a toe-to-toe fight. Grimm he would overwhelm, no question.

"There's no end of ugly rumors about him," Bordeaux was saying, "and he won't hesitate to fight dirty. But there's no question he's a capable commander. So much so that they gave him command of the first of the four armies formed by the recent reorganization. So relax! You're in good hands." Then he gave a great guffaw, back to his usual humor.

"R-right, sir," Grimm said, then muttered, "I better ask this charm Carol gave me for more luck…" He held the charm in his hand and murmured a prayer.

A glance showed that Carol had given him a pendant—a locket with something inside.

"A present from a girl, huh? Color me impressed, kid. What's in it?"

"Um, I gather Carol got it from whoever it is she serves. Inside is…a flower, I think? A pressed flower. It's so yellow and elegant, which kind of seems like it would suit her—"

Grimm waxed maudlin as he showed the locket to Bordeaux. As he did so, Wilhelm was startled when he caught a glimpse of the flower inside.

It was, without a doubt, the same kind of yellow blossom as those attended by the girl in the poor district.

"We're about to go into combat, here. What is *wrong* with everyone…?"

His concentration was ruined. Were they specifically trying to throw him off? He pushed down his explosive rage and tried once more to collect himself, when—

"Zergev Squadron, form up. We're going to meet with the other squadrons to discuss positioning, so… Is something wrong, Wilhelm?"

"Nothing at all!"

—to top it all off, Pivot showed up, forcing him to postpone his meditations once again.

"Damn it all," he muttered. "If this goes wrong, don't blame me…!"

Swept up in the flow of soldiers marching out, Wilhelm looked up at the sky with distaste. Night was ending; dawn would soon arrive. The operation would begin first thing in the morning, hardly a few hours from now. Wilhelm always strove to become one with his sword and not let unnecessary things interfere. But now he was walking into the jaws of combat without his focus.

Many destinies would be decided at Aihiya Swamp. The battle loomed over them all as they marched.

THE LOVE SONG OF THE SWORD DEVIL

Fourth Stanza

1

Aihiya Swamp, which occupied a large area along Lugunica's southern frontier and formed part of its border with the Volakia Empire, was extremely dangerous territory. In the four years since the start of the civil conflict known as the Demi-human War, there had probably been no other battle on the scale of Aihiya, nor any other time when tensions had been so high.

"We're already constantly fighting skirmishes with the Volakians. Massing this many troops on their border... I hate to think what the Empire might do if it gets skittish."

Distant war cries echoed through the air, and the rumble of stomping feet reached them. The knights had the battlefield under their very boots, but they were tormented by impatience. The clash between the royal army and the Demi-human Alliance had already begun, but they had been ordered to hold their position.

"Being the rearguard sounds glorious, but it's a short straw to draw."

"Take care of who hears you say that, Razaac, sir," one of his subordinates cautioned. The knight who had complained nodded calmly.

He had previously been charged with teaching the new recruits, but as the war worsened, he had been returned to the front. As he became more renowned and more skilled with the sword, he had been given command of a squadron, but with greater responsibility came greater restrictions on his actions, and he found it boring at times.

Especially now as he turned away from the raging battle and glared in the direction of the Empire.

For the battle at Aihiya, the royal forces had been split into four armies. Three of them would engage the demi-humans, while the remaining group would continue the staring contest with the Volakian troops across the border.

"...You don't suppose they'll do anything, do you?"

"I doubt it. If they took advantage of the demi-humans' actions to attack us, they would invoke the wrath of the Holy Dragon Volcanica. As long as our nation is under the protection of the Dragon, the Empire won't move against us."

"Then why are we standing here just looking at them?" Razaac sighed deeply. "Short straw."

It was awful to wait, motionless, as his comrades died on the battlefield. Razaac was a knight's knight, a man whose friends and country meant everything to him—all the more reason being here hurt his heart and niggled at his pride.

"My comrades...come home alive, if you can. If not, then at least make the final sacrifice with honor. Don't be defeated by shameless foes who have forgotten what they owe to this kingdom, like the demi-humans."

Razaac's barely repressed pain could be seen on his face. His subordinate nodded at him, sympathy in his eyes. Razaac was a knight's knight. Like so many of the soldiers of Lugunica, he clung to a frank contempt of the demi-humans that clashed with his otherwise high principles.

This was why almost no one, including Razaac, had noticed.

This subconscious prejudice was the greatest reason the demi-humans could never surrender.

2

His attack sliced off his enemy's hand, cleaving the bone neatly. As he brought his blade back, he cut off the screaming man's head. He turned, the gushing blood splattering onto his back, and buried his steel in the face of a lizard who had tried to get behind him. Brains spattered everywhere. The corpse's eyes rolled up in its head; he kicked the body off the end of his sword.

"Riiiyaaahhh!"

Beside Wilhelm, a demi-human fell to the ground, knocked back by an impact. The source was Grimm, holding up his shield. He had used it both to block and then answer the enemy's attack. His defensive abilities were unparalleled. He had perfected them just behind the vanguard, making the ideal complement to Wilhelm's talent as the vanguard itself.

But there was no time to admire him. Wilhelm stabbed the demi-human in the heart.

Grimm jogged up to him. "Wilhelm! Are you okay?"

"See for yourself."

"I thought so. I was just asking. I think we're about done here. The captain is—"

He glanced back. An enemy soldier's limbs were hurtling through the air, the result of a brutal blow from an ax. A halberd so terrible must belong to Bordeaux. A war cry like the howl of a wild animal echoed around the area.

"This is over," Bordeaux shouted. "Let's link back up! Go on to the next battlefield."

"I hope they put up more of a fight at the next one," Wilhelm said.

"Not me," Grimm said. "I don't want to die. I want to get back alive." His hand searched at his neckline, finding the locket. Ignoring the gesture, Wilhelm looked at Grimm in perplexity. No matter how many battles they survived, he never changed. He claimed he didn't want to die, yet he would rush headlong into the fight. He said he wanted to get back alive, yet he could deflect the murderous enemy with his shield and then beat them to death.

He's a paradox.

"So are you fighting because you want to die?" Grimm asked.

"—"

"I don't think you are," Grimm went on. "You don't strike me as the type to have a death wish. But I don't think you're in it for the killing, either. If anything, I think you want to live more than anyone else here."

Grimm appeared to have seen directly into Wilhelm's innermost thoughts. And that irritated him. Wilhelm clicked his tongue and started walking faster. Fast enough, he hoped, to leave behind the young man scrambling to follow him.

Bordeaux saw them as they were coming back and exclaimed, "Well, if it isn't Captain Killer and his friend the Watch Dog! How's the enemy, Wilhelm?"

Wilhelm pointed his blood-drenched sword in the direction of the battlefield and said, "Not so tough. We should make for the center. We can trim all the leaves and branches we want, it won't make any difference. We have to pull this problem up by the roots."

"How about you, Grimm?" Pivot asked. "No bad feelings?"

"No, sir, nothing. I'm not a fan of intense fighting, but I agree we should keep moving."

This recommendation was enough for Bordeaux. He hefted his battle-ax and nodded. "Right, let's do it, then! I was getting tired of all these small fry. In battle, just like in the hunt, the true warrior goes after the big game! Come on, Zergev Squadron, follow me!"

"Wait, young sir! Shouldn't we consult the general for his instructions? Lady Mathers is with him, I believe."

"Don't be stupid, Pivot. If we go back, Viscount Bariel is only going to use us like the tools he thinks we are. We cut our way in there and let our success in battle speak for itself! That's the ultimate comeuppance, Bordeaux-style!" He held up his battle-ax for emphasis.

"Comeuppance, is it? How very like you, young sir. But I can hardly…"

Pivot went quiet, a troubled expression on his slim face. Bordeaux laughed good-naturedly to see his second-in-command in such a state. "Just do what you've always done, Pivot, and follow me! Hell, what've you got to lose? Anyway, don't forget our beloved general made a fool of Wilhelm before the battle. We've got to return the favor, don't we?"

Wilhelm scowled at this. "Hold on. Don't drag me into this. I told you not to make a big deal about it. And if he's going to get paid back, I want to be the one to do it. Myself."

"And because we can't let you go by yourself, the whole squad's coming with you." Grimm met Wilhelm's grimace with a shrug.

The resigned gesture made Bordeaux and Pivot laugh with merriment and acquiescence, respectively.

"Grimm's learned how to handle himself, huh? What do you think, Pivot? Still worried?"

"...I give. You are here, young sir, and Wilhelm is here, and Grimm. This is Zergev Squadron. I am with you."

"Don't forget, Pivot, you're here, too," Bordeaux said. "All right, men, now we go for real!" He lifted his halberd to the sky. Everyone else in the unit raised their weapons as well and cheered. The squadron set out, the giant man at their head. Wilhelm let out a breath as the only one who didn't feel the same spirit.

"I get dragged into one thing after another," he muttered.

He wanted to be steel. He wanted to be a perfect blade, free of impurities. But this wish was continually undermined by the distractions and frustrations that seemed to flock to him daily. Ruminating angrily, Wilhelm tried to work his way to the front of the ranks.

That was when he noticed it: a red flower bobbing inconspicuously in one corner of the battlefield. Flowers bloomed even in war.

"Don't be stupid!" he said to himself.

He couldn't imagine why he was suddenly picturing the field by the square.

3

The Battle of Aihiya Swamp. Lyp Bariel, viscount of the south, was in charge.

"Magic circles have been discovered in two more locations on the north side of the swamp, sir! That makes eight spots total!"

"Mark them on the map. Carefully, be precise."

The breathless messenger drew two red marks on the map on the wall. The map, depicting Aihiya Swamp, already bore nearly forty others like it.

In the roughly six hours since the battle had begun, reports of magic circles had flooded in from the battlefield. The royal forces had been prioritizing magic circle countermeasures since the loss at Castour Field, with the result that the demi-humans had never duplicated their success with magic circle traps since that battle.

"Admittedly, this number is unusual," Lyp said, glaring at the map.

"Maybe another ensnarement really was their plan," a subordinate offered.

"Now? When our countermeasures are so widespread? I would be just as happy if the enemy's renowned strategists turned out to be so lump-headed. But I doubt they are, and I doubt they'll do the same thing twice."

"They are just demi-humans, sir. They're half beast."

Lyp stopped in his tracks, fixing the man with a cold stare. "And so what? Is that a reason to underestimate our enemy? If you think overcoming a beast is so easy, go catch me a white whale or two right now!"

"Er, ah…"

"Idiots should keep their mouths shut. If you've forgotten how to use your mind, there's no reason to have you here at headquarters. Maybe you'd prefer the front lines?"

"M-my apologies, sir! I've overstepped myself!"

The man shuffled out of the tent, hanging his head. Lyp snorted and turned back to the map. Someone came up beside him—a woman with indigo-colored hair and wearing a military uniform. Roswaal.

"Your tongue is always so sharp," she said. "I'm suuure he was just offering a thought."

"Are you saying good intentions deserve a reward? Ridiculous. All things are rewarded according to their outcomes. If a hasty act sullies your reputation, some of what you have is taken away from you. Do you have a problem with that?"

"Nooo, not especially. I don't love incompetents myseeelf." She shook her head.

Lyp gave a vaguely satisfied cough. "Very wise," he said. "I want the opinion of an expert. What do you think of this arrangement of magic circles?"

"It's rather unuuusual. Not only the number but also the place-ment. Following the logic of this arrangement, I expect there are other circles here and here, as well as this area."

"I thought as much. Anyone could have guessed that. What do they think this trap will gain them?"

"We have to destroy the circles, regardless. They give me a bad feeling... There's something I'd like to check. Would you allow me to examine one of the projected sites?"

"You have that woman knight to look out for you, don't you? I'll assign ten men to the two of you. Avoid any active battle locations."

She had permission now to go to the blank—the expected place of the magic circles—closest to headquarters. Roswaal offered an elegant bow to Lyp, who hardly even bothered to glance up as she left the tent. Carol met her outside with concern written on her face. Roswaal smiled at her.

"I want to have a look at something. We'll be on the fringes of the battle, so I'm counting on you to keep me safe."

"I understand. But I see you plan on personally going somewhere dangerous again."

"Nooothing so dangerous as where your little boyfriend is. Com-pared to the front, we'll be teeerribly safe."

"G-Grimm is not my boyfriend!"

"I don't recall mentioning his naaame."

Carol's serious face turned red at having given away how she felt. This evoked a smile from Roswaal. Then she turned her one yellow eye to the battlefield, full of rumbling and smoke.

"I know you're there, Sphinx. What are you planning?"

4

Zergev Squadron worked in concert, slicing their way toward the center of the battlefield. Every demi-human who stood in their way was cut down. Between the whipping ax strikes and the expertly wielded shield, the enemy had almost no chance to hit back, but one person stood out even in this distinguished company. That was the swordsman—no, the Sword Devil—whose blade was like a whirlwind.

Flashes of silver sent hands and feet flying, and thrusts found throat and heart; every move was ruthless, and every blow fatal. He shredded his enemies when they approached from the side; when they tried to keep their distance, he would close the space in the blink of an eye and skewer them. One demi-human after another met their end, swallowed up by the maelstrom of this swordsman's spirit.

"Wh-what in the world is that? How are we supposed to fight it?"

They would shrink away, having lost their appetite for battle. Before he approached, they could see his overwhelming power, and when they fought him, they were simply buried, gaining nothing. A young demi-human quivered at the scene, but he found a hand on his shoulder.

"You should withdraw. There is no purpose in challenging an opponent you can't defeat. Far be it from me to allow any to call such an action cowardice."

The owner of the voice, this person who would show kindness to terrified soldiers, stepped forward. He was so tall most of them had to crane their necks to see his face. He was covered in scales and had a head like a snake's. In his hand was a double sword—a central grip with a blade on either side.

"You there, swordsman," the snake called in a cracking falsetto, "stop where you are! You seem to be quite capable. Allow me to oppose you personally!"

The whirling form came to a stop. Wilhelm lowered his blood-soaked weapon, his breath coming hard. The utter force of his aura struck his enemies as if he were already attacking them; his glare alone was enough to set the demi-humans trembling.

But the snake gave a snorting laugh and said, "You want to kill me. How charming. There's something to you, boy. I'll be happy to be your playmate!" Then the serpent leaped at Wilhelm, his two-bladed sword at the ready. Wilhelm rushed in as well, and the distance between them closed in an instant.

A dodge, a sideways swipe. A lightning-fast attack sought its enemy's head, but a rising blade met it from below. With a screech and a shower of sparks, the deflected blade returned for another strike...

"Ah-ha!" the lizard exclaimed. "So you can't match my speed!"

"Hrrr!"

Wilhelm bent his head back, the twin blade passing right in front of it. It had come up at his chin, and the quick follow-up attack had pressed him hard. There was only one enemy, but two weapons; its moves were simultaneously offensive and defensive.

As they exchanged close strikes and near misses, someone shouted, "It's Libre Fermi! The Viper! One of the pillars of the Demi-human Alliance!"

Now everyone knew who the opponent was. The demi-human— Libre—only smiled wider, his long tongue emerging conspicuously from his mouth.

"Pillar? I don't know that I like that. People will think I'm as fat as one! I'm far too lithe for such a word!"

"Lithe? You? Maybe in my nightmares!"

"Oh, how cruel. Flippant children. I could eat you up...literally."

No sooner had he spoken than Libre's face took on a new cast. His pupils narrowed, and the hiss of a snake warning its foe came out of his mouth. The speed of his movements increased further.

"Wilhelm!"

In the storm of steel, everything happening too quickly to see, Wilhelm was fighting a defensive battle. He was finding himself cornered. Somebody had called his name. Grimm? Bordeaux? It didn't matter. It didn't matter, as long as they didn't do anything. This fight, this enemy, was his alone.

"Ha...ha-ha..."

"Are you...laughing?" Libre asked.

He couldn't hold it in any longer. "Ha-ha-ha! Ha-ha-ha-ha-ha!" It wouldn't stop. This was joy itself welling up in his heart. The emotion encouraged him, guided him into the flow of the next attack. This caused Libre to slow for an instant, and Wilhelm's sword came at him. The snake threw himself to one side, dodging the blow—and then he felt a kick.

"Hrr—gg!"

He bent nearly double with the unexpected strike, and a knee rose to catch his face as it came forward. He was bleeding. The sword arced toward his exposed Adam's apple, seeking to cut off his head.

"Gracious! You are skilled for one so impertinent and young!"

He brought his left arm in to block the blow. The scales resisted the steel for just an instant, and then his hand was severed at the wrist. But in that instant, Libre sank low to strike Wilhelm in the gut with his powerful arm. The boy's ribs cracked, and his internal organs compressed as he was thrown backward. The ground dealt him several unpleasant blows as he rolled, but he was still alive. He spat out a mouthful of blood and bile.

"Wilhelm!" Grimm shouted. "Damn it, I'm joining you!"

"D-don't be st-stupid…! This one is mine…and mine alone!"

"That's where you're wrong. That snake is an enemy of our nation. Which means all of us!" Bordeaux said, positioning himself along with Grimm in front of the sputtering Wilhelm. The other members of the squadron moved to surround Libre, cutting off his escape.

"Goodness gracious," Libre said. "Attacking a wounded, heartbroken lady all at once? Aren't you worried about your precious honor?"

"Take a look. Do we seem like much for honor to you? We're all out of knightly virtues."

"And besides that, Libre Fermi, I happen to be aware that a missing hand or foot is no great loss to a snake person. You simply grow it back."

"My, my, an expert. It is awfully tiring, though."

Pivot, who had spoken, stood outside the circle. Libre held up his handless left arm. The cut was clean.

The edges of the wound began writhing, and then the flesh assumed the shape of a hand in a spectacular display of regenerative power.

The snake's eyes looked in one direction and then another; everywhere, demi-humans were being dismembered and slaughtered. Libre looked sadly at the ground, then gestured at the squadron surrounding him.

"You lot speak the language of power. You've trained yourselves to the utmost. And that boy there… Could he be the Sword Devil, I wonder?"

"Oh-ho!" Bordeaux said. "So even the demi-human commanders know the Sword Devil. You're moving up in the world!"

"Please don't call me a commander. There's no allure to that title; it's not suited for me. Titles reeking of such manliness would make idiots like Valga happy." Libre crossed his arms and let out a long breath. Then he looked up at the sky. "I suppose even I am not quite a match for Zergev Squadron by myself."

"You and me, then! I'll knock that head right off your shoulders—!" Wilhelm, breathing hard, stepped forward to demand the continuation of their fight. But Libre only shrugged and raised his twin blade.

"I would love to share this dance…but I believe the moment to call an end to things is coming. If you'll so kindly pardon me."

"What are you—?"

But he never got to *talking about.*

He felt it first as a change in the air. The atmosphere of the battlefield, thick with bloodlust and the smell of iron, became something moist and clinging.

An instant later, his hands and arms were underwater.

"Wha?! What in the—!"

"You were all much too worried about magic circles. Carefully getting rid of them one by one. Suppose someone knew you would do just that? Wouldn't it only be logical to make it the crux of a trap?"

"Magic circles? How—?"

Ever since Castour Field, the elimination of magic circles on any battlefield had been a top priority over the royal forces. Zergev Squadron was careful to destroy any that they found; they had even removed one circle from this very battlefield.

"Magic circles work by imbuing the circles with meaning and then running magical power through them. You're terrified of the effects they might have—but these circles were active from the beginning."

Libre's voice grated against Wilhelm's eardrums. His limbs were heavy, as though he'd jumped into a pool of water fully clothed, and he was even finding it hard to breathe. It wasn't just him; everyone around him seemed to be experiencing the same thing. But Libre showed no sign of being affected.

"Those magic circles had power stored up in them. And you destroyed every last one! You released the energy in them, allowing it to charge up the hidden, true magic circle—and you see the result."

"Why all the games...? Why not just start with the...true circle?" Pivot asked, his voice straining.

Libre replied as if he had all the time in the world. "Would you ever have come anywhere near the swamp if it had a gigantic spell trigger on it? Instead, we left you a little trail of bread crumbs to follow. And think of the future. When you see a magic circle on some other battlefield, you'll have to wonder—to destroy it or not?" It was one of Valga Cromwell's strategies, one that took into account not only this battle but others to come.

Libre looked up. The others followed his gaze to find a reddish-purple sky above them. The strange color extended all over the battlefield—most likely marking the magic circle's area of effect. In other words...

"I always believed humans and demi-humans were divided only by their appearance and their blood. Now I see that that's more than enough to split the world in two." He paused meaningfully. "We will push back against you, beginning now. You'll see."

5

"Lady Mathers...! What is happening?!"

"We've been haaad. All the magic circles today—no, aaall the circles since Castour Field—have been decoys, leeeading us to this moment."

Carol had sunk painfully to her knees; beside her, Roswaal frowned at the magic circle.

It happened after they'd left headquarters to investigate. Even as they were examining the diagram, it had activated, and the entire battlefield had been enveloped in this magical effect. Her whole body felt like it was stuck in some syrupy liquid, hard to move and inhale.

"I can hardly breathe…and my body…so heavy…," Carol groaned, sweating. All the other soldiers Lyp had sent with her felt the same way. The effect seemed to manifest slight individual differences, but all of them were on their knees, moaning.

"If this is happening all over the battlefield…"

"I ceeertainly suspect that's the case. I presume the demi-human side is unaffected. It's as if they get to fight on land and we have to move underwater. Perhaps you, Carol, might emerge victorious?"

"Heaven…help us. If this is the work of magic, then could you…?"

"It's pooossible I could decode the ritual for the circle and undo it. But that…" Roswaal paused, looking up at the discolored sky. She narrowed her heterochromatic eyes as something slowly descended toward the ground. "…is whyyy you are here," she concluded.

"If there is any chance of stopping this circle, you of all people would figure it out based on what you've seen. And I put too much effort into this magic to have you destroy it."

The owner of the calm, even voice landed on the earth—a young girl in a white robe. The fabric ensconced a witch of terrifying malice—Sphinx.

"What a surpriiise that you should worry about me. I'm so touched I could vomit."

"Those with a high degree of specialized knowledge are valuable. If possible, I had hoped you might cooperate in making me complete."

Sphinx looked at Roswaal curiously, but Roswaal steadfastly rejected the witch. "My teacher's principles were a barrier to progress. You're just a failed experiment from an earlier time. And I *will* get rid of you."

At Roswaal's answer, Sphinx raised a hand and pointed at one of the agonized soldiers.

"Were you able to respond to what I did just now?"

A beam of light had glanced toward, then through, the soldier's neck in the blink of an eye. His head evaporated. She had done it again and again until six soldiers lay on the ground.

"Ah... Ahhh..." Carol, still unable to move, made a noise of astonishment at this slaughter. Even if they hadn't been constrained, it had happened so fast it would have been almost impossible to evade. On a visceral level, she understood that if that finger happened to point at her, it would be the last thing she ever saw. Her carefully honed sword technique, the ideals she held so dear—none of it meant anything in the face of this monster.

"I ask once more. Will you cooperate in completing me?"

It wasn't a request; it was a threat. Her heart, her body—something would surely give in.

But even as that finger with such devastating potential pointed at her, Roswaal shook her head.

"I told you," she said. "I *will* kill you."

"A shame." Her words were dispassionate. And then her finger glowed.

As Carol watched, the beam of light shot straight at Roswaal.

6

Screams and death rattles reached Wilhelm's ears from all around the battlefield.

His knees shivered, and his breath was harsh; he was barely remaining on his feet. His head was heavy, and his hands and feet seemed to move too slowly. No matter how greedily he gulped the air, he couldn't seem to get nearly enough oxygen to fill his lungs.

The same phenomenon was afflicting Bordeaux and the others; presumably, it was occurring all over the field of battle. It appeared to be affecting only the royal army—the human forces.

"I told Valga that even if he gave ten times as good as he got to the humans, we would still lose," Libre hissed, flicking his twin blade. "I suppose this is his answer. If he hurts you a hundred, two hundred times as badly as you hurt us, you'll sing a different tune!"

"Don't be stupid!" Bordeaux bellowed, supporting his weight with his battle-ax. "You could slaughter each and every soldier on this field, and we still wouldn't give in to the likes of you!"

Libre frowned at the noise and indicated the gasping soldiers with a twitch of his tongue. "Pride is all well and good, but will you not be satisfied until both sides are completely annihilated? This is why I hate brutish, barbarian men. It's impossible to have a productive conversation."

"Are you trying to suggest you're looking for one?" This remark came from Pivot, whose face was slowly turning blue. A cold sweat was running down his cheeks. "What is it that you want from the outcome of this battle?"

"What else? Peace. Not to be mercilessly picked out and murdered and trodden underfoot. We demi-humans want to know we'll be able to live out our days in peace. That's why we fight."

"...That's not what we've been hearing from Valga Cromwell."

"That fool's little speeches are altogether too extreme! ...But he talks that way because of you humans. And I pour all my sympathy upon the flames of his hatred. It's one more reason why we will see you defeated and force you to come to the bargaining table."

On one level, Libre seemed willing to have a meeting of the minds, but he also wished for the demi-humans' victory. The snake turned away from Pivot's gaze and pointed his weapon at Bordeaux.

"I despise the idea of killing immobilized knights, but I am going to use you heroes to break the will of humanity. When they hear Zergev Squadron has been destroyed, their morale will die with you."

"...You think...we're going to go that easily?!" Bordeaux rasped.

"I assure you, it pains me to do this. But I am Libre Fermi. I embody the anger of the demi-humans, and I shall show you humans my fangs regardless of my personal wishes! Bordeaux Zergev, this is where you die!"

Libre's sinewy body leaped at Bordeaux. His twin blade spun

overhead in a deadly storm and closed on the huge human with the intent to end his life. Without meaning to, everyone looked away.

That was when the Sword Devil's strike came in from the side.

"Grrrahhhhhhhhhh!"

"You can still move…?!"

Aware of the constraints on his body, Wilhelm's attack cut through the air with minimum possible movement. Libre quickly deflected it with his twin blade, but the Sword Devil's frenzied assault would not be denied. He struck out with his sword at the serpent's feet as they came to earth, at his head as it dodged back from him, and at the stomach that sought to evade him. Sparks and the screech of steel were everywhere; the pair engaged each other in a murderous dance.

"You may act strong, but you're too slow! Too sluggish! Too weak! As you are now, you can't defeat me!"

Wilhelm was being pushed back. Of course. This was an opponent he only had a fifty-fifty chance against on even terms, and now he had to fight while struggling in invisible water. He shouldn't even have been able to give battle in this state; he certainly had no chance of winning.

But Wilhelm refused to simply lie down and die without offering any resistance.

"I respect your loyalty to your friend, diving in to save him, but this is where it ends!" Libre shouted.

The words lit a fire in Wilhelm's heart. "Don't make me laugh! This isn't about loyalty to anyone!" But the movements of his arm wouldn't follow the dictates of his rage. The twin blade deflected his sword, following up with a stab at his exposed belly. His blood ran cold, certain that he was about to be slit open.

An instant later, he felt a gentle impact and a spray of hot blood.

"Ahh. Good lord. I always have the worst lot in life."

"Pivot!"

Pivot made a ghastly scream, as if vomiting blood. Then Wilhelm saw him, right before his eyes, cut deep and falling to the ground. A long diagonal slash ran from his left shoulder across his body.

He had thrown himself in the path of Libre's strike. He had saved Wilhelm.

As he fell supine, Pivot shouted in a voice louder than they had ever heard from him, "...Do not...let Wilhelm die!"

The yell inspired the other members of the squadron; they fought their immobile bodies to confront Libre and his twin blade.

They had no hope of victory. Their dulled movements succumbed to Libre's dancing weapon, and one by one they spilled their blood upon the battlefield.

"...Stop..."

Wilhelm had fallen to his knees. Pivot had protected him, but he was still injured. The swordsman watched Zergev Squadron being dismantled one man at a time in front of his eyes, and he couldn't even stand up.

"STOOOPPP!"

He howled with all the emotion that roiled within him. Was Libre its true object? Or was he shouting at his squad mates, protecting him at the cost of their own lives? He himself didn't know.

His voice echoed cruelly as the twin blade continued carving up his squadron. The pile of bodies grew.

"You're good men, all," Libre said. "...Why has it come to this?"

"Damned if I know. But I'm sure of one thing: We won't let Wilhelm be killed. Because he is the sword of the Kingdom of Lugunica!" Grimm tossed aside his own blade and raised his shield, blocking Libre's blows. This was the fruit of all the time he had spent on the defensive, and Grimm was able to resist far longer than any of the other squad members.

But it was all relative. If it had taken only a single attack to fell the other men, it took five to reach Grimm.

"Ghhgh—"

Grimm couldn't move his shield in time, and the twin blade dug into his throat. Grimm's eyes went wide at the critical blow; he dropped his shield and collapsed to the ground. Blood frothed from the wound, and the limbs of the Defender of the Shield twitched helplessly. And then a merciless blow descended from directly above him...

"Hrraaaaahhhh!!"

Possessed by a killing rage, Wilhelm flung himself at Libre. The serpent was slow to respond to this unexpected counterattack, and the two of them tumbled to the ground, tangled together, and fell into a hollow.

As up and down switched places, they beat at each other until they reached the bottom of the depression. Spitting blood and giving animal howls, the Sword Devil and the snake rolled to the place of their final battle.

7

The beam of light flew at Roswaal almost faster than the eye could see. It moved so quickly that Carol could make no move to guard her mistress; somewhere inside she resigned herself to watching Roswaal explode. But her despair turned to amazement.

"...Well. Well..."

"Didn't I tell you? I am the one who will kill you."

Sphinx was clutching her abdomen, which had been hit. For the first time, she was breathing with pain. The source of the injury was Roswaal, who had dodged the beam of light and stepped in to deliver a punch.

She shook her indigo hair, raising her hands as if ready to box. "Not everyone is affected by a magic circle in the same way. It's a difference in our mana cycles. Simply put, the more adept you are at sorcery, the more susceptible you'll be to a circle's effects. It makes things simple. The worse of a sorcerer you are, the more normally you'll be able to move."

"I had heard you were a specialist in magic, but this..."

"I know more than anyone. I juuust can't put it into practice. This generation, Roswaal J. Mathers, is completely and totally unable to use magic. That's why I can kill you."

As she spoke, Roswaal took out a pair of steel gauntlets and put them over her hands. Her fists became weapons of steel; she was prepared to literally beat the monster before her to death.

"From my youngest days, I was trained in the fighting arts, all for this moment. I hope you have a chance to admire my technique before I finish you off."

Roswaal stepped in with intensity, her blows slamming through the air. Any one of them, had it landed, would have been strong enough to crush a boulder, and Sphinx quickly found herself completely on the defensive.

Carol gulped, enraptured by Roswaal's fighting. The way she used her fists and the way she held herself unmistakably marked her as an accomplished practitioner, a genius whose natural talents had been honed over twenty years to forge the tremendous pugilist Carol saw before her. Roswaal had not been boasting nor exaggerating when she said she had trained since she was a girl. It was a fact.

A kick that could have split a large tree in half caught Sphinx squarely, sending her light body flying sideways. Her youthful face slammed into the ground, and soon after, a gauntleted fist sought to pulverize her skull.

"...This is beyond...what I imagined. My observation was insufficient." In the blink of an eye, Sphinx was off the ground as she leaped into space. She wiped the edge of her mouth. Perhaps she had some internal injury, for fresh blood trickled relentlessly from her mouth.

Roswaal's lips twisted down contemptuously as she watched her opponent float in the air. "You're going to run?"

"I could also take pot shots at you from up here where you can't reach me."

"—"

Sphinx must have seen something in Roswaal's glinting eye, because she decided to let caution prevail. "But let us cease this. I presume you have some plan prepared to knock me out of the sky."

The young witch danced through the air, leaving Roswaal and Carol farther and farther below.

"Lady Mathers!" Carol exclaimed. "That villain—the witch—is getting away!"

"I can see that," Roswaal said, remaining calmer than her bodyguard. "But it's no use chasing her. And don't call her 'the witch.'"

She took off her gauntlets. Instead of pursuing the fleeing enemy, she stepped on the magic circle, which glowed with a surfeit of magical power.

"This complicated design isn't about enhancing the effect of the magic so much as making it harder to dispel. They seem to think quiiite highly of me. And they've *still* underestimated me." As she muttered, Roswaal got down in the dirt beside the glowing circle and began scratching something into the earth. She pointed a finger at the circle and closed one eye. Her yellow iris flickered weirdly, and an instant later, the design under her feet shattered with the sound of breaking glass.

As the magic vanished along with it, their breath returned, and their limbs lightened. The angry red sky remembered its normal color, and the world was tinted twilight. Carol got to her feet.

"I can move…! Wait, Lady Mathers. What damage did we sustain from this circle?"

"In battle, it only takes five seconds for the tide to turn, let alone ten minutes… Who can say what's happened?"

"Grimm…" Carol immediately thought of the one she loved and whispered his name.

Beside her, Roswaal watched the sky regain its color. "I thought I might not be able to destroy that thing here at Aihiya. So the final battle will be elsewhere…"

8

Wilhelm was on top by the time they landed at the bottom of the depression.

His face hit the damp ground, and he spat mud and dirt out of his mouth, baring his teeth at the same time. Libre was reaching out as if to pull him up, and Wilhelm bit off the serpent's fingers. He planted a knee in the snake's stomach as he came down from above.

He suddenly found his body had returned to normal. He adjusted his grip on his beloved sword and pointed it at Libre. The snake-man rose, readying his twin blade. The two stared at each other.

"I guess this means our magic circle is done for," Libre said. "Just as well. As I said, I have no desire to murder a helpless opponent!"

"Shut your mouth, you son of a bitch! I'll never forgive you for what you did!"

"Are you mad that I killed your friends? So it seems the Sword Devil has human feelings after all."

For just a second, Wilhelm found he could say nothing in response to Libre's taunts. A white-hot rage rose in his chest, as if it were not blood but magma that ran through his veins. But even he didn't know where this tremendous anger came from. He could only deny it.

"You've got some nerve! I'm only a sword! Just one sword! Loyalty and friendship have nothing—"

Steel was beautiful. Never angry. Never complaining. Complete within itself. That was why Wilhelm wanted—

"I see. I think this makes sense to me now. You, at this very moment, are being reborn."

Wilhelm caught his breath.

"Come at me, immature one. I shall teach you how a newborn first cries."

Wilhelm brazenly sprang at Libre with everything he had. And in response, the strongest warrior in the Demi-human Alliance raised his twin blade.

9

"Pivot! Pivot, wake up! Don't you die on me!"

Pivot's breath came in short gasps. Bordeaux held him in his arms, shouting desperately. The lean man's eyes fluttered open, and he looked at Bordeaux, his pupils clouded. A weak smile worked its way across his face.

"Y-young…sir…what an un…becoming face you're making."

"Don't try to talk! No, wait—keep going! Don't die! If you go unconscious, that's it!"

Pivot clung to Bordeaux's neck, his breath growing short. His face was colorless, and the flow of blood from his wounds was abating. Anyone could see that his condition was fatal. The only person who refused to admit it was Bordeaux.

"Young…young sir, you must be careful…to correct…your failings."

"Picking up my slack is supposed to be your job! This is a dereliction of duty, and I won't allow it!"

The collective difficulty of breathing had eased at last, but many had fallen in addition to Pivot. How many of them were left to enjoy the free air again?

"Y—ng…ir… It's been…an hon…or…" The vice captain let out a long breath, and the strength left his body.

"Pivot? Pivot, come on! Stop being stupid! Open your eyes! Pivot!" Bordeaux slapped the man's cheeks, tried to force his eyes open. But Pivot's body didn't move. His life was gone. Even Bordeaux could see it. The battlefield had taught him what corpses looked like, and now Pivot was one of them.

Yet no matter how much time passed, he couldn't admit it.

Suddenly, Pivot's remains gave a single great shudder. "—"

"Pivot?" The astonished Bordeaux looked down at the body as though he couldn't believe it. The corpse's eyes drifted open. The pupils focused on Bordeaux.

"Pivo—!"

The captain was just exclaiming at this miracle when two hands wrapped around his neck. His head snapped back in pain and surprise, then two arms rose and encircled his torso in an attempt to break his spine. It was as if the departed Pivot was trying to take Bordeaux with him.

"Hrggh— Gah—"

As the corpse throttled him, Bordeaux felt his consciousness slipping away. It was inconceivable that Pivot would betray him. He of all people would never do that. What had happened? An instant before the world faded from view—

"*Hrrr!*"

Grimm knocked Pivot's body away, his shield at the ready. The two of them tumbled to the ground, practically on top of each other.

Grimm didn't get up. But Pivot did, and he reached out for the unconscious boy with a howl like a wild animal's. The merciless fingers sought Grimm's weakness, stretched out to take his life...

"Yaaaaaahhhhhh!"

With a rush of air, Bordeaux's battle-ax caught the defenseless Pivot square in the middle of the back. This was a weapon that could slice through even armor like paper. It cut its foe nearly in two; he fell to the ground and was still at last.

A corpse. This time he was well and truly a corpse.

"____"

Bordeaux stood poised with his battle-ax, and all around him stood the deceased members of Zergev Squadron. Faces he knew, now drained of life, pierced Bordeaux with their empty gazes. Their former commander began to laugh.

"Ha... Ha-ha...ha-ha-ha! Ahhh-ha-ha-ha-ha-ha-ha!"

These were undead puppets. A little parlor trick of the witch Sphinx. Bordeaux knew it, the moment her hatefulness entered these once-proud warriors in an attempt to profane them in death.

"That witch...! That witch, thatwitchthatwitchthatwitchthatwitch-thatwitchthatwitchthatwiiiiitch!!"

Shouting the words almost like an incantation, Bordeaux swore revenge against the true evil, the one that was doing all this despite not being present. And then he and his battle-ax set to work butchering all his newly deceased subordinates. As he cut down the encroaching zombies, sending them back into death, Bordeaux laughed. He laughed and laughed.

The howls went on and on, until they mingled with sobs. The echoes reached every corner of the battlefield.

10

The dance of death and steel was reaching its climax. Wilhelm wielded his blade with a chilling clarity, growing ever faster and more nimble. Libre's responses with his twin blade were balletic, but his injuries were increasing as he found it harder and harder to avoid Wilhelm's blows.

This startling display of swordsmanship was the result of a mind-boggling talent combined with Wilhelm's own sweat and tears. Libre had lived a long life and knew few who could challenge him in combat. He could only feel admiration at having found a challenger in a boy so young.

This was ominous, he thought. He felt that not only the boy's sword technique boded ill, but also the quality of his humanity. He was incomplete, imperfect. Immature. He was still young, and had not yet mastered himself.

He said that he wanted to be steel. To be the swipe of a sword.

Perhaps that was the task he had set himself and the motivation that had driven him. The weight and quickness of his strikes could have been achieved through halfhearted effort. But as he dodged and deflected the blows with his twin blade, Libre could feel that the torrent of emotion contained in the attacking sword was not that of steel.

The emotions burned hot, and steel did not heat itself. It was the way of the human heart to be swayed by feelings, but it was those same emotions that gave intensity to their fighting. This devil who wished to be a sword—was still human.

"Heh-heh."

"What's so funny?!" Wilhelm demanded of the chuckling Libre. Wilhelm's face was covered in blood.

"Oh, nothing," Libre said. "It's simply that even as we try to kill each other, I simply can't get excited about fighting a wooden opponent. If I'm going to pit my way of life against another's, I want it to be someone who bleeds, someone who weeps!"

The commotion was immense. The flash of sparks, the clang of clashing blades, their stamping across the earth all added to the cacophony. Life bloomed in every blow, emotions were expressed in every strike, and all the noise cried out for more combat.

He wasn't steel. He wasn't a demon. Here, he was just a boy named Wilhelm. Libre's opponent was just a single human, and Libre himself was just a single demi-human—the whole war was encapsulated in the two of them.

Wilhelm just managed to find an opening from above, spinning to bring his sword toward Libre's neck. The serpent raised his weapon and caught it—and then the blade shattered, and Wilhelm's strike found its mark.

Libre's vision went red. But the blow's power had been blunted, and the sword was unable to pierce Libre's scales. With the sword half buried in his neck, Libre brought up the remaining end of his twin blade to sweep at Wilhelm.

The difference between them as species, the difference in the abilities they were born with, decided this battle. It was, indeed, the reason for this entire civil war.

"In the end…maybe we are different," Libre mused. "Maybe we can't understand each other. For just a moment, I almost thought I had gotten through to you, if ever so little. Did I imagine it?"

Wilhelm fell back, clutching the wound on his chest. Libre thrust with his sword. But even as death approached, the boy's murderous eyes refused to admit defeat. Sadness flooded Libre's heart. Such intense vitality did not deserve this fate.

"You really are human, aren't you? So utterly human, it brings me sorrow. But it doesn't change the fact that you're a threat to me and mine. I regret to say that this is good-bye."

The boy could not be allowed to live. Libre might be taunted; it might be said that his own humanness had been exploited in combat. But his affection for a given individual and his pride as a demi-human were different things.

Libre Fermi was not in a position to give precedence to his personal feelings. He knew that all his actions must advance the demi-human cause. And so—

"When this is all over, I shall put a flower on your grave. A blood-red one, full of the heat of passion."

Then he raised his halved twin blade, hoping to offer the Sword Devil at least a painless death.

The next instant, a beam of light pierced Libre's chest from behind.

11

The moment before death came to him, Wilhelm's life did indeed flash before his eyes.

"Hrrk! Haah!"

Blood accompanied Libre's long tongue as it slid out of his mouth; trembling, he looked behind him in amazement. There stood the witch Sphinx, who had appeared suddenly, her glowing finger pointed in their direction.

"What…do you think…you're doing?"

"Right. I have been injured more severely than I planned and am currently retreating. While I do so, I wished to request the protection of the most capable person I could, and you were near at hand, so I have selected you."

Libre looked down at the hole in his chest, touched the bloodless wound, and smiled.

"Is that so…? I must say, this hardly looks like a request to me."

"I do not have time to negotiate, so I have decided simply to kill you and make you my puppet immediately. Do not fear. Valga has told me of how desperately he needs you. Thus, although I will turn you into an undead warrior, I plan to take every measure to prevent you from rotting. This requires careful thought."

"Valga… That fool. I told him…we couldn't control you…"

Brandishing his broken blade, Libre turned toward Sphinx. She cocked her head at this behavior. "Based on your injuries and level of fatigue, I conclude that resistance is futile."

"Futility is no reason for inaction. I…am the pride of the demi-human race. Libre Fermi! Do not underestimate me, you little bitch!"

Fangs bared, Libre sprang forward. His movements and speed would never have betrayed that he was on the edge of death.

"I didn't want to hurt you too much, but you give me no choice." A storm of white light assaulted the oncoming Libre, piercing his chest, knees, and neck. Blood sprayed everywhere; countless coin-size holes opened in Libre's body, and he toppled to the ground.

"Damnable…witch… You shall ne…never have…m-m…"

"—"

"V—Valga… The rest is…up to…y—"

These two unfinished imprecations were Libre's last words as a beam of light struck him in the head. And so the strongest of the demi-humans fell dead, a great hole in the middle of his face.

As his chance to settle things with such a fine opponent was stolen from him, Wilhelm said nothing. He watched as Sphinx placed a palm on Libre's remains.

"I will tell Valga you died honorably in battle. My study suggests that report would make you happy. Now, then…"

"W-wait…"

As Sphinx began to rise, Wilhelm stopped her, murder in his eyes. But the way she looked at him suggested that, to her, his hatred was nothing more than a gentle breeze.

"Fear not; you are safe. I have no intention of harming you. I wish to leave this place promptly and make ready for what is next. This requires preparation."

"Don't mock me! You're…letting me live? Why? Fight me… F-fight…me…!"

Sphinx's formerly expressionless eyes widened. "I am most surprised to hear you say such a thing, in your present state." Then she nodded several times, surveying Wilhelm with interest. "You clearly are unable to do battle. Yet you seek combat. I do not understand. Perhaps because my emotions are incomplete. I see that you, too, require observation."

"Observation…?"

"Valga, who burns with hatred, and Libre, who wielded his sword with sadness, were both objects of study. You, the vessel of an anger that supersedes death, are one, too… I am eager for the next chance to observe you."

With that, Sphinx turned around. Wilhelm wanted to call out, stop her; he tried to rise up, but his limbs wouldn't move. Instead—

"…Libre."

The corpse of Libre Fermi, the light gone from its eyes, stood up.

Libre now wore the empty expression of an undead warrior, and he spared no attention for Wilhelm as he followed after the departing Sphinx. The tall serpent and the diminutive girl vanished into the distance, leaving Wilhelm alone.

"Damn it all," Wilhelm growled, gritting his teeth so hard he thought they might crack and cursing his immobile body. His eyes were open wide, and he lay curled in the corner of a battlefield scorched by the flames of war, voicing his hatred to himself like a spell.

"You'll pay... You'll pay! I'll make you regret this... You'll regret leaving me alive! Damn it! Damn it all to helllllll!"

His last word turned into a wrenching howl of despair, and the Sword Devil's personal defeat underscored all that had happened that day. Wilhelm's regret and anger burned until the royal army found him and long after. It was clear to everyone that the flames would not be doused until he cut off the head of the witch.

12

The Battle of Aihiya Swamp went down as the worst defeat since Castour Field.

The blow was not as one-sided as Castour, but the royal army had sacrificed nearly twice as many men, the greatest loss of life in a single battle since the start of the civil war. All the royal troops involved had been simultaneously weakened by the effects of the magic circle around the battlefield, and casualties were reckoned at greater than 60 percent.

The weight of this defeat was felt keenly at general headquarters, and responsibility was pinned on the mid-level eradicators of the magic circles—in other words, on whoever had nullified the most magic circles on the field. As a result, Lyp Bariel, viscount of the south, found his name marred as a war criminal.

Lyp protested mightily, demanding a retrial from general headquarters. Not only was he a suspect in the death of his predecessor, but also Lord Crumère, his former commanding officer, was only too happy to report his bouts of violence and irrationality. Ultimately, he was unable to regain his honor, and his suit was denied.

The viscount was only the first of many officers to become scapegoats; the majority of the units in the royal army had suffered losses, and the postmortem went on without mercy. Among those whom the battle had badly bloodied was Zergev Squadron, a unit renowned for its heroism. Its survivors numbered just eleven.

These included Bordeaux Zergev and Grimm Fauzen; Wilhelm Trias was soon added to the list. Zergev Squadron's casualties, including Vice Captain Pivot Anansi, numbered sixty-nine. Each and every one of them had become undead warriors and been dispatched by Bordeaux.

Later, history would see this as a convenient point at which to mark the beginning of the final phase of the civil war. It would change not only the course of history but all those who participated in the conflict.

Bordeaux Zergev was now solidly on the side of demi-human extermination, moved by his profound hatred for the witch.

Grimm Fauzen's wounds cost him his voice, setting his kindhearted lover adrift on a sea of sorrow.

As for Wilhelm Trias, that battle was the day he began to wonder about the path of the sword and question his very way of life.

He could not find the answer to that question alone. But the day he found the answer would come before long.

THE LOVE SONG OF THE SWORD DEVIL

Fifth Stanza

1

More than a month had passed since Aihiya.

There had been no major battles in the kingdom during that time, and on the surface, all seemed quiet. But a look at the nation's domestic politics showed that such an assessment would earn more than a roll of the eyes from those in the know.

The losses at Aihiya had cost the kingdom more than 40 percent of its fighting power; the army was undergoing a massive reorganization and was concerned about how to deal with this dramatic reduction in force.

Zergev Squadron was not immune from the effects of this. Nearly 90 percent of the long-standing members of the unit had been killed, including Vice Captain Pivot. The squadron was in tatters, and whether it was even possible to rebuild was an open question. Zergev Squadron was famous for its strength of spirit. Wilhelm and Bordeaux returned miraculously safe, but while they had not been severely injured physically, the same could not be said of their hearts.

There were wounds in that battle no armor could protect them from and that pained them even now.

"You somehow seem even more fearsome than before," the girl said suddenly as she watched Wilhelm silently lose himself in his blade.

They were in a corner of the poor district, in the plaza next to the field of flowers. Due to the ongoing restructuring of the army, Wilhelm had no specific assigned unit. Neither was there any battle to fight. His days mounted with depression and anger. Recently, he had been coming here daily to work with his sword.

That, of course, meant more opportunities to see the girl who spent her time here. He had even become used to her periodic interjections during his practice.

"Feh."

"Oh! You clucked at me just now!" The girl sounded put out.

Being used to her comments didn't make them any less annoying, and Wilhelm had made no attempt to hide his noise of frustration.

"I just hate it when you make it so obvious," the girl said. "Could you stop?"

"It's my choice where I practice my sword and my choice where I click my tongue," Wilhelm said. "Even if you happen to be nearby, wasting your time doing nothing."

"Don't say that. I'm admiring my flowers and expanding my heart... Won't you put it that way?"

"You should be glad I said *wasting your time* and not *wasting your life*."

It was their custom to trade barbs like this, without looking at each other. They each came here to relax, but they ended up in these childish arguments. It was silly, yet neither wanted to give in by going somewhere else. And so the two of them saw more and more of each other.

"I'd have to say it's you who's wasting time," the girl said. "And it looks like soldiers have plenty of time to waste. You're always hanging around here these days."

"...The military is reorganizing. I won't be going anywhere for a while. You really think this is what I want? And I'm not 'hanging around.'"

"You think? Even though you're having so much fun swinging

your sword? ...I guess you haven't been enjoying yourself much recently, by all appearances."

"What do you know?" Feeling she had seen through him, Wilhelm attempted to conceal how much it bothered him with a mean remark.

He didn't swing his sword for fun, but there was no denying Wilhelm enjoyed the time he spent absorbed in his practice. Indeed, for him, those times were the very fulfillment of his life. And the girl was right that now, he found he could no longer face the sword with purity of purpose.

Libre's words from Aihiya Swamp reverberated in his head.

Come at me, immature one. I shall teach you how a newborn first cries.

Wilhelm had been an instant from the end of his life back then. If Sphinx hadn't intervened, he would be dead right now. But their fight had been interrupted, and his battle that day would remain forever unresolved.

"Frowning *again*! You're too young to let your face get stuck that way."

Suddenly, the girl was standing in front of the silent Wilhelm. He was startled to realize he hadn't noticed her, and he grabbed his own face in an attempt to force the frown away.

"The way you go around scowling and glaring and looking all prickly, I bet everyone is too scared to come anywhere near you."

"Shut up! What's it to you? What do you mean, 'too young,' anyway? How old do you think I—"

"Eighteen. Same as me. Right?"

The girl was pointing at him with a wink. Wilhelm couldn't make a sound. She was right. And he wasn't so shameless or concerned with trivialities to try to hide that fact.

"See?" she said. "Wouldn't it be embarrassing to get frown lines at that age? If you have to get wrinkles, why not get laugh lines from smiling at flowers?"

He looked away, but the girl seemed to take this as an answer and giggled prettily. Then she spun around in a little dance, and Wilhelm found his attention stolen by the way her beautiful red hair fluttered in the wind. And as the strands vanished from his peripheral vision, they were replaced by a field of yellow flowers.

He had seen that field over and over, every time he had met the girl. So he was used to her proud look as she showed him the plants, as well as the question that came next.

"Do you like flowers?"

What kind of answer did she want? Nothing had changed. Wilhelm shook his head and replied, "No, I hate them."

2

"You been to the castle town again?"

Bordeaux's towering frame blocked Wilhelm's way back into the soldiers' barracks. His beefy arms were crossed, and he glared down at Wilhelm.

The swordsman clicked his tongue. "What if I have? Some sort of problem with that?"

"Damn right there is. We may be in the middle of a reorganization, but you never know when or where those demi-human bastards might strike. The military has to be ready for anything at any time. I don't care if you're on your day off or what, you'd better—"

He stopped in the middle of this unusually logical argument, closed his eyes, and began again slowly.

"Ahem. That's what's expected of you and me."

"—"

Wilhelm felt a chill pass down his spine. His commander was completely right. Normally, such careful logic would have come from Pivot, not Bordeaux. Bordeaux would have slapped Pivot on the back and shot him down.

Bordeaux Zergev had changed since the battle at Aihiya Swamp, though he had no obvious visible injuries. The difference was internal, as was amply evident in his attitude and behavior. He had begun trying to speak more properly, as he had done just now, and strove to say things befitting his position. It was as if Pivot's departed hollow, his spirit, were whispering to him.

But the biggest difference of all would be evident to anyone who spent time with him. Of course Wilhelm, who had known Bordeaux for more than three years, would notice it.

"The kingdom can't spare your abilities right now. Practice as much and however you like. But keep in mind to stay where you can be called to action at any time. That's all I ask."

Bordeaux's face as he spoke was all darkness and doubt. There wasn't so much as a hint of a smile or laughter, and that was the most drastic change.

"After all, I'm pretty sure I don't have to give you a direct order to kill those barbarians."

The old Bordeaux would never have revealed the depth of his anger and hatred so openly. These displays gave Wilhelm a strange tightness in his chest. He disliked the feeling of his own weakness and determined to avoid Bordeaux even more than before.

"There'll be another big battle soon. That's what Lady Mathers says. Be ready."

Wilhelm hadn't spoken at all and didn't break his silence. Bordeaux clapped him on the shoulder and then opened the path to the barracks. The way Bordeaux came to speak to Wilhelm himself, rather than sending some lackey, gave Wilhelm the impression that Bordeaux had not lost all his old directness. But he quickly discarded the feeling.

After meeting the girl in town and Bordeaux in front of the barracks, Wilhelm's emotions were in shambles. He went inside. As he headed back to his quarters, he passed the barracks captain. The man looked about to ask what had happened, but Wilhelm silenced him with a glance and walked quickly into his room.

The royal army had military dormitories in each district of the capital, and the building Wilhelm was assigned to was one for the upper staff. This was the highest treatment for a foot soldier who had not attained the rank of knight, and he appreciated life in a private room that minimized his chances of running into other people. So much so, in fact, that he was apt to get angry at uninvited visitors.

"You were up bright and early this morning."

"Why the hell are you here?"

"When I showed him who I was, the barracks captain let me in here. Even though I told him I could wait downstairs."

"You're overstepping."

He thought back to the pathetic face of the barracks captain he'd passed in the hallway and clicked his tongue, although the captain was long gone.

Carol had been waiting in Wilhelm's room. She was in normal women's clothes rather than her knight's armor, and it made her a bit less intimidating. It reminded Wilhelm that she was, after all, a woman. Not that he was stupid enough to say that out loud—it would only earn him a tongue-lashing and make this encounter longer than it needed to be.

"You know," Carol said, "I've known you for three years, and this might be the first time I've gotten to sit and have a quiet chat with you."

"There's not going to be anything quiet about it. Get out of here."

"You haven't changed. Or...maybe you changed a little and then went back to how you were. You have that look in your eyes that reminds me of a stray dog—or a mad one."

"Did you come here just to pick a fight? I'm impressed you'd go to all the trouble on your day off. Fine, I'll oblige you."

Their respective warrior spirits clashed briefly before Carol frowned and sighed.

"I didn't expect you to be happy to see me," she said. "Once I'm done here, I'll leave immediately."

"Oh, so you were looking for something else besides trouble?"

"This is about Grimm, of course. What else do you and I have in common?"

Wilhelm made a disgusted grimace at the mention of Grimm's name. Ever since his injuries, he had been shut up in a medical center. Wilhelm, naturally, had not gone to visit him once.

After all, why would he? A visit would serve no purpose, and anyway, the relationship between them wasn't like that.

But to find Carol going out of her way to come to his room like this—

"I came to tell you that Grimm wants to see you."

It was exactly what he'd expected her to say. It wasn't lost on Wilhelm that Grimm and Carol shared the bond of a man and woman. Well, they could care about each other if they wanted. But they shouldn't push it on him.

"All right, you've delivered your message. Congratulations. But I don't have any intention of listening to you. Going to see him would be a waste of effort."

"Why, you—"

"But I'm impressed you were able to bring me a message from someone who can't talk. I didn't know he was literate enough to write down—"

"Don't get too pleased with yourself, Wilhelm Trias." Carol's intensity rose again as though to resume their contest earlier. Wilhelm narrowed his eyes. Carol's empty hand was clenched in a fist. "Grimm may forgive all the humiliating things you say about him, but I will not stand here and allow you to demean him."

"You're talking about the sort of thing friends do. Don't try to force it on me."

The two of them stood exchanging dangerous stares.

Carol looked away first. Wilhelm scoffed.

She shook her head slowly and headed for the door, but then she said, "I brought you his message, even if it's hopeless. Just once, try doing something decent by a friendship forged in battle."

"Since when are he and I friends?"

"Grimm sees you as his brother in arms. I thought maybe I could, too." Carol left the room, an intimidated-looking Wilhelm behind her. He heard the door close, then he threw himself down on his bed in frustration.

He exhausted his swordsman's spirit glaring at the ceiling. After that, only emptiness was left in his heart.

3

The place was filled with the stench of rot and blood. Valga frowned at the stomach-turning odor as he entered the little building. But though his old face might have been frowning, he would not turn away from any of this. All the tragedies he witnessed were the result of his own decision. It would be unthinkable not to look.

"...Sphinx. How's your progress?"

He didn't even greet the small, hunched figure before flinging out his question. The robed girl stood up when he spoke, wiped her face with the blood-stained fabric, and turned around.

"It will require ongoing observation. One thing I have concluded, though, is that it doesn't smell nice. It may indeed be too much for me, as the incomplete creation of my mother, to reconstruct a spell missing its most crucial element."

"Awful lot of whining for a so-called witch... I'm sorry. I'm just angry." He let out a long sigh and looked past the girl, Sphinx. Standing behind her was a snake-man covered in green scales—what was once Libre Fermi.

"So there's nothing left of you. It's a real pity, Libre."

Once the strongest warrior among the demi-humans, the light of life was gone from Libre's eyes. Yet he still stood and fought at the behest of the witch—the result of a spell that could cause the dead to move. But he was an undead warrior now, capable of following only simple commands. He could no longer fulfill Libre's role.

"So many of our fellows have surfaced after our victory at Aihiya. And the blow we dealt to the humans was severe. To think, this may be our greatest opportunity since this war began, and—!"

"Isn't it enough that you're here? Or couldn't this undead warrior act the part you have in mind?"

"...No. It's not enough. I don't have the facility to stand at the head of our allies. And no empty corpse is going to be able to muster the charisma of Libre's leadership!"

Valga glared at the undead Libre, then put his thick palms to his face.

The strategy at Aihiya Swamp had gone exactly according to plan, a major blow against the royal army. This should have been an opportunity to decimate a broken enemy, but Libre's death in battle was completely outside Valga's calculations. As much as he hated to admit it, Valga knew that Libre's influence on the Demi-human Alliance was even greater than his own.

Sphinx had at least succeeded in collecting the body and reanimating it as an undead warrior, but no spell, no matter how unholy, would truly bring Libre back.

"Though the flesh is revived, the soul does not reside within it," Sphinx said. "Reconstructing the Sacrament of the Immortal King is difficult indeed."

"How to continue the civil war without Libre...? We don't have many options left."

"But we have some...?" Sphinx narrowed her eyes.

Valga gave a deep nod. Of course, he had considered the possibility that he or Libre might not survive this war. He had hoped Libre might outlast him, but it had been the serpent who went first—such was their fate.

Now I can do what I could never have done with Libre here.

"He hated the thought of the world gone to hell. He would have stopped me, possibly by force, from sending this world somewhere even lower."

"And what is it that you wish from me in this hell?"

"I will open the gates of the netherworld and comfort the souls of our departed comrades with the humans' screams and death rattles. And you yourself will lead the way. All the kingdom's warriors shall be burned to ash in the flames of my wrath!"

The anger blazed within him; it never faded and never would. Every provocation would feed it until it razed everything to the ground.

The flames would never be quenched. This, if nothing else, Valga knew to be true.

"Libre is gone and I remain. Consider it testament to my undying rage."

Valga began a terrifying set of calculations of what would become the fuel for the flames. It was the beginning of the most crucial battle in the whole of the Demi-human War.

"...This requires observation."

And it was the beginning of the end that would settle the doom of many, including the witch Sphinx.

4

The demi-humans continued intermittent attempts to wreak havoc in the capital.

"Wha?! Y-you're the Sword Devil...!"

"Ruuuahhhh!"

Wilhelm threw himself at one group trying to cause trouble on the capital's high outer walls around the city. Some of this simplistic mischief was simply the work of ruffians caught up by the idea of demi-human superiority.

The reorganization of the army was behind schedule, and Wilhelm had been assigned to a unit of military police. He had already cut up several such groups of ne'er-do-wells.

One of the men held the fatal wound on his torn belly, spitting blood and contempt. "T-to think our fight would end like this... Cur—curse you, you animal...!" But Wilhelm was accustomed to such abuse. He readied his sword to grant the man a mercifully quick death.

"Quit your yammering, you idiot," he muttered. "If you're so afraid to die, learn to use a sword."

"...You think so...? Then take your...famous sword... Soon tongues of flame will lick the whole nation... Even the capital will not escape destruc—"

"—?"

These were strange words with which to greet death, but it didn't matter. Wilhelm struck off the demi-human's head before he was finished speaking.

Wilhelm had sent the body tumbling over the wall with a kick and then finished off the group by the time the other guardsmen arrived. They were nearly speechless at the scene before them.

"A-are you the notorious Sword Devil, Wilhelm...?" The man's voice cracked as he said the nickname, even though they were supposedly on the same side. His friends were as scared of him as his enemies. That was something else he was used to.

The name of the Sword Devil, as well as Wilhelm's, were now inextricably associated with blood and death.

That was why...

"I'm Theresia. All right? Call me Theresia. And you are...?"
He'd stayed silent.
"You are...?"
"—?"
"Oh, come on! I'm sure you understand. I'm asking you to tell me your name, obviously!"

She puffed out her cheeks and stamped the ground; the girl in front of him—Theresia—was clearly frustrated.

They were in the square as usual, and Wilhelm had just finished his daily practice. She had gestured him over. He hadn't been able to refuse. As they were looking at the flowers, she had suddenly said in annoyance, "I'm not *hey you* or *girl*. Call me by my name."

Wilhelm had replied that he didn't know what her name was. Her eyes had gone wide. They had known each other for three months now, and it was a little late for introductions.

She had coughed, then quietly said, "Theresia..."

He thought it was a fitting name. Always smiling like the sun, sometimes annoyingly talkative and yet—charming. Her mood was dangerously prone to sudden swings, but still—*Theresia*. Yes. It was a better thing to call her than "Flower Girl."

"Hey! Why aren't you saying anything? Are you even listening to me?"

"...Yeah. That's a pretty nice name, I guess."

"Oh, uh... Y-you think so? Well, I do appreciate your saying so..."

"I mean, I've been calling you 'Flower Girl' all this time."

"Whaaaat?"

He just had to go and add a little too much information. Theresia's expression changed completely, her cheeks red at going from happiness to anger so quickly. Wilhelm dodged all her attempts to step on his foot.

"Ahh!" Theresia exclaimed. "You are the worst! Anyway, aren't you about ready to answer me?"

"—?"

"Why are you acting like you don't know what I want?! I'm asking you to tell me your name!"

She stamped the ground again. Wilhelm wondered what the problem was—and then questioned himself for wondering. All he had to do was tell her his name. It was only polite, and Wilhelm had no reason not to.

Not even if it would provoke her terror and disgust.

"It's Wilhelm Trias."

If Theresia knew that the royal army called him "the Sword Devil" and what they said about him... The girl who loved flowers would revile him. The thought brought a strange ache to his chest.

"Wilhelm. Yes. Wilhelm, Wilhelm, Wilhelm."

"...Stop saying that."

"Huh. That's a pretty nice name, I guess." Her eyes glittered mischievously. Perhaps she thought she was paying him back for earlier. "It sounds very like you, Wilhelm."

Wilhelm was silent at this; he was feeling too many things at once to know how to respond.

"Still, it's a little strange."

"Yeah?"

"I mean, it's been three months since we met each other...but we're just now getting introduced." Theresia stuck out her tongue and smiled shyly. At the sight, Wilhelm felt the confusion of emotions in his chest evaporate. His body felt strangely light.

"Why should we have known each other's names?" he said. "We

The Love Song of the Sword Devil   127

didn't have any interest in each other. We both just happened to show up here at the same time to do what we wanted to do."

"Really? I had a little interest in you. And it's not like I don't know anything about you, Wilhelm. You hate flowers, don't you?"

"…Yeah, that's right. And, Theresia, you love them."

"Yes! See? We do know something about each other. We wanted to know."

She puffed out her chest triumphantly, and Wilhelm found the corners of his mouth turning up slightly of their own accord. It was rare for him: a smile that was neither ironic nor grim.

"By the way, Wilhelm. Do you like flowers?"

The question came at him unexpectedly, while he was trying hard to stiffen his cheeks to hide the involuntary smile. It was the same question as always—and yet, it meant something a little different today.

"No, I hate them."

Even so, Wilhelm's answer didn't change. There was nothing to be gained by looking at plants. Certainly not the things that mattered to Wilhelm.

"Oh? If that's the case—"

Normally it stopped with the question and the answer. But today it didn't. Holding the hem of her skirt, Theresia turned away from him, so Wilhelm couldn't see her expression.

"—Why do you wield your sword?"

"—" She had never asked this question before.

In the three months they had known each other, there had always been flowers and a sword. But until this moment, Theresia had not once broached the subject of his weapon. Now that she knew his name, she was trying to find out what was inside of Wilhelm.

If it wasn't Theresia asking, if it had been anyone else, Wilhelm would have simply pushed them away. But he found he could answer her with an unusually calm heart.

"…Because this is all I have."

The question was about his sword. Why he wielded it. In his heart, the answer was very simple—it was all he had. This was what Wilhelm, more than anyone else, had come to believe.

"—"

Theresia was silent, saying nothing in response to Wilhelm's answer. Just as she said nothing to his answer to her flower question. She talked too much and flitted from topic to topic, but she always repeated this one unchanging question, as though she were trying to solidify their tenuous relationship.

Wilhelm, too, kept quiet. He was not so foolish as to offend the moment by speaking.

5

I never thought you would actually come.

Grimm, his eyes wide, scrawled the words on a piece of paper as he sat up in bed, and showed the paper to Wilhelm.

They were in Grimm's room at the Royal Hospital, although it was actually a very large area full of injured people. One could tell how busy the hospital was from the number of beds with patients in them.

"Just on a whim. I was on my way to do something else," Wilhelm answered tersely. He stood beside Grimm's sickbed with his arms crossed.

It was close to a miracle that, after parting ways with Theresia, he had found his feet pointing him toward a visit to Grimm. He was telling the truth—it was nothing more than a whim. It was his first day off duty, and just going to his room to sleep would serve no purpose. That was all there was to this.

"Anyway, your woman will never leave me alone if I don't."

Please don't talk about Carol that way.

"…This writing is a pain. Can't you do anything about it?"

It took Grimm time to respond to anything Wilhelm said. Paper for holding these conversations was not an abundant resource, either. Grimm kept using one sheet until it was almost completely black with letters.

In the face of Wilhelm's annoyance, Grimm gave a pathetic smile and pointed to his throat. A long white scar ran across it, a sign of the damage to his speech organs. He could make a scratchy sound with his breath, but he would never speak again.

I was at least lucky to escape with my life.

"...Given that we were fighting Libre, you probably were."

Where's Carol?

"What, you think we're friendly enough to show up here together? Don't make me laugh."

He really had come here on an absolute whim. Just the thought of bringing Carol along, someone whose company he didn't enjoy in the least, was enough to make him choke. Encountering her was something he dearly wanted to avoid.

"I'm not visiting again. You make sure she knows I was here, okay?"

I've got it. I'll tell her.

That helped him relax a little, at least. Now maybe he wouldn't have to worry about Carol coming around to harangue him. If she had left him alone, he never would have bothered coming to see Grimm.

How's the captain doing?

"It's like he's possessed by the ghost of Pivot. I don't like it. 'Do this. Kill the demi-humans.' That's all you ever hear from him these days. Supposedly things have quieted down recently, but he's only gotten louder."

Apparently Bordeaux had come to visit once as well but had quickly left again on business. The royal army was in total chaos, and the commanders had a lot on their plates. Bordeaux was no exception.

"—"

Suddenly, Grimm stopped writing and gazed into the distance. Wilhelm recognized the expression. It was the way Grimm had looked at the royal army's cemetery, when they had said their last farewells to their fallen comrades. Wilhelm knew that he was lost in his memories of all those in Zergev Squadron who had died at Aihiya.

Wilhelm, arms still crossed, walked over to the window and thought back to the swamp himself. He had ruminated on that battle many, many times—always so that he wouldn't forget his rage at the unresolved conflict with Libre or at Sphinx, who had stolen that chance from him.

This time, though, was different. This time, Wilhelm thought back to a different moment in the battle…

"…Why did they protect me?"

He remembered Pivot, who had given his life taking a blow meant for Wilhelm. He remembered all the others, who had stood against Libre at Pivot's dying command and been cut down themselves.

Grimm, too. He was among those who had faced Libre in Wilhelm's place, and for his trouble he had received a wound he would bear forever and lost his voice.

He didn't understand why. None of them had had a hope of winning. If the effect of the magic circle had continued, Wilhelm probably also would have met his doom there. What meaning could there have been in their actions?

"You, all of you, challenged a foe you could never beat. Pivot died, all of you died, and I—"

If it hadn't been for Sphinx's intervention, Wilhelm would have died, too. And if he had, all of Zergev Squadron's sacrifices would have been for nothing. And then—

There was a quiet noise from behind him.

"—"

"Are you…laughing?"

As Wilhelm looked down at him, Grimm was reacting in an unusual way. His shoulders shook, his breath scratched from his throat, and he made a sound like he was coughing. It almost looked like laughter.

This totally unexpected answer left Wilhelm at a loss. Grimm took up his writing utensils.

I'm sorry for laughing. I never thought you'd respond that way.

"That's my line. I never took you for the type to find matters of life and death funny."

Me neither. I didn't think Pivot's death or the deaths of our comrades meant anything to you. And to think you're even upset that no one is blaming you...

"—?!" Wilhelm reached the end of what Grimm had written, and the unbelievable sentence immediately made him angry. But Grimm shook his head.

Nobody blames you, Wilhelm. My wounds and Pivot's death are not your fault. I'm sure the captain doesn't hold you responsible for Pivot, either.

It was the truth. Each time they saw each other, Wilhelm could tell how different Bordeaux was. Yet he never spoke ill of Wilhelm nor blamed him for Pivot's death. Nor did Grimm consider Wilhelm to be the reason he'd lost his voice. Knowing as much should have been a relief to him. Should have been.

Wilhelm. You're the sword of our Zergev Squadron. If you aren't defeated, we won't be, either. Everyone believed that, and that's why they put their lives on the line.

"You're making things up. My sword is mine, and I am my own."

That's true. I guess that's enough. Your intense way of living is yours alone. Well, it was—but it isn't anymore.

"I don't know what you mean."

Your way of living is an ideal. Describing it in words makes it sound cheap and thin, but only those who have really dedicated themselves can live like you. The rest of us couldn't do it.

Wilhelm couldn't quite grasp Grimm's emotion as he poured the letters onto the page. Wilhelm had always hated when people said they couldn't do something. Above all, he hated the look in a person's eye when they said it. He despised the look of people who thought they were making a smart choice as they gave up and made excuses.

But nothing in Grimm's expression as he looked at Wilhelm was anything like that. He was saying he couldn't. He was making excuses. His face was that of a man who had given up. Yet his eyes were neither resigned nor regretful. Wilhelm found Grimm's gaze very unsettling.

Wilhelm, I've always admired your strength. When we saw Tholter as an undead warrior at Castour Field, I could tell how different you and I were, and I thought you were amazing. So did everyone in the squadron. It's hard to see from a distance what makes you special. But up close, you can tell.

"...Don't go giving me a weird reputation."

Sorry. But you tend to do whatever you want to, you know. Maybe us independent types just tend to run into each other. I have high hopes for how far you can go.

How far could he go? He could swing his sword, become a sword—and where would he end up? He finally understood the inexplicable emotion he saw in Grimm's eyes. It was expectation and hope. It was envy toward someone he knew could keep going, even though Grimm himself had given up.

I would have liked to tell you, at least once, before I lost my voice. I guess it's a little late for that.

"—"

Thank you for that time. Thanks to you, I'm here now.

Grimm spoke all this without a word, then bowed his head toward Wilhelm with a smile. It was unmistakably a smile of brotherhood.

Wilhelm could hardly bear it.

6

"Do you like flowers?"
"No, I hate them."

"Why do you wield your sword?"
"Because this is all I have."

After he had learned Theresia's name, after Grimm had confessed his envy, things went on without any real change. The royal army was still moving slowly, and with the reorganization yet ongoing, he continued to wield his blade on behalf of the capital's police force. When he wasn't doing that, he was in the plaza having his absurd conversations with Theresia.

The questions about flowers and why he wielded his sword became an immutable touchstone for them. Wilhelm's answers and Theresia's reactions never changed, either.

Or rather, they weren't supposed to. But at some point Wilhelm noticed how the exchanges made him ache. He did still feel the same way about flowers—there was no way that would ever change. But being asked about his sword hurt his heart. Each time, the question made him uneasy and irritated. His chest throbbed with the emotions Pivot had shown him at Aihiya, as had Grimm in his hospital room.

"Wilhelm...you're staring at me. Is something wrong?"

"No...nothing."

"Oh? You shouldn't look too intently at a woman's face, then. It's rude."

"What? Don't you think you have a face worth looking at?"

"Wha? Wh-what does that mean...?"

"—?"

"Why do you act like you don't know what I mean?!" she said. "Don't you know how to have a conversation?"

He also started to notice that talking with Theresia in the square gave him the same sense of calm as swinging his sword. And finally, he saw that he was no longer able to lose himself in his sword practice the way he once had. Just swinging the sword should have been enough for him, but now, facing that blade made it hard for him to breathe.

It was almost as if he was—

"It's as if your sword is crying."

"—!" He had been swinging his blade out of sheer habit when Theresia said this. Instantly, Wilhelm felt a storm of emotion; he whirled on Theresia and glared at her.

"...Wh-what's wrong?" she asked.

"You—! What do *you* know about my sword...?!"

His unfocused pain had found an outlet. Wilhelm regretted the words, but they couldn't be taken back. Theresia frowned and said, "Wilhelm...you're right. I'm not qualified to talk about swords. But I can see by looking at you that using your blade right now is hurting you."

"Don't act like you understand. Nothing's hurting me. I—"

"If it's that painful, why don't you stop?"

"Stop...?"

He frowned; he had never so much as thought the word.

Right, Theresia nodded. "If you really hate it, there's no point in going on. It might seem irresponsible, but why keep going if you have to destroy your own heart to do it? Or..." She paused and looked at Wilhelm, who stood bolt upright. "...Does it mean something else you, to pour yourself into your sword like that?" *Something beyond the sword itself*, she meant.

She asked as though it were the same question she always asked, but it wasn't.

Wilhelm wielded his sword because the sword was all he had. But the meaning of it—what was it that drove Wilhelm Trias to do so?

"Even I don't know the answer to that," he said.

"In that case—"

"But putting it down would be unforgivable."

This time it was Theresia's turn to fall silent. He couldn't be allowed to put down his sword. What he wanted didn't figure into it.

"Unforgivable? So...you mean to go on using your sword forever, no matter how much it hurts you? No matter how painful it is?"

"That's right. I don't have to know why I'm doing it. I just have to." Wilhelm had no way of finding any other answer than that, anything other than the sword. He grabbed hold of the hilt of his weapon as if clinging to a lifeline. Theresia exhaled when she saw it.

"I see. So there was a meaning. To keeping you alive."

"A meaning to keeping me alive...?"

He was stunned by the words. They almost suggested that she knew about Pivot and all the people of Zergev Squadron, and how he had been saved from death. But he didn't see it in her eyes. Two clear blue irises looked at him.

"Yes," she said. "As much pain as it causes you, you can't let your sword go. I..." Theresia looked down, her expression sad. Wilhelm noticed the change but was unable to give an immediate response. Her words were still ringing in his ears.

"I hope you find it," she said. "Your reason."

"My...reason...?"

He wondered if perhaps those words might, in truth, be the key to resolving the problem in his heart. Then again, he could have told her it wasn't so easy and not to say such stupid things. But Wilhelm didn't do either of these.

"Yeah," he answered. "If I even have one." He nodded at Theresia.

It was the meaning of letting him live, the reason Pivot and the others gave themselves up, the answer to Grimm's envy. Or perhaps the thing that would turn Wilhelm into steel once and for all.

"Don't worry," Theresia said. "I'm sure you'll find it. You of all people can do it." She had no basis for saying so, but she smiled gently. And Wilhelm, for some reason, found himself unable to argue.

The chance to find his answer was coming, as if Theresia's words had summoned it. It would be a great battle that Wilhelm Trias, the Sword Devil, could not avoid.

A critical moment in the Demi-human War, a bloodbath at Lugunica Castle, would soon arrive.

THE LOVE SONG OF THE SWORD DEVIL

Sixth Stanza

1

A mass uprising of the demi-humans all throughout the kingdom engulfed the nation in the fires of war.

The royal army, still reeling from their earlier losses, was put on the defensive by the armed uprising of demi-humans and the mass of undead warriors who accompanied them. As casualty reports flooded in, army headquarters was thrown into chaos, and the defense of each region was left to those in charge on the ground.

"That's the general gist of what I'm hearing, anyway, but I haven't gotten any details," Bordeaux said quietly. "If they had put us out there somewhere, we might at least have been able to help prevent some casualties."

Zergev Squadron, fully armored, was gathered at a guard station. The members present were the newcomers, the ones who had helped fill out the squadron after its old cohort had been so cruelly reduced. With the reorganization ongoing, official reassignment papers hadn't yet been issued, but everyone he had spoken to ahead of time had come. Among them, of course, were Grimm, now out of the hospital, and Wilhelm.

"Grimm!" Bordeaux said. "You might've lost your voice, but I hope you can still fight like you used to! This is your chance to show us what you've got."

Grimm could say nothing to this attempt to inspire morale, but he pounded his shield in response. Bordeaux nodded at the display of spirit, then gazed out of the guard station. "I expect we'll be dispatched to the nearest battlefield soon. Frankly, I'd like to rush out there right now, but it's worth remembering that the bigger they get, the slower they are."

As Bordeaux counseled patience, Wilhelm was silently readying himself for battle. He would meet the oncoming fight with the over-whelming spirit of the Sword Devil. On the field, in the midst of a life-and-death struggle—he could forget the confusion he felt about fields of flowers. Where the sparks of life flew in sprays of blood, his spirit could give itself wholly to the sword, and he didn't need to feel lost...

"An armed uprising, though," Bordeaux said dispassionately, still looking out the window. "That's a bold move. Valga Cromwell came up with it, I'm sure, but I have to admire how he was able to get all the demi-humans in on it." He ran a hand through his short hair and frowned grimly. "But unfortunately for him, the capital was too vigilant for his plan to work here. The rest of the country may be burning, but he missed the most important part. I guess that's all you can expect from a bunch of stupid savages."

His words reflected more than a little of his personal animus, but Wilhelm largely agreed with him. Rebellions had occurred all over the nation, but the capital alone was untouched.

Wilhelm had spent several years in the capital now, even if he hadn't especially wanted to. He didn't want to see the city turned into a battlefield, nor did he desire all the casualties that would result. Including Theresia and her field of flowers...

"Wait." This felt wrong to Wilhelm. And not in the depths of his heart as Theresia had revealed to him. Something was off. And one word Bordeaux had used brought it together.

"Burning…?"

Wilhelm had heard something very similar recently. He wracked his memory, trying to recall when it had been—then bolted immediately to his feet.

Soon tongues of flame will lick the whole nation… Even the capital will not escape destruction.

The words belonged to one of the demi-human vandals he had apprehended. Of course, they could be dismissed as bravado—but it had also described Valga Cromwell's plan.

The capital was a volatile place. Wilhelm knew that from his time with the local constabulary. Would Valga ignore his potential allies here and leave the capital out of his plans?

It's not possible. He wouldn't forget this city.

Which had to mean the uprisings were—

"Bordeaux! All these uprisings are just a diversion! The real target is the capital—the royal castle!"

"What?!"

After Wilhelm's intuition led him to the answer, he ran up to Bordeaux, his voice ragged. A dark look came across his commander's craggy face.

It angered him, but he was sure. He knew the enemy would seek the royal forces' most vital point.

"Think back to Castour and Aihiya! The battles where the royal forces suffered their worst losses! Both times, we went for the obvious bait and fell right into Valga Cromwell's traps!"

"And that makes you think these uprisings are a decoy, while the real aim is the heart of the kingdom?"

"Yes! You know this, Bordeaux! We dispatch soldiers from the capital to put down the rebellions, then they concentrate their forces on the undefended capital. They'll conquer the kingdom!"

Depending on how things went, the choice the squadron made now could determine the future of the Dragonfriend Kingdom of Lugunica. They had no sure proof, but Wilhelm trusted his instincts. If he hadn't trusted those same instincts on the battlefield, he would never have survived to see this day.

"Hmm." Bordeaux crossed his arms and assumed a look of deep contemplation. Wilhelm could only grind his teeth.

The same thing had happened before. At the Battle of Castour Field, when they had encountered the first magic circles and had been trying to decide what to do with them, Wilhelm had urged the captain then to push forward. He had said it was the only way to survive. But his opinion had been overruled, and he and Grimm had ended up the last living members of their unit.

The same thing was happening again now. If Bordeaux wouldn't listen to him, then even if Wilhelm had to go alone, he would—

Someone patted the increasingly agitated Wilhelm on the shoulder. He turned around to see Grimm nodding at him and raising his hand to Bordeaux.

The commander noticed the gesture. He stared at Wilhelm and Grimm. Then he gave a deep nod, and a wide grin, the first they'd seen in a long time, came over his face.

"Well, how about that? Leaving Zergev Squadron to stew in the capital might turn out to be headquarters' smartest move! Now things are getting interesting!"

Bordeaux slammed the butt of his halberd against the floor. The metallic noise rang throughout the guard station, and all the members of Zergev Squadron responded with one voice. "Yeeeaaahhhh!"

In an instant, everyone was eager for battle, the room shaking with their cry. The noise surrounded Wilhelm, but he wasn't caught up in it. Bordeaux, resting his halberd on his shoulder, grinned at the swordsman.

"What's wrong, Captain Killer? You don't look yourself."

"We've got no proof. You're going to trust me?"

"The final decision is mine, and I'm not going to let anyone stop me. Plus...my instincts agree with yours. Let's shred this demi-human plan—call it a parting gift to Pivot and the others!"

Bordeaux gave Wilhelm a shove in the chest; Wilhelm stumbled backward until Grimm caught him. The silent shield bearer smiled at him in a way that seemed to ask, *How about that?* Wilhelm waved him away.

"All right, here we go! Zergev Squadron is the sword of the kingdom!

That makes it our duty to bring justice to any barbarians who would go against the flag of our nation! Anyone disagree? Anyone object?"

"No! No one! How could we?"

Bordeaux gave a shout, raising his battle-ax, and the soldiers shouted back. Their leader listened to them with satisfaction, then turned to Wilhelm again.

"Wilhelm! Wilhelm Trias, the Sword Devil! The enemy is after—?"

"What else?" Wilhelm answered. "The castle—the royal castle of Lugunica!"

Bordeaux pointed his ax at the distant castle. Then he sucked in a breath and howled like an animal. "The enemy is closing in on the castle! Zergev Squadron, move out!"

2

As Zergev Squadron approached the castle ready for battle, the castle's defenders prepared themselves to die. They were sure the murderous-looking mass of soldiers approaching them was an enemy contingent bent on their destruction.

"What? What's this?! Is this how defenders of the realm comport themselves?!" a knight shouted at the trembling men. The cruel-looking knight stared down the onrushing squadron, then gave a disdainful click of his tongue.

"Well, if it isn't that idiotic stray... Halt where you are, Bordeaux Zergev!"

"Is that Lord Lyp Bariel?" Bordeaux called back, gaping at the man who stood in the midst of the defending soldiers. It was the viscount, the same knight they had encountered at Aihiya Swamp.

Zergev Squadron came to a standstill. Lyp moved to stand in front of Bordeaux.

"Don't you know we're at war, Bordeaux? What do you think you're doing?! The kingdom is in crisis, and you're playing pranks? This is practically rebellion!"

"I apologize for startling you all. But we aren't here on a friendly visit. Time is of the essence—the fate of the kingdom hangs in the balance!"

"Oh, it does, does it?"

Lyp frowned at Bordeaux's declaration. Then someone stepped forward out of the battle-ready crowd to stand beside Bordeaux. It was Wilhelm. Lyp looked at the young man who radiated a swordsman's aura, clearly displeased.

"You again, Sword Devil."

"Call me what you like. I have no time to argue with you. The enemy is targeting this castle."

"You mean to say the armed uprisings are a diversion? Do you have any proof?"

Lyp was nothing if not intelligent. From Wilhelm's curt remark, he had guessed what the demi-humans were really up to. But the only way they could respond to his request for certainty was with a shake of their heads.

"So on the basis of an educated guess, you descend upon the castle like an avalanche?" Lyp said. "I request you withdraw, Zergev Squadron. At present, the defense of this castle is my responsibility."

"Valga, Libre, and Sphinx," Wilhelm said. "You mean to take them all on yourself? You must be pretty confident."

"Again? How many times must I tell you not to talk back to your superiors!"

With a sharp *tsk*, Lyp lashed out at Wilhelm with his metal gauntlet. But whereas the blow had landed at Aihiya Swamp, this time Wilhelm simply turned his head and avoided it easily.

"Who gave you permission to dodge me—?"

"At Aihiya, you were my commanding officer, but not now. You have no reason to strike me and no reason to stop us. If you get in our way, we'll just push past you."

Wilhelm rattled the hilt of his sword pointedly. The other castle guards cowered at his spirit, which hit them almost like a physical force. Even Lyp looked somewhat cowed for once. The situation seemed set to explode at any moment.

"Weeell, then," a new voice said. "How about an order from me? I rank higher than any of you. I officially command Zergev Squadron to join in the castle's defense."

The woman's voice came from the direction of the castle. The collective gaze turned to see two figures approaching—Roswaal, dressed in her military outfit, and her attendant Carol.

"Roswaal J. Mathers…!" Lyp gasped.

"So we have the war's anti-magic specialist—that's me—and a self-indulgent gate guard—that's you. Shaaall we compare our positions to see which of us ranks higher in your precious chain of command?"

Lyp ground his teeth angrily, but Roswaal only shrugged. What she was saying was completely true, and the reality was as pitiless as a snake. As much as he hated it, Lyp could only shut his mouth.

"Ohhh, don't be like that. All isn't lost. Being here today may yet give you your chance to bring honor and glory to your name. Consider all the possibilities." Her words weren't much consolation, but they effectively took Lyp out of the equation.

Then Roswaal spotted Wilhelm. She brushed her hair back behind her shoulders, smiling sweetly. "I kneeew you'd be here. It was the right choice to focus on all of you—well, on you specifically—at Castour."

"I still don't understand a word you're saying," Wilhelm said. "But we can come into the castle, right?"

"You could at leeeast learn how to talk to a woman. Of course you can come in."

Wilhelm told her, as bluntly as always, that he had no interest in lengthy talk. Then he turned to Bordeaux. The man known as the Mad Dog nodded gravely.

"Aaall right, then! Zergev Squadron will now enter the castle! Make sure we reinforce all the crucial points in the building! We'll split into ten groups, just as we planned." He pounded the ground with the butt of his battle-ax, and Zergev Squadron separated into ten groups. They would shortly assume their assigned roles and set themselves to the complete defense of the castle.

"Lord Lyp," Bordeaux said, "you stay here. Zergev Squadron will patrol the inside. Make sure you don't let any demi-humans inside the gate."

"—! I know my business! We wouldn't let a fly in here. Now get lost, you pack of mongrels!" The viscount was not a very gracious loser. Nonetheless, Wilhelm and the others trooped into the castle. Roswaal came trotting behind them with obvious interest.

"The unit's split into groups," she said. "Can I assuuume you will act on your own regardless?"

"You've got Grimm to keep an eye on you," Wilhelm said. "You'd only be trouble, anyway." He spared a backward glance. It was an act of kindness on his part toward the wordless Grimm, who walked alongside Carol. Apparently, they were capable of having a conversation when only one of them could actually talk. Wilhelm scoffed a little at that.

As the members of Zergev Squadron walked through the castle, they found hallways silent and rooms abandoned. "Looks like you're short on soldiers," Wilhelm muttered. This was the first time he had been in the royal castle of Lugunica since he had been invited to the meeting at general headquarters. That day, the castle had been stuffed with more people than it needed, but now it was practically empty.

"After the losses at Aihiya, the command staff has been dispatched to battle lines all over the country," Roswaal said. "And His Majesty personally ordered that troops be sent where the impact of the rebellions is greatest."

"But that's—"

"A royal command is nooot something you can ignore. Not eeeven if it plays into the enemy's hands."

Lugunica's royal family were a sympathetic lot, but they were figureheads unsuited to national government. So much was widely rumored—and it seemed there was some basis for it.

"So there's no one protecting the castle?"

"A minimal contingent of the royal guard and defense units like Lord Lyp's. That's about it, I suppose. I admire His Majesty's refuuusal to prioritize his own safety, but it's just a sliiight problem when he occupies the most crucial building in the nation. Perhaps it's time to start praying to the Dragon for the kingdom's peace."

"I might admire your patriotism if you didn't end by saying we need to beg for help. But—wait."

Wilhelm's intuition was nagging at him again. If the demi-humans were after the castle, then their ultimate goal would be the heart of the kingdom—the king himself. And after causing the uprisings, they had a sure way of capturing their target. There was one place the king of the Dragonfriend Kingdom of Lugunica was certain to go when his country was in dire straits.

It was almost as if Valga Cromwell was inviting him there.

Bordeaux was heading upstairs. "Wilhelm! I'm going to go protect His Majesty! The throne room—"

Wilhelm cut him off with his own view of things. "Bordeaux! I'm going to the chapel! Objections?!"

Bordeaux looked startled at the way everything about Wilhelm suggested that he was going to follow his own instincts, but then he grinned.

"None at all! Whatever happens, just don't forget what Zergev Squadron stands for!"

"You know I never gave a damn about that."

"Then we should ask Grimm. Grimm! Don't let Wilhelm out of your sight!"

The vigorous pounding of a shield came in answer. Wilhelm frowned. Bordeaux hefted his battle-ax, wished them luck, and rushed off.

"What are you going to do?" Wilhelm asked Roswaal, who apparently intended to follow him down to the castle's basement chapel. "Why are you with us, anyway?"

Roswaal winked. "I have my own objective. Wheeether it will show up here is a biiig gamble, but I think I'll trust the judgment of the man I'm head over heels for."

Grimm and Carol exchanged astonished looks at Roswaal's teasing words. But Wilhelm, the man in question, only gave a thoroughly exasperated cluck and shifted away from Roswaal.

"Don't come whining to me if you get killed," he said. "I'm not nice enough to be looking behind me while I'm trying to fight."

"...I think you've changed, though. You wouldn't have said that befooore."

"Me? Changed? Even if I have—"

Even if he had, it was only to advance along the path to becoming an unfeeling sword. It was, he believed, the answer he had found in his blade.

Wilhelm gritted his teeth and forced away the image of Theresia that floated through his mind. If she hadn't kept asking him, he would have stopped believing it long ago. He dashed forward, as if to escape the fact.

3

When Bordeaux entered the audience chamber, he could physically feel the air thicken. It was the tingling sensation of a great battle about to begin—a confrontation with an absolute opponent. He had been right to come here alone. He suspected only he among his men could bear this.

"I'll never be able to thank Wilhelm enough," he muttered. Although they rarely fought now, his duels with Wilhelm on the training ground had accustomed him to such an overwhelming aura of battle. He was frightened, yes, but the fear was familiar.

There were few opponents whom Bordeaux would recognize as genuinely stronger than himself. It wasn't just that he hated to admit it. He was, in fact, a tremendous fighter. He had been around weapons since he had been a boy and had used his natural physique and intellect to pursue the path of a knight. Between his family's social standing and his own gifts, Bordeaux's life went almost exactly as he would have wished. Accompanied by other disciples who seemed like annoying older brothers, the wind had always seemed to be at his back as he advanced day by day.

A change had come into his life in the form of Wilhelm. Bordeaux could remember many times he had been at a loss as to how to handle the impertinent and rebellious boy. But Bordeaux had saved Wilhelm, which was enough to justify all the work.

Wilhelm had gone from a boy to a young man, and his sword had become indispensable to the kingdom. Pivot had understood that. It was why he had given his life to save him. Pivot had seen that Wilhelm would be essential in determining not just the kingdom's future, but Bordeaux's.

And here, now, Wilhelm's presence did indeed make the difference between life and death for Bordeaux.

A twin blade came at the hulking man, dyeing the audience chamber's red carpet even darker with blood as it did. His enemy's eyes were lifeless, his putrid breath ragged. It was the snake-man, Libre Fermi, but with no hint of who he had been in life. Yet even as an undead warrior, his aura of the greatest demi-human fighter remained.

"No Sphinx, eh? But at least I can get revenge for Pivot. You dirty little reptile!" Bordeaux inflamed his own lust for battle by taunting his enemy. Otherwise, he might have been swept away by the enemy's aura and lost the initiative.

The difference between them—in the power of their spirits as warriors—was unmistakable. The reason Bordeaux did not succumb was because he had already been on the losing end of such exchanges dozens of times. Wilhelm Trias had acquainted him with it more than well enough.

"I'm not about to be intimidated by an enemy who's on the back foot. Have at, Libre Fermi!"

He spun his battle-ax above his head and howled like an animal, stomping across the carpet. His huge body sprang forward, and the snake-man met him with the twin blade. Sparks flew, and the room filled with the ringing of steel on steel. The battle between the Viper and the Mad Dog had begun.

4

In front of the huge door of the chapel lay the headless bodies of several royal guards. They were the few that remained to provide security for the castle. They had fought valiantly but futilely, as evidenced by the weapons that lay scattered around and the array of sword marks. Usually, Wilhelm felt he had no sympathy to spare for the dead—that was, the weak. But this time, he found a strange emotion welling up within him. Perhaps it was because he knew what these corpses had been fighting for.

"—"

He cut the emotion off, and with his beloved sword in hand, Wilhelm opened the massive door. It moved slowly with a great creak, and a fresh breeze blew from the chapel into the hallway.

Magical, bluish-white lights illuminated the chapel in the basement of the castle. It was a place of grandeur and solemnity. On either side of the entrance ran rows of benches, and the crest of the Holy Dragon, the crest of the nation, was carved in the far wall. And at the altar, where prayers were offered to that carving, stood two figures.

The figures, one huge and one a small girl, spoke in hoarse voices.

"In this chapel, the people of the kingdom pray to the Dragon," the larger shadow said. "Empires worship power, and holy kingdoms worship the spirits. I don't know about the western city states, but I suppose they must have someone who offers up prayers."

"So then, what do you all pray for?" the girl asked. "What do demi-humans pray for, and to whom?"

"Hmm. If I were to pray, I suppose it would be to the souls of my comrades and ancestors. I, at least, have no other reason to pray."

Then the two figures turned around.

The girl, of course, he knew well by now. It was the witch Sphinx. And the giant standing next to her—he was the greatest enemy in this war, the leader of the demi-human tribes...

"Valga Cromwell."

The man nodded when Wilhelm spoke his name, but Wilhelm couldn't see his expression. Valga had wrapped himself entirely in a white sheet, as though he was trying to hide his identity at this late stage.

"Indeed I am. And you must be the Sword Devil. Yes, I see... The hostility in your face radiates an exceptional spirit. Even I am not immune to it, and battle is my everything. No wonder you were able to kill Libre."

"What are you talking about?" Such a description of the outcome at Aihiya could only be intended to humiliate him.

The witch, who had twisted the facts in her report, ignored the Sword Devil's gaze and focused on Roswaal. "If you are here…it must mean the king isn't coming." Her voice was emotionless.

Roswaal, her hands encased in metal gloves, responded, "I didn't have any special reason to tag along. I just haaated the thought of giving you what you wanted. I reject everything about you, and I will eventually stamp out your life under my heel." She gave a wave of her wrist and assumed a fighting stance with more flourish than was strictly necessary. Behind her, Carol drew her sword, and Grimm readied his shield.

"Brave people, all of you," Valga said. "For the four of you to try to stand against us…"

"No, that would be the two of you, coming into the heart of the castle," Wilhelm retorted. "Too bad for you, one of your friends has loose lips and gave away the surprise. We're putting an end to this, here and now."

"…I thought I had taken the utmost care in whom I told about my plans, but I see someone found himself talkative at the prospect of death. Never mind. I will not bear a grudge against a fellow demi-human. We've made it this far. Our plan is going well enough."

"True, to the extent that you were able to sneak into the castle. What were those stupid guards doing?"

"We took a hidden pathway through the sewers. No one knows of it now—you humans don't live long enough to remember."

Valga stamped his heel against the ground, opening a hidden tunnel. Perhaps he was so frank about it because Wilhelm had explained how he knew Valga's plan. Someone gave an involuntary click of the tongue.

"Back before the covenant with the Dragon, demi-humans were among those who helped construct this castle. Trying to speculate about the relations between humans and demi-humans in those days is a fool's errand, but it is rather ironic. It was those times that allowed this moment of reprisal."

"Nice talk, but bad troop choices," Wilhelm said. "The way I hear it, you're only good in a battle of wits, not a contest of arms. Apparently, your witch there is the only one with real fighting power."

"...Yes. As I am now, I suppose that is true." Valga's voice grew quiet.

Wilhelm raised an eyebrow at this portentous whisper, and the demi-human gave a rumbling laugh.

"If all had gone as I wished, the king would be here now. In order to reach him, I would have had no choice but to defeat the royal guard. Do you think I came unprepared for that task?"

"You never do anything the simple way."

"You are an emotionless man, aren't you?" Valga said curtly. Then he turned to his companion. "Sphinx, the spell."

Sphinx looked up at the huge man beside her and cocked her head. "Are you sure? Once I begin, it will be difficult to stop. Impossible, in fact."

"I don't care. I knew all along that if I wanted to properly avenge my comrades, I wouldn't return alive!" With a bellow, Valga tore away the sheet that was covering him. Hidden underneath was an old man with a bald head and a face like a demon. But his armor-like muscles, a unique trait of the giants, showed no age. His body was like a sheer cliff, and drawn on it was a purple sigil that began to glow—a magic circle.

"A magic circle on a living body?!" Carol exclaimed. "What kind of spell is this?!"

"I told you," Valga said gravely. "You humans pray to your dragon. I will pray to my ancestors and my fellow demi-humans."

The spell began to take effect on his aged flesh, and as the glow intensified, Valga pulled something out of a pouch—a small box.

"O bones of my forefathers, testament to the days when the giants were truly feared...!"

"The Sacrament of the Immortal King cannot construct an undead warrior from a pile of bones," Sphinx said. "But with a living descendent who shares the same blood and a tremendous amount of mana, things are different."

"You think you're going to bring back the old giants using the body of Valga Cromwell?!" Wilhelm said.

"The pride and the anger of the demi-humans you shall see with your eyes, feel with your flesh, and carve into your souls, damnable humans!" Valga shouted, and then he shoved the bones into his own chest. Immediately, Sphinx's ritual, amplified by the magic circle drawn on his body, did its awful work.

"Hrrraahh— Ahhhh— Ahhhhhhhh!"

Valga's howling voice got louder and louder, and the body it came from grew larger and larger. His lungs expanded as his body swelled to twice its original size, then twice again. Seconds later, the light of the spell faded.

Carol's trembling voice filled the chapel as she stared up at the looming form: "Is—is this what the giants used to be? You're nothing but a monster...!" Her words carried no small amount of terror. No one could have blamed her for it. Valga's head now reached the ceiling; he was easily more than thirty feet tall. He had grown so much, in fact, that he had to kneel to fit in the chapel.

Suddenly, the huge form stretched out its arm. The movement was nonchalant, yet it occurred with a violent quickness.

"Look out!" Wilhelm shouted, dodging to one side of the incoming fist. Roswaal was able to avoid it as well, while Grimm faced the blow head-on and protected Carol. Trying his best to judge where to hold his shield, Grimm took an impact like that of a rampaging animal. Instantaneously, he and Carol were both launched backward out the door and into the hallway.

"Oh no—!"

"That idiot threw himself backward to blunt the impact! But never mind that—here comes Valga!" Wilhelm called to the worried Roswaal. He refocused with his blade in hand and stared at Valga, whose battle aura had grown with him, and at Sphinx, who was floating in the air.

The witch paid his glare no mind, looking up at the ceiling the giant had shattered. "Valga, perhaps I could leave this to you? I believe the next step will require going elsewhere."

"Do what you want. As for me, I'll take revenge for Libre."

"So be it, then. Valga, I require your good fortune in battle."

"Right. I appreciate your help. Although I'm not sure about all the details."

Sphinx, given leave, cocked her head at Valga's parting words. But then the witch floated up through the destroyed ceiling without saying anything further.

"Sphinx…!" Roswaal shouted angrily.

Wilhelm gestured to the hallway with his sword. "You follow the witch. Bring those kids catnapping in the corridor."

Roswaal's eyes widened with a glance at Valga's hulking form.

"You mean to take Valga on alone? Like that? I don't think thaaat's possible, do you?"

"We can't let the witch get away. And you're not going to fight Valga with your fists or a shield. Carol specializes in deflecting things with her blade, and that won't help, either. You have to get in there and cut him down. He's mine."

Wilhelm, his sword now pointed once more at the giant, exuded an immense battle aura.

"You really are something. If we both make it back safely, I might practically kiss you."

"Forget the creepy chatter and just go."

"So cold, though. Perhaps your heart belongs to someone else?" Roswaal said, ignoring the circumstances long enough to tease Wilhelm. He only snorted. He certainly wasn't going to tell her that, just for an instant, the image of a red-haired girl had flashed through his mind.

"Best of luck," Roswaal said.

"Yeah. You be sure to kill her."

With these deadly words, the two vowed to fight, and then Roswaal retreated quickly from the chapel. Wilhelm assumed she had grabbed their two companions from the hallway and gone upstairs to battle Sphinx. Whether or not the three of them could best the witch depended on them.

Wilhelm didn't realize that this was, in its own way, a kind of trust.

"I don't have time to be worrying about anyone else, anyway," he muttered, sinking into a fighting stance.

"Don't overestimate yourself, boy," Valga replied. "Do you think one as lowly as yourself can really stop me from getting what I want?" He made a sweep with one gigantic arm. The Sword Devil dodged it, trusting in his own skills. The corners of his mouth turned up.

"If you're strong enough, you'll get by me. If you're weak, I'll crush you. That's all there is to it. The strength of your ideals has nothing to do with it."

5

He stepped in and brought the ax down with all his might. One end of the twin blade caught the blow and then cracked under a force that it couldn't withstand. The ax bit into the serpent's body, sending scales and blood flying. Libre reeled backward.

"Grraaahhhhhh!!" Though the wounded creature made not a sound, Bordeaux flew at him with a cry. He swung the heavy battle-ax like an extension of his arms, cutting with the blade and following up with the hilt. The undead warrior that had once been Libre resisted these attacks with all the skill that was still left in him.

He dodged, defending with the twin blade. Bordeaux was thrown off balance, and a strike found him. It grazed his shoulder and abdomen, but Bordeaux held his ground despite the flow of blood.

This was without a doubt the strongest opponent he had ever faced. It was hard to believe that this was how he fought, even with his lessened capabilities as an undead warrior. The thought of what Libre must have been while alive made Bordeaux shudder—whether from fear or a lust for battle, he didn't know.

"My blood! My blood boils, Libre Fermi!"

Whichever it was, at this moment he told himself it was the urge to fight. Despite being drenched in blood, Bordeaux continued to shout; he looked into Libre's lightless eyes. The serpent showed no reaction to the yell and only twirled the twin blade in his hand to continue the battle.

It was a deadly dance as Libre Fermi's twin blade began a ballet that was sure to kill.

"Hrrgh— Yaaaaaahhhh!"

Bordeaux's heart quailed at the storm of blows. But as he was driven back, he could feel the trembling from below through the soles of his boots. They were the shocks of a tremendous battle, and imagining the deeds of his comrades inspired him.

Pivot's last words were not to neglect what was below me.

What would Pivot say if he saw Bordeaux taking heart from his friends fighting literally under his feet?

Of course.

"You'd just laugh and tell me that wasn't what you meant, wouldn't you, Pivot!"

Bordeaux howled. His emotions stirred by the incoming dance of death, he hefted his ax and charged in. He didn't have Wilhelm's technique or Grimm's ability to block a blow, nor was he as nimble as Carol or as thoughtful as Roswaal. Instead, Bordeaux Zergev gambled everything on what he did have, the body and abilities he'd been given.

"Rrraaahhhhhhh!!"

The twin blade assaulted him like a tempest, scoring his body; everywhere he felt burning pain and flowing blood. Still, he raised his ax and brought it down squarely on the snake-man with shattering force.

The strike slammed home. And finally…

6

The burning light was a beam of death, evaporating everything it touched as it carved a trail along the floor and the wall. This rain of destruction came from a peerless demon in the form of a young girl.

Sphinx had retreated through the ceiling of the chapel up to the ground floor of the castle, but she was stopped by a woman in a military outfit, who had chased her.

"You are quite persistent," Sphinx said. "You require extermination."

"Is that sooo? If you would hurry up and die, I could go back to being a normal woman." Roswaal kicked off the stone wall, vaulting into the air and punching at the levitating Sphinx. The girl dodged left and right, but Roswaal pushed off the wall again, her long leg tracing a beautiful arc in the sky. The kick connected with the witch, bringing her to the ground.

"Grimm, with me!"

"—!"

Carol and Grimm slammed into her from opposite directions in the corridor. Sphinx spun to meet the double attack, creating a shield of magic to defend herself against Carol's sword, the more deadly of the two instruments.

"Hrk!"

But of course, that left her to take Grimm's shield blow undefended. The girl stumbled at the strike from behind and was thrown into the large, open room beyond the corridor.

"We did it!" Carol whooped.

"No, nooo. We slipped. I was hoping to keep her here, where space is tight." Roswaal frowned at her failed ploy. Along with the wordless Grimm, the three of them charged after Sphinx.

A second later, the beam rained down upon them, turning the exit of the corridor a glowing white.

"This requires caution," Sphinx said, floating in the air of the large room, well above the ceiling of the hallway. "However weak, prey may turn vicious when cornered." Her timing was perfect; she had her enemies trapped with no escape. She was confident they could never have dodged her light.

But then… "—? What trick is this?"

"Ohhh, it's not so haaard to understand," Roswaal said as she and the others emerged unharmed from the hall through the smoke. In answer to Sphinx's question, she flung aside the cape she had been wearing. "My cape was woooven with a spell that allows it to resist any magic at all, one time."

"I see. So that's how you protected yourself and your allies. I commend your thoroughness. You truly do want to kill me."

"But of course. Still, I thiiink you still dooon't understand how much."

Sphinx may have had an air of superiority as she stared Roswaal down, but Roswaal was undaunted. Carol stepped out from behind her, holding her sword in a low stance.

"My apologies for the trouble, Lady Mathers," she said. "May I leave your side for a moment?"

"Yes, do what you want. Maybe you could do something that rattles her nerves."

Sphinx cocked her head, mystified by this exchange between a master and servant who had known each other a long time. "She is considerably less powerful than you. Do you not merely send her to her death in vain?"

"Base creature. Do not make light of the sword technique of Remendes, my house, which serves the Sword Saints," Carol said sharply. She raised her sword and, with a light-footed leap, jumped into the air, throwing herself at the witch.

Sphinx met this sudden, direct assault with a glowing finger. "A futile death indeed. You would have required innovation to reach me."

The beam lanced out. Carol, hanging in midair and with no wings to fly, could not avoid it. Surely she would be pierced by the light and turned into smoldering ash.

And yet she wasn't.

"Hrm?"

"I told you, don't underestimate the Remendes family!" Carol said to the surprised witch, having neatly dodged her attack. Though she had been in midflight, Carol had kicked off of thin air to accelerate herself upward. Then she came down with a crescent strike, cleaving the witch's undefended left arm in half.

"Haaagh!"

The arm went flying, and a spray of blood erupted from the girl as she fell to the ground. Carol attempted to follow with another blow, but her opponent's remaining arm flung out another beam. Carol kicked the air again and just managed to avoid it. But this was not the end of the witch's troubles.

"I've been waiting twenty years for this, witch! Take this!"

Roswaal was directly below the plummeting Sphinx, and her fist came up in a whirlwind of air. It impacted the girl's body, the power of it coming through the metal glove, breaking bones and rupturing internal organs. The sound could be heard throughout the entire room.

"—!!"

Even Sphinx could not remain unperturbed in the face of such power. The deadly force drove blood from her mouth and distorted her sweet face with pain. She tried to speak, but her words were lost as she vomited. Her body tumbled to the middle of the huge room.

The blood loss from her left arm and the heavy damage to her organs from the punch would have spelled the immediate death of any normal human, but with a witch, even that might not be enough.

"Until I've crushed your skull and torn out your heart, I can't be sure," Carol said, lowering herself to the ground and eyeing the witch. She came down from the sky less out of an abundance of caution and more for personal reasons. She would be the one to finish Sphinx.

She advanced on the girl, ready to strike one decisive blow...

"You sur-surprise me. I never—*cough!*—expected to be brought so low..." Sphinx sat up, still coughing up blood. Her face had gone pale, and she should not have been able to move. But she could still evoke an unspeakable terror.

"I'm glad it was...my left arm you cut off..."

Roswaal moved in, looking to crush the witch's head with another punch before she could do anything. But Sphinx was faster, pulling off her robe with her remaining arm. The cloth tore away with a soft rip, and there beneath, on the girl's white, exposed skin, was a purple design. The same one that had been drawn on Valga.

"*Al Ziwald.*" She intoned the magic for the ultimate form of Ziwald, her death ray.

The beam that had previously come only from the tip of her finger now burst from her entire palm. It was as if her hand was reaching out to annihilate everything in its path.

The destructive ray speared diagonally across the great hall, and death drew nearer by the instant. Even Roswaal would be hard-pressed to dodge it; she found herself hardly able to speak with astonishment.

Similarly silent was the young man who brought up his shield and met the beam head-on.

7

The blows smashed the floor and ceiling of the chapel with the force of an oncoming wall. The giant's strikes looked powerful enough to send a person flying, even if the hit only grazed him. But Wilhelm, the wind from the swipes rustling his hair, avoided the attacks as narrowly as he could, then struck back.

"It's hopeless, boy!" Valga crowed. "Do you think a cheap little sword like that can bring down a giant?"

The Sword Devil's attacks merely bounced off the massive creature, who was strong enough to punch through steel or rock. The recoil flung Wilhelm back, and the giant's other arm came for him. He danced away from it, but the speed of his evasion only put him further off balance, providing a critical opening.

"I like your talk—but this is the end!"

"Gwah?!"

Wilhelm was caught in midair, and Valga brought his hand down as if swatting a fly. Wilhelm defended immediately, but against the overwhelming force of the attack it was meaningless. The blow hit his entire body all at once. He bounced off the chapel floor and

slammed into a row of pews. He was pinned under the rubble of the shattered seat, and silence descended.

"A trifle. Now to destroy the entire castle and—"

"Don't get ahead of yourself."

"Hrm?"

The giant's inquisitive grunt rumbled throughout the room. Wilhelm leaped at him from out of the mountain of debris. The Sword Devil was soaked in blood, but still his eyes burned with the lust for combat. Valga quickly brought up his right arm to block, but Wilhelm ducked around it. The left arm was late in coming, and he dodged it. He dashed up Valga's arm and drove his sword into one of the giant's astonished eyes.

Giants' skin could withstand steel, but their vital points were as fragile as a human's. Wilhelm pierced the eye easily, and vitreous fluid gushed out, covering him.

Valga roared in pain. "Hwoooahhhhhh!"

The Sword Devil pulled out his blade with satisfaction. As Valga convulsed in agony, Wilhelm grabbed on to his shoulder and laughed. His own body groaned from the earlier impact; the moment of inattention had cost him several broken bones and ruptured internal organs. If he wasn't careful, the blood would block his throat. The burning pain made him regret even having to breathe.

But *now*—now this was his battlefield.

"Ruuuahhhhhh!"

With a shout, Wilhelm targeted Valga's fingers as the monster pressed a hand to his wound. He scored a hit against a joint. It felt hard under his sword, and he couldn't sever it. But that was no reason to admit defeat or lose hope.

Carrying the momentum of the deflected blow, he buried the tip of his sword in one of the howling lips. He broke through skin, pierced flesh until he felt the blade collide with a row of teeth. Valga bellowed again at this violence to his mouth. He lashed out blindly, trusting his strength to make up for his lack of precision, and scored a lucky direct hit. Wilhelm went spiraling through the air and slammed into the ground.

Wilhelm planted his fist into the ground to stop himself from rolling. Legs trembling, he stood. But once he was on his feet, the Sword Devil gave a click of his tongue at his own powerlessness and stared up at the giant. The sword buried in the side of the creature's mouth seemed impossibly far away.

"So this," Valga growled, "is the pain of battle...the suffering of my fellows as I sat in the shadows, concocting my little schemes. How self-important I was!"

As Wilhelm stood gritting his teeth, Valga took his hand away from his wound. As Wilhelm watched, red steam drifted from his ruined left eye, and the wound healed itself. This was accompanied by an intensifying glow of the symbol on Valga's chest—the fearful effects of the Sacrament of the Immortal King.

"But I shall not be defeated while the anger and humiliation of my comrades remain unexpiated! However strong you may be, you will learn you are nothing before the pride of—"

"Blah, blah, blah. I thought I told you. I don't give a damn how idealistic you are!"

Valga howled again and raised both arms high. He whipped them about, yet despite the display of deadly power, Wilhelm boldly stepped forward in hopes of reclaiming his sword. His opponent was a monster with immense endurance and the ability to regenerate himself. Wilhelm would not be able to defeat him unarmed.

Valga was an amateur when it came to combat; he relied entirely on his strength. That gave Wilhelm a glimmer of a chance.

It was true. Ideals were meaningless in battle. It wasn't the demi-humans' collective anger or pride that had allowed Valga to corner Wilhelm. It was simply that giants were powerful.

"What a pain in the ass!" Wilhelm shouted. "Everyone wants to drag me into some ridiculous...*thing*!"

He wanted to throw himself into being a single sword—yet he encountered so many unnecessary intrusions. Everyone wanted him to have a reason, or an ethos, or a faith, or pride, or dignity. What was so great about having a reason to fight? Did there have to be a meaning to using the sword?

*   *   *

Do you like flowers?

No, he hated them. He was sure he did. To him, it was all superfluous emotion.

Why do you wield your sword?

Because it was all he had. It was all he needed. It was enough.

Because he had been taken by the beauty of steel, enthralled by its vitality, and so had hoped to become a sword himself.

"Your ruination is upon you, human! The death of the Sword Devil will be an appropriate footnote to the destruction of this kingdom!"

"Everything...that's mine...is *mine!*"

"No one but you believes that now! You and I are both—!"

Two giant arms and harsh avowals assaulted Wilhelm as he tried to draw closer. The physical strength shattered the floor, the words pierced the Sword Devil as well as the giant. Anger against anger, pride against pride—it was neither of those, certainly. What each of them brought to the battle was too different. The gulf between what each of them wanted was too vast.

Still, as two people who fought, they waged a battle. And so it would not be luck that decided the outcome. The result would be down to who was stronger.

All this was what Wilhelm believed, the source of the strength that the Sword Devil trusted in. So perhaps the outcome was a foregone conclusion.

Because the Sword Devil, who believed his strength was as steel, had impurities within himself.

"Gah... Haah..."

"*Now*, your end has come."

Wilhelm had taken a direct hit, unable to avoid the blow. It threw him back against the wall, where he slid to the ground. His left arm was a wreck, and his mutilated forehead was pouring so much blood into his eyes he could barely see. The giant made a fist and raised it over his head, taking aim at the now immobile Sword Devil.

Wordlessly, Wilhelm watched the fist float over his head. When it came down, it would crush his body and turn him into nothing more than a bloody lump of flesh.

Death itself was before him. Death, which he had visited on so many others. He had no sword. He hadn't even found the reason he clung to his blade. And now he was going to—

"Meet your end, Sword Devil. Perhaps Libre and I will see you in hell!"

The fist came down. The end of Wilhelm's life came barreling toward him.

"Grimm! Now!!"

"—rrrr!"

In that final instant, he heard the voice of a woman, and of a man whose voice was hardly a whisper. The impact shook the entire chapel.

8

Grimm threw himself between Roswaal and the beam of light an instant before it annihilated her.

"—"

He hadn't been sure he would win or even survive. Until now, neither victory nor survival had influenced Grimm's life as bad luck had, so what came of his blocking the light with his shield was also a gift of his "bad luck."

"With a mere shield…"

This was not like stopping any normal attack. This was the light that had decimated the castle's great hall and all but evaporated the royal guards who now lay dead in the corridor. It could pierce armor; it should certainly have been able to do the same to a shield.

"Grimm!" Carol shouted as the attack hit home. She could be cool, but deep down she was kind and pure. Her fragile heart was surrounded by a shell like glass. So although she could appear hard, she was in fact quite delicate. She wanted to support Grimm—even if he, who had relied on her help so much lately, might have thought that was ridiculous.

Even so, in the days before this battle, her thoughtfulness had been his salvation.

"—"

Grimm felt the grip of his shield heating up under the beam's assault. It burned as though he had put his hand to a hot soup pot, but he refused to let go.

He couldn't use a sword. He had no voice. He would not relinquish his shield.

"My Al Ziwald. He—?"

Across from Grimm, the witch could hardly speak for amazement. Grimm's shield was catching the beam from her hand, reflecting the all-consuming heat up to the ceiling of the great hall.

The heat was the only thing that affected the shield; there was no further damage to it. The shelter had saved Grimm and Roswaal.

On the back of the shield was the crest of the House of Remendes, Carol's family. It was an heirloom Carol had given to Grimm to celebrate his survival. And in doing so, she saved his life.

"—*rrr!*"

The heat burned his hand, and the pain forced a scratchy sound out of his throat. Deflected by Grimm's defense, the beam destroyed the ceiling and brought down the floor of the room above the great hall.

That room happened to be the audience chamber, where the Mad Dog and the Viper were fighting.

"Wh-what the—?!"

Two humanoid figures fell with the rest of the rubble as the floor suddenly vanished from beneath them. The shout belonged to a badly wounded Bordeaux. He pushed the butt of his battle-ax against the wall to lessen the force of his descent. It allowed him to avoid a fatal impact, even though he still hit the ground hard.

"Hrrgh... Th-the great hall? How did I get here...?" Bordeaux shook his head and looked around in confusion.

But the shape next to him, despite having had nothing to soften its landing, stood up slowly as though it didn't feel its wounds. This other person was tall and covered in scales—it was without a doubt the serpent Libre Fermi.

"I believe this is what they call 'turning the tide of battle,'" Sphinx said. Her magic had been deflected, but as a result, she had gotten reinforcements in the form of her most powerful undead warrior. The witch moved to Libre's side and thrust out her right arm in front of the silent warrior. She pointed at Grimm, who had fallen to one knee, and at Roswaal, who stood with her fists up.

"You have the numbers, but I have the strength. Libre. This requires your attention. Starting now, you will fight, and I will support you as you—"

Sphinx found herself cut off before she could finish giving orders.

The reason was a sword blow. And it came from the most unexpected of places—right beside her.

"...Wha?"

Her right arm, which had been pointed at Roswaal, went tumbling freely through space. She had never expected to lose her other arm in this way. Now the witch was truly hemorrhaging. She turned toward Libre.

Brandishing the twin blade, the undead Libre Fermi looked at the witch and dropped his weapon. Now they could see he had a gaping, critical wound in his chest, inflicted by a battle-ax.

The zombie Libre Fermi had already been defeated by Bordeaux Zergev.

"Impossible...," Sphinx breathed. "In your last moment, did you fulfill...your final vow...?"

No sooner had she spoken than Libre lost what remained of his existence. The slender body crumbled into dust, leaving only its robe, and the flesh was now nothing more than a pile of ashes. The strongest of the demi-human warriors, who had been used and exploited even after his death, was at last well and truly gone.

"Looks like the tide's turned back, Sphinx," Roswaal said coldly.

"—!" The witch had now lost both her undead warrior and the arm she had been using to cast her magic. She had no more options, and for the first time, something like panic entered her face. She did the only thing she could still do—she used her levitation magic to float from the great hall toward the corridor to escape.

"—! We can't let her—!"

"She has nooo hope of getting away at this point. Leave her to me." Roswaal stopped Carol before she could give pursuit and moved to finish the witch. Just before she disappeared into the hallway, Roswaal turned. "I thank you, Grimm Fauzen. Without you, I would never have been able to accomplish my mission. I apologize for having made light of you before. And, Carol, I'm sorry to you, too."

"—"

"Y-you needn't apologize to me! J-just deal with that *thing*!"

Grimm couldn't have spoken at that moment even if his vocal cords had been in working order. Carol, for her part, turned red at Roswaal's jibe.

Roswaal nodded with her usual slightly detached look, then tapped the floor with her fingers. "I can still hear something from downstairs. You two go join our dear Wilhelm. I'll meet you all later." Then she sprinted into the corridor after Sphinx.

Behind her, Grimm and Carol nodded at each other and then went over to Bordeaux.

"So Libre and the witch are taken care of?" he asked. "What about Wilhelm? What's happening with him?"

"He's in the chapel fighting Valga Cromwell, who was turned into a massive giant by a spell," Carol told him. "Honestly, I'm not sure he needs our help, but..." She seemed to have complicated feelings about the matter. She wasn't being stubborn and refusing to help Wilhelm. Rather, she seemed to be speaking from a genuine knowledge of how powerful the Sword Devil was. But that didn't change the fact that the two of them didn't get along. It was possible that her excessive hostility had caused her to misjudge Wilhelm.

"—"

"...Hmph. Cheeky punk. But I guess that's what makes you part of Zergev Squadron." Wordlessly, Grimm was holding out a hand to the kneeling Bordeaux. He smiled broadly, took the proffered hand, and lifted his huge body to its feet. Hefting his battle-ax, he nodded at Carol, who looked at him wide-eyed. "You're right. Wilhelm—the Sword Devil—he's more powerful than any of us. Much as I hate to admit it. But I don't care. If he says he doesn't need us, then we get to enjoy the show. But on the off chance he's bitten off more than even he can chew..."

"Yes? What then?"

"We'll finally get to lend him a hand. The rest of us owe him more than enough favors!"

Then Bordeaux thumped Carol happily on the shoulder and set off for the chapel at a run. Grimm followed him, smiling at the befuddled young woman.

And then…

9

"Grimm! Now!!"

"—*rrrr!*"

Two figures flung themselves between him and the fist as it came rushing down. The point of a sword found the spaces between the giant fingers, and a shield came up to meet the blow. And, shortly after, a battle-ax arced in and delivered a tremendous strike.

"Hrrrgh!" Bordeaux gave a low groan as the ax connected right below the knuckles of the slowing fist. The skin was too tough for the ax to cut through it, but it couldn't diffuse the force of the impact. There was a sound like a falling tree, and the middle and index fingers of the hand bent backward.

"Guh… Ahh!" Valga shouted with pain as the digits broke. He pulled his fist back, and Bordeaux laughed. Baring his teeth madly, the huge man saw Wilhelm crumpled against the wall, and his smile widened.

"What's the matter, Wilhelm? Something wrong? This isn't like you! Have you given up? Do you think that's becoming of Captain Killer of the glorious Zergev Squadron?!"

Wilhelm, lying on the ground, didn't say a word at the mockery, but his hand curled into a fist. He coughed up the blood in his throat and braced himself against the wall, trying to stand.

"Keep it…to yourself. And I don't recall…asking you to save me."

"Bwa-ha-ha-ha! You never were a gracious loser! Ahh, now I'm glad I didn't die. I wish Pivot and the others could hear this!"

There was no malice in his words. Wilhelm could find nothing to say. Bordeaux was right. Wilhelm had once again been saved from death. It was just like with Pivot and Zergev Squadron—Wilhelm had been left alive.

Wilhelm couldn't say anything, but Valga looked at Bordeaux, Grimm, and Carol and shook his head.

"Reinforcements? No…if you lot are here, it must mean Libre and Sphinx are finished."

"Libre Fermi has turned to ash, and the witch Sphinx will soon find herself in hell, courtesy of Lady Mathers," Carol said, pointing her sword at the giant. "Valga Cromwell, you are the last of the Demi-human Alliance's leaders."

Valga put his bloodied hand to his face, and for several seconds, he was silent. Then a rumble began in his throat. The sound echoed on and on through the air. Unbelievably, it was laughter.

"Why do you laugh?!" Carol demanded.

"You humans understand nothing," Valga said. "For even now, after all this killing, you fail to grasp our purpose, our principles!" His yell, as loud as an explosion, echoed through the chapel. The wind of his anger shook the basement air. Rage was on Valga's face. He spread his arms wide and ground his teeth. "It will not stop, this war. Let Libre and Sphinx be dead, and let the lot of you kill me here. It will not extinguish the anger of the demi-humans. The hatred will not fade."

"—"

"Even if we fail in this battle today," Valga went on, "the demi-humans' rage will one day burn this kingdom to cinders. As long as you humans refuse to understand my anger, along with that of my fellow demi-humans and all our dead—!"

Confronted with Valga's furious pronouncements, Carol and Bordeaux fell silent. The emotion in his words was more than enough to suggest the truth of what he said, that the fighting would not end.

Many more would be hurt, the country would be exhausted, and even then it would not stop. Precisely because Bordeaux and the others had such a broad perspective, they understood how serious this possibility was.

But there was one person in the chapel who didn't share their view.

"Don't you ever shut up?" The interruption came from Wilhelm, who now exuded murder from every pore of his body. The Sword Devil wiped the blood roughly from his face and, his breath ragged, glared at the giant. "Stake everything on this moment. Who cares about what'll happen after you die or how this war will go? What you do right here, right now, is everything you are!"

"How simplistic... Indeed, how stupid! Your vision is too narrow! Your thinking is softheaded! You say the fight is all?! Well, you've overreached yourself in this battle—what will you do when it's over?"

Wilhelm's reply was simple. "I'll keep running and killing everything I can. I'll keep cutting and killing until it's all over."

Valga Cromwell found himself at a loss in the face of such a shallow, immature, foolish response. But it wasn't astonishment that kept him from answering immediately. It was because this was a pronouncement. Wilhelm Trias's words were as serious as serious could be.

"There's nothing else," Wilhelm went on. "I don't know any other way. So I'll keep killing."

There was nothing, had never been anything else Wilhelm could have done. He had been left alive, first by Pivot and his squad mates, and now by Bordeaux and his comrades. If there was to be meaning in having survived, if anyone expected anything of Wilhelm—the only way he knew to answer was by fighting.

Valga gave Wilhelm a tired shake of his head. "...There is no more value in talk. There is no need to speak here. I hardly need to say it."

Now the giant and the Sword Devil symbolized the total rupture between humans and demi-humans. Neither expected the other to ever understand him, and so their battle resumed.

Wilhelm's cherished blade was still lodged in Valga's lip. The

Sword Devil would have to dodge Valga's attacks long enough to steal back his sword before he could join the battle in earnest.

"Do you truly believe you can win, human?!" Valga Cromwell, the giant, howled.

"Win, lose, I don't care," Wilhelm, the Sword Devil, answered. "Just so long as I get to cut you down."

And then the final battle began.

10

He twisted to dodge the fingers. He was exhausted, every inch of him wounded. His endurance and strength were near their limits, yet he seemed more agile than when he had been in perfect health. Like a candle that burns brightest before it goes out, everything that was not necessary to his life had been stripped away, and he felt polished, clean.

His doubt had been dispelled. He had shrugged off all those invisible weights, and Wilhelm's heart and body both felt light.

"Ha-ha!"

It was a good feeling. A good way of being. His heart and mind were both focused on combat more completely than ever before. Here, on the cusp of life and death, only he and Valga existed.

Bordeaux and Grimm, although they had come to the chapel for this fight, showed no sign of intervening. Wilhelm was grateful to know that the purity of his battle would not be tarnished, but he also knew that the battlefield was his and his alone.

The fingers tore up the floor, and a hand swiped at him, but he kicked off the wall and jumped to dodge it. The instant he hit the ground, he crouched low and began to run, putting the series of attacks behind him as he closed distance. He put worthless thoughts behind him, too, throwing himself undiluted into a contest of life and death.

"Stand still, you stinking human—!" Valga yelled, unable to take precise aim at his constantly moving enemy.

The basement room was sturdily constructed, but already no trace of its former elegance remained. Rebuilding it would no doubt take time and effort. The only part of the room that remained undisturbed was the wall behind Valga, on which was carved the seal of the dragon.

It was not only the chapel that had suffered. The battle with Sphinx and the undead Libre would have caused destruction throughout the castle. Wilhelm had wanted to personally repay both of them, and he wasn't pleased to have had vengeance snatched from him by interlopers. But if Bordeaux and Grimm were both safe, then perhaps he could live with it.

Valga's voice trembled. "Do you think you have the time to be looking at your friends, you sniveling—"

"I was just making sure they were out of the way. Don't get all bent out of shape."

Wilhelm eliminated the last impure thing within him. Now, the Sword Devil's awakening was complete.

"It's time for you to pay!" he bellowed, spinning to dodge an enraged backhand. The move carried him closer to the giant. The monster's hand reached out to grab Wilhelm as he drove at the creature's chest, but the Sword Devil used the huge fingers as stepping-stones to jump closer still. At last, his outstretched hand reached Valga's lip, grabbed the trapped sword, and made a sideways cut.

The Sword Devil landed on the ground amid a rain of blood. Valga howled in pain and struck out at his enemy. Well aware of the incoming fist, Wilhelm changed his stance and took another swing.

The horizontal swipe got under three of the nails on Valga's right hand. Each fingernail was almost the size of a person's head. With his sword lodged between the nails and the fingers, Wilhelm pushed, shattering the fingertips and tearing the nails from the hand. Valga could hardly make a sound, his throat constricted with agony, but as his body pitched backward the Sword Devil jumped in.

His target was none of the vital points above the neck—he was aiming for Valga's exposed chest. Buried in that chest, at the center of the glowing purple symbol, were the bones that had allowed Valga to grow so large.

"Ru—ahhhhhhhhh!"

Holding his sword in a reverse grip, he brought the blade down with all his strength. The blow smashed Valga's collarbone, piercing into the flesh beneath—and a second later, the sword arrived at the scattered bones.

As soon as he felt the sword strike something hard, Wilhelm kicked off Valga's chin, driving the weapon down with his body weight. The sword acted like a lever, tearing through the flesh, though it was still caught in the bones.

"Daaaaaaamnn youuuuuu!"

Finally realizing Wilhelm's intention, Valga brought both hands blindly to his chest, as hard as he could. But the Sword Devil kicked off Valga's abdomen, flipping completely upside down and executing a spin that finally dislodged the bones. A blinding light filled the chapel.

"Hrrraaghhh!"

Without the bones of his ancestors, Valga lost the source of his immense size. Immediately, his strength began to dwindle. The symbol on his chest was still glowing, but the power it was feeding into him was too much for his normal body. He was caught between his weakening flesh and the increasingly powerful magic circle, and his body couldn't withstand it.

"Ah—ahhhhh!"

Blood began to spew out from all over his body, and Valga fell to his knees. His thirty-foot-tall body was audibly shrinking.

"—"

Valga glared at Wilhelm, tears of blood streaming from his eyes. Wilhelm, whose sword had remained at the ready the entire time, stared unflinchingly back.

Valga took his hands from his wounds and formed them into fists.

"...Victory hinges on this moment now."

"...Damn right." The enemy had not lost his will to fight but saw one final confrontation—and it was this to which the Sword Devil responded.

"Have at, human."

"Come at me, demi-human."

With these quiet declarations, the last exchange between the giant and the Sword Devil began.

Valga did not spare even the effort to utter a battle cry; he brought both his arms, as large as trees, down with all his might. The blow shattered the floor and caused not just the chapel but the whole castle to tremble on its foundations.

But the blow had not landed on Wilhelm.

"Shhhhhhyaa!"

Wilhelm barely dodged Valga's attack, moving in toward the giant's feet. His fervent shout was accompanied by a strike of his sword, which cut into Valga's shins. Wilhelm could feel the resistance as the weapon cleaved flesh and bone, but he was able to wound the weakened body. As he brought the sword back, it sliced up through the femurs.

"Hrrraaaghhh!"

The attack came through the thighs, continued through the hips, and then Wilhelm turned to bring his sword across Valga's abdomen. Finally, he reached the chest and, launching himself through the air, the shoulders, and then the multitude of lacerations exploded with blood.

The silver flash devastated the giant's body and finally hewed at his neck—all in a single, uninterrupted move.

"Remember this, human." As he struck the ground, Valga spoke quietly to Wilhelm. He made no effort to attend to his plethora of wounds. The Sword Devil stood with his back to the giant. "Remember that this will not bring an end to the demi-humans' rage."

Then his massive body lost all strength, slumping to the ground before falling face-first into the floor. The impact was the last straw for the cracked chapel floor beneath him, as it gave way. The castle basement opened into an even deeper darkness, and Valga's body was swallowed up by the void.

"…Well, let them come at me, then," Wilhelm said, stepping up to the edge of the hole and looking into the inky blackness. He was covered in blood. Behind him, on the wall of the chapel, was the kingdom's crest. "So long as I have my sword, I'll fight them. I'll cut them down until there aren't any left."

Those words marked the end of the contest between the Sword Devil and the giant, Wilhelm and Valga.

11

The items she pulled from her pouch were steel balls small enough to roll around in the palm of the hand. Made of solid metal, they were heavier than they looked. If one were to carelessly drop it on a foot, it would easily break a toe or two. And of course, at full force, it would hit almost as hard as a sword strike.

"Gah... Haah..."

Two of Roswaal's metal balls buried themselves in Sphinx's body, one in the lower abdomen and one right in the back. Sphinx groaned at their power and, unable to maintain her altitude, collided with the wall. The witch continued to slide along until she reached the floor, where she was struck by another metal ball. Bones broke, and blood flowed.

"Are you quiiite done trying to fly away?" Roswaal asked the cornered Sphinx, rolling the next steel sphere around in her hand.

Sphinx had left the great hall and flown madly through the castle in an attempt to escape. But without her arms, she couldn't use her magic, and the dribbling blood left an easy trail to follow. She'd had no hope. Roswaal had calmly attacked her with the metal balls from a distance, tormenting her with them.

"Are these...steel balls...your plan for defeating me...?"

"Quiiite something, aren't they? They started out as a by-product of the thing I'd prepared to kill you with. Unfortunately, my scrawny arms aren't enough to do you in by themseeeelves. Having said that, I'm just about out of rounds. I think it's time we finished this."

As she approached the witch rolling on the floor, Roswaal loosed the next ball, shattering her bones. Roswaal looked down at the groaning Sphinx and made a fist in preparation to end the witch's life.

But then Sphinx spoke. "You are worse...than Valga...it seems... This requires caution..."

"Oh? Are you giving me a warning? How amusing. And what is it I should be cautious of?"

"That the rug isn't...pulled out from under you," Sphinx replied emotionlessly. Then she rested her head on the wall. Her pink hair, now drenched in blood, brushed against the stone. As Roswaal looked at the witch in perplexity, a quiet sound reached her.

Then the device hidden in the hallway activated, and Sphinx was whisked away by the spinning floor.

"—"

Even as the girl disappeared, Roswaal realized this had to be one of the castle's many hidden passageways—the very ones that allowed the demi-humans entry in the first place.

"But it won't buy you much time," she said.

Roswaal carefully scrutinized the place where Sphinx had disappeared and quickly figured out how to activate the device. She did so and dropped into the secret tunnel herself.

She landed on her feet and strained to see into the darkness around her. A faint sound of water suggested that this tunnel was home to one of the underground streams that ran beneath the castle. The only light came from the softly glowing minerals in the walls. The path didn't offer steady footing, but Roswaal set off following the scent of blood.

She could smell it; she was close. But in the middle of the trail, the smell turned to something else unpleasant, and the change inspired an anxiety in Roswaal. She began moving faster and found herself deep within the tunnel.

"Who's there? Is that you, Lady Mathers?"

The man's hoarse voice brought Roswaal to a stop. Someone emerged from the dimness, someone she thought she had left behind at the castle gate: Lyp Bariel.

"I thought so," he said. "You came down here to chase that demi-human as well, did you?"

"So we find ourselves set to the same task, I suppose," Roswaal said.

Assured of Roswaal's identity, the knight returned his dagger to its sheath. She didn't recognize the weapon. Most likely it was a mitia, a magical item capable of tremendous power. Roswaal made no mention of this and looked past Lyp.

"Sphinx, the main force behind the demi-humans, ran this way. Have you seen her?"

"The witch, is it? Well, you can relax," Lyp said. "I finished her off."

Roswaal's breath caught in her throat at this. When Lyp saw her reaction, a cruel smile spread over his already mean visage.

"I helped mop up the demi-humans who got into the castle. A few of them ran. I followed them here. I never imagined there was a place like this underneath the castle—but regardless, I ran into the armless witch not long ago. I didn't ask any questions. I just burned her to death."

"You burned her...? Where is the body?"

"She turned to ash. Don't ask me how, but this was left over in the cinders."

Lyp dug in his pouch and took out a necklace. It was nothing more than a roughly woven cord with a ring on it, just something to dangle from the neck, but to Roswaal, it had profound importance.

"Perhaps you would be so kiiind as to let me have that?"

"What?"

"It may have magical value. I would dearly like to investigate it."

Lyp went quiet. But soon after, he flung it at her with a snort.

"Take it, I don't care. But when they pass out the honors, I expect you to testify that I, Lyp Bariel, arrested the flight of the witch Sphinx at the water's edge, and that it was I who put an end to her."

"...Yes, of course. I'm in your debt, Lord Lyp." Roswaal gave no further answer as she stood with the necklace—the ring—clutched firmly in her hand. So long as it was hers, she had no further business here. She was surprised that someone else had killed Sphinx, but if the witch was dead, then it was no problem for her. Everything was going according to plan.

Caressing the ring tenderly, Roswaal J. Mathers murmured, "Master, I've finished cleaning up. What comes next is for the future."

It was impossible to see her face clearly in the darkness, but she was smiling with the most serene expression.

*   *   *

Lyp Bariel snorted as he watched Roswaal grow smaller in the distance.

"What has she got in mind?" he muttered to himself. "That woman gives me the shivers."

Now that she had the ring, Roswaal apparently intended to get out from underground as quickly as possible. That was convenient enough for him, but it didn't make complete sense. It was as if the ring was all she had ever really wanted.

"Well, who cares? What a she-fox like that wants is nothing to do with me."

What mattered to Lyp was whatever advanced his own ambitions and nothing more. Ever since the defeat at Aihiya Swamp, he had been encountering a headwind. Once a commander of scores of troops, he was reduced to the gendarmerie. They were even considering taking away his noble rank.

It was inconceivable. How could the weak and the incompetent flourish while capable men like himself languished in the lower ranks?

"But I'll get it all back. No—I'll get back more than I lost."

He would do anything to accomplish that goal. Even forsake his loyalty to the kingdom. Lyp was his own kingdom. He was his own world.

Saying nothing further, Lyp turned back. Lying on the ground in the tunnel behind him was a small form wrapped in rags. He picked it up. Without arms, the body was quite light. He had hidden it in these wrappings, and now he was careful to take a different path out of the underground than Roswaal had.

This betrayal was the first act of Lyp Bariel's long-lived ambition.

12

The attack on Lugunica Castle had been perpetrated by just a few elite demi-humans. Although the destruction of the castle was narrowly avoided, severe damage had been done to the building, and in addition, there was the discovery of the tunnels that had allowed the demi-humans access in the first place. It would take a long time to deal with all of this.

It only made sense to entrust much of the cleanup to Zergev Squadron, which had once again distinguished itself in battle. However, Wilhelm foisted many of his chores on Grimm and fled the castle.

"Like I have the time to hang around with them..."

Stripping off bandages and looking utterly drained from combat, Wilhelm headed for the now-quiet castle town. With the demise of Valga and the other main movers, the rebellions throughout the kingdom had subsided, and peace had returned to the capital. This evoked an unusually strong feeling in Wilhelm, and there was only one place he wanted to go.

Even he didn't fully understand why he was pushing his exhausted body just so he could go there. After all, it had only been a day since his ordeal. The capital might have been less violent, but many shops had chosen not to do business that day in deference to the destruction at the royal castle, and the streets were still largely deserted.

A sane person would probably have stayed inside, fearful of getting caught up in any trouble. That meant that today, at least, all the people shut up in their houses were showing themselves to be in their right minds. To be out for a little walk on a day like this, as if everything was normal...

"I look like I'm crazy..."

Wilhelm hurried through the poor district—so quickly it almost seemed he'd forgotten about his wounds—and arrived at the plaza. He could detect a faint scent of flowers on the breeze blowing through the square, notifying him of the presence of the field.

And there, in the very middle of the plaza, stood the red-haired girl.

She had her back to him. At the sight of her, Wilhelm stopped cold. The confused welter of emotions swirling in his heart was at once good and bad. The confidence that she would be there overlapped with astonishment at the same fact. It all turned into a tightness in his chest.

At the same time, he felt a kind of melancholic distaste at the thought of their usual exchange.

She was safe. That was what he had come to find out. Wilhelm was just considering whether he should turn on his heel and leave without anything further when Theresia noticed he was there. She turned around. Her blue eyes widened slightly in surprise, and then they narrowed. Finally, her lips formed the half circle of a smile.

"Wilhelm."

She said his name with such familiarity and affection. It sent a feeling bounding through Wilhelm's heart that all was right with the world. He completely forgot any notion of turning around and going home. His pulse raced with joy at meeting Theresia, and the warmth and relief spread through his whole chest.

"...Ah."

No sooner had he realized what he was really feeling than his heart, with no warning at all, trembled. It was a moment of sudden and totally unexpected self-awareness. Wilhelm understood that Theresia's smile brought him a feeling of well-being. He had a feeling of accomplishment at having protected her smile, her person, their time together.

Thanks to Theresia, standing there with her back to the flowers, he felt something that made him think there might be a greater joy than felling an opponent with his sword and proving his own swordsmanship superior.

The instant this realization struck him was accompanied by a torrent of emotion, a flood Wilhelm thought he had long ago left behind. Caught up in its force, Wilhelm put his hands to his face.

"—"

The insides of his eyelids grew hot, and his nose prickled. He suddenly felt his throat go dry, and his head felt heavy, as if his blood was pumping too fast. There and then, his soul shook; he thought it might drive him to his knees.

A light that Wilhelm had almost forgotten filled his mind.

No—he hadn't forgotten it. It had always been in his heart, never fading. He had never forgotten its beauty. What he had forgotten was what used to draw him to that light.

He remembered the first day he had taken up a sword, pointing it to the sky. If he had the light, if it was real and, could be real—with that power, he could protect everything. That was what he had believed. That day, a powerless young man had picked up a blade for the first time. That day, he had wished for something.

"Wilhelm…"

As Wilhelm stood with his hands to his face, consumed by emotion, Theresia's voice reached him. How absurd must he have looked to the girl standing in front of him? She couldn't possibly understand what was going on. She had just been having a normal day when suddenly, the boy she saw from time to time stood quaking with emotion before her.

He was embarrassed, something he hadn't been for a long time. He was so ashamed, it made him tremble. He wanted to run away immediately. He didn't want anyone to see his shame, but least of all Theresia. This was about the worst thing he could imagine.

And yet his feet didn't move. His heart wouldn't let them—almost as if this was what his soul desired.

"—"

Time passed as both of them stood silently. Then, suddenly, Wilhelm felt a tickling sensation of soft fingers on the backs of his hands. It was Theresia, reaching out and gently touching the hands Wilhelm had placed over his face.

His breath caught at the heat of her thin fingers. He had never realized another person's body could be so warm. The heat from her fingers made Wilhelm feel like a piece of steel in a forge. And as hot metal is shaped in the fire, Theresia's heat hit him and began to transform him.

Only now did he realize he had been exposed to that heat every time he came here. Every time he saw her, talked to her, and left without promising to come back. All that time, the sword called Wilhelm was being forged.

No. In fact, it wasn't just her. It was everything and everyone who was a part of every day that he had survived.

Theresia, Grimm, Bordeaux, Roswaal, Carol, Pivot, and the whole of Zergev Squadron. Valga, Libre, Sphinx, and all the enemies he'd cut down. Everyone who had crossed paths with Wilhelm the blade had left their mark.

Now, at last, he realized it.

As he stood there silently, seeing how he had been molded, a question was asked of Wilhelm:

"Do you like flowers?"

No doubt that question, the same every time, had been seeking some change in him. And Wilhelm saw at last that he had indeed been transforming.

"…I don't…hate them."

Now he had no difficulty and no anxiety speaking those words. When he saw flowers on the battlefield, walked by them in his daily life, or saw them in the field by the plaza, surely he would feel something different than he had before.

Theresia's questions went on. "Why do you wield your sword?"

This was the question that had bothered Wilhelm for so long. But now, at last, he remembered. He could recall what he felt when he had first picked up the blade.

"Because it was…the only way I had of protecting people."

A sword was power. The most beautiful, finely honed, and purest power. A power to be respected. But how it was used, what ends it was put to—that was controlled by the person wielding it. Wilhelm had forgotten this most basic thing. But now, he remembered. He recalled the beginning, how he had felt when he loved the sword.

"—"

Wilhelm removed his hands from his face and took Theresia's outstretched hand. A small "Oh" escaped her, but she didn't draw back. The gesture was too one-sided to be called holding hands, but each could clearly feel the other's warmth.

"—"

Neither of them said anything, and only looked at each other. Partly they didn't know what to say, and partly there was no need to say anything. Like when two sword fighters face each other in combat, words were too crude a vehicle for what was passing between them.

"____"

Theresia simply smiled gently at Wilhelm. It was the soft expression she always wore when looking at her flowers, now directed at him.

Wilhelm felt his heart pound, the rhythm taking over him. He couldn't put the feeling into words. He wanted to share it with the girl before him—but he held back.

Still, though, one small sign of the flood of emotions did make itself known.

That day, for the first time, Wilhelm gave Theresia a completely heartfelt smile.

13

The uprisings that had shaken all of Lugunica subsided as suddenly as they had begun. The reason for their end was the deaths of the three main leaders of the demi-human peoples—their strongest warrior, Libre Fermi; their strategist, Valga Cromwell; and the witch, Sphinx. The three of them had been killed in battle by the humans. The resistance had failed.

With the Demi-human Alliance thus losing its main support, it was widely believed that the civil war itself would soon show signs of ending. However, contrary to that expectation, demi-human resistance throughout the land grew more and more fevered. It was, as Valga had said in his last moments, the inferno of their hatred, which was not to be easily extinguished.

And so the humans began to understand. Despite the loss of their leading lights, it was natural that the Demi-human Alliance should continue to fight. However terrible the humans believed the demi-humans' unchecked hatred was, they had never yet truly faced their enemies' anger.

This was the beginning of the final stage of the Demi-human War, the civil conflict that rocked the kingdom.

It was, too, the story of the meeting and parting of the Sword Devil and the Sword Saint.

THE LOVE SONG OF THE SWORD DEVIL

Seventh Stanza

1

At that time, a certain subject was frequently discussed by the members of Zergev Squadron. It was a matter that struck at the very heart of the squadron, one every member felt deeply and personally concerned about. It would not be too much to describe it as a dramatic change.

"Laslow, fall back!" Wilhelm ordered the soldier, catching the battle-ax with his sword. Until a second earlier, the man he had spoken to had been all but cornered by the enemy's brutal attack. When Wilhelm saw this, he was there faster than the wind, intercepting the enemy's blow and ordering Laslow to safety.

As his squad mate gulped down air, Wilhelm forced the enemy back. Overwhelmed by the Sword Devil's sheer force of will, the ax-wielding beast-man took a stab to the thigh, howling as he toppled to the ground. This was the moment for Wilhelm to leap on him, strike the finishing blow—

"Give me your hand. Get to the rear as quick as you can, idiot."

But Wilhelm didn't pursue his crippled foe. Instead, he gave his wounded ally his shoulder to lean on. Surprised by the strength in his small frame, the hulking soldier stuttered out an apology.

"I-I'm sorry, Vice Captain!"

"If you have time to apologize, use it to train better. Then we won't have to leave a hole in our front line."

His words sounded harsh, but he moved carefully as he supported the wounded man. Other squad members covered their withdrawal, and once he had deposited Laslow safely in the rear, the Sword Devil went back to the battle with all speed.

Then, cutting a swath through the enemy forces, he shouted, "Don't act like a bunch of green rookies, Zergev Squadron! Look them in the eye and fight!"

With this exhortation to both himself and his comrades, Wilhelm dashed forward. Countless silver flashes followed, each one felling an enemy soldier, the Sword Devil single-handedly raising the morale of his men.

The name of Wilhelm Trias, the Sword Devil, was so widely known and respected that it was said to be the hope of the royal army and the despair of the Demi-human Alliance.

"I can't believe the change in that man… It makes me a little ill."

"Ah, don't be so hard on him, Miss Carol. It just goes to show that even Wilhelm has a good side. But I've seen him grow up, and I have to admit, it does feel a bit strange!" Bordeaux laughed heartily. With the help of his battle-ax, he had decimated the enemies in one part of the frontline.

Carol all but ignored Bordeaux's guffaws, fending off an encroaching enemy soldier with her sword.

"I've known him since before he changed, too," she went on. "I'm not trying to be cold. I just wonder what he's planning, acting like that…and when he'll show his true colors."

"__"

Carol had a look of disgust in her eyes. Beside her, Grimm pounded his shield as if to speak. His usually friendly face was full of reproach as he shook his head at Carol.

"I'm sorry, Grimm. But I just can't get used to it…"

"There's lots of opinions about the new Wilhelm in the squadron. But at the end of the day, everyone pretty much agrees with me and Grimm. It's a real sudden change…but not a bad one."

"…I do know that."

"Heck, they say 'fire and a hammer are all it takes to temper steel.' He can be prickly, but I guess he can also change pretty quick when he has a reason. It'd be interesting if that reason were a woman…"

"Erk…"

"What's wrong? You know something I don't?" Bordeaux gave her an intrigued look, but Carol shook her head vigorously, a troubled expression coming over her neat features.

"I don't know any— This puts me in a difficult position vis-à-vis my assigned duties. Please understand."

"What you mean is you *do* know something about it. But I get it. I won't press you."

"I'd appreciate that. Even so, I just can't get used to it…"

Carol watched as Wilhelm continued to protect his allies and cut down the enemy. In the midst of violent sword battles, he would help his squad mates and deliver words of advice. It was a profound transformation.

If it had caused him to lose his focus and had negatively impacted his abilities in battle, that would have made it a problem, but Wilhelm's prowess had not faded in the least—if anything, he might have been even more capable than before.

"—"

"I know, Grimm, I know! We'll keep pushing the enemy back."

Let's not let Wilhelm show us up, Grimm had said. The two of them advanced to the front line. Bordeaux watched them go, resting his ax across both shoulders.

"Speaking of changes," he said, "I don't think you're the same person you were when you first met Grimm, Miss Carol. But I guess maybe you don't realize it. Ahh, damn it, you're all so *young*!"

Bordeaux laughed wildly and looked to the side, hoping for someone to agree with him. But it was just force of habit; the man he half expected to see standing just a step behind him wasn't there. Bordeaux touched the wounds on his face and cracked his neck. Then he bellowed, "Hey, save some for me! We'll destroy all these barbarians!"

After the fight at the castle, Bordeaux Zergev had continued to improve his technique with his ax. Now, he showed the fruits of all that practice, wading into the fight even though he was himself a commander. It was a battle that encapsulated both what had changed about Zergev Squadron and what hadn't.

2

After their assigned period of defensive duty ended, Zergev Squadron returned to the capital for the first time in two weeks.

They arrived in the city late at night, and most of the squad members would probably spend their first day of leave asleep. But Wilhelm, who had perhaps fought harder than anyone else in the squadron, woke early and left the barracks.

He walked through the crisp, cool air, his beloved sword hanging at his side. When the town guard saw him, they straightened up and gave respectful salutes. Wilhelm waved a hand casually at them and headed for the castle town. Soon he would be at the plaza in the poor district. They had no set date or time. They didn't know what their plans would be, and Wilhelm himself had no specific days off.

Hence, it was down to luck whether the person he was looking for would be there or not. And on this day…

"Oh, Wilhelm. You made it today."

Theresia, who had arrived first, turned around when she noticed Wilhelm. The wind picked up her long red hair, and she smiled at him. Wilhelm raised an eyebrow. The source of his bemusement was the place she was standing: right in the middle of the field of flowers.

"I know that look," she said. "'What's this girl up to?' you're wondering."

"Well, thank you for putting my feelings into words. What *are* you up to, 'this girl'?"

"I'd say that's just the question. What am I up to?" Theresia said innocently. Then suddenly, she raised one bare foot. The hem of her dress shifted with the motion, revealing a pale thigh. Wilhelm quickly averted his eyes.

"What's this?" Theresia said. "Is that too stimulating for a pure-hearted young man?"

"Stop playing tomboy, dummy. I told you before, this place isn't safe. If you leave yourself vulnerable, you'll pay for it eventually."

"Oh, I'm not worried about that. After all, I have a big, bad swordsman with me, don't I?" she said with a wink. The gesture caused Wilhelm's voice to catch in his throat. He ran a hand nervously through his chestnut hair as he dutifully approached her.

"Okay, out with it. What is it you're doing? Rediscovering your inner child and playing barefoot in the dirt?"

"H-how rude! I can rediscover my inner child if I want. And anyway, I'm not playing in the dirt! You're completely wrong! Blind! Insensitive!"

"Gosh, why'd you have to lay it on so thick?"

She really was a woman of intense emotions. She laughed from the heart, but she got sincerely angry as well. He genuinely believed he would never get tired of her laughter and shouting, her smiles and her frowns. The thought left even Wilhelm a little exasperated with himself.

"The correct answer is…I'm planting seeds for some new flowers!"

"New seeds?"

While he'd stood transfixed by her profile, Theresia had grown impatient and had blurted out the answer herself. But it only caused Wilhelm to regard her curiously.

Theresia pointed at the field and said, "Yes, that's right. The seasons will change soon, so the flowers have to change, too, don't they? I'm sorry to see my flowers wither, but I can raise new ones for the new season."

"Raise them? I've never even seen you water this thing."

"I-it's true I mostly let them take care of themselves, but I'm the one who gave them that first push! And I plan to take good care of them this time. So maybe you could be so kind as to not sneer?"

Theresia always had to give back double what she got when she felt she'd been wronged. At the end of this tirade, however, Theresia gazed at the field and added, "Besides. If there aren't any flowers here, I won't have an excuse to come anymore."

"__"

Wilhelm caught his breath. *An excuse.* It had been their unspoken understanding when they met here.

"__"

Theresia was coming to check on her flowers, Wilhelm to practice his sword work. But their facade had already all but broken down. They more or less neglected their alleged objectives—Theresia mostly, and Wilhelm entirely. It was not, of course, that Wilhelm had any less reverence for his sword. It was simply that now his reason for coming here was Theresia.

Both of them knew it, surely. Yet they never said it aloud, and continued to meet this way. It must have been from fear of change.

Even now, as he continued to be pounded like steel, to be reshaped, he didn't seem to realize.

Wilhelm turned away, unable to bear her gaze any longer. "You know...there's something I'd like to report to you, too."

"Report?" Theresia looked at him quizzically.

He could feel her eyes on him. "Yeah," he said. "They recognized my deeds in combat. There was talk of some award or something, and...I'm a knight now."

"__"

He could sense her holding her breath. At her reaction, Wilhelm made a fist, careful to keep it where Theresia would not see it. The decisive factor in his promotion to knighthood was that he had helped thwart the demi-human attack on the castle. The change in Wilhelm's behavior after that, along with a recommendation from Bordeaux, had sealed the promotion.

In the past, Wilhelm might have turned down this award, but now he accepted gratefully. He took pride in this proof that his achievements had been recognized. Neither would his conscience let him disdain the efforts of Bordeaux and his other companions to get this for him.

Then there was the fact that being a knight pleased him in his heart of hearts.

"Oh? Congratulations. I guess this brings you one step closer to your dream."

"My dream?"

The thought had been so secret that Theresia's remark took him by surprise.

She put her hand to her mouth as if Wilhelm's wide-eyed look amused her. "You use your sword to protect people, don't you? And a knight is someone who protects people." She looked quite certain about this, and her lips turned up, for some reason, with what he thought was pride.

Finally, it made sense to him. He etched her smile into his memory so that she would always be among those things he was fighting to protect.

3

After visiting Theresia, the sun now high in the sky, Wilhelm headed for the merchants' quarter. The kingdom might have been exhausted by the ongoing civil war, but it didn't seem to make a dent in the avarice of the merchants who went in and out of town. In the whole of the capital, only the commercial quarter still had the same bustling activity as before. The familiar little restaurant was no exception.

"The usual," he said to the girl at the door, then went to a corner seat far in the back. The person he'd come to meet was already sitting there, just pouring himself a drink.

"Drinking at this hour? Pretty ballsy, even for a day off."

Wilhelm took the seat across from the man. Despite Wilhelm's rough words, the man laughed voicelessly and began pouring a drink for the newcomer. He shook his head, and the serving girl brought him water. The man across from Wilhelm raised his glass insistently. Frowning, Wilhelm indulged with a clink of their glasses.

I never thought the day would come when you and I would sit down and drink together.

Once Wilhelm had wetted his lips with that first sip of water, the other man pushed a paper at him with those words written on it. Wilhelm had become accustomed to this, but there was no denying it was inconvenient. He tapped the paper with one finger.

"Me neither. But I'm not drinking. Who would want to drink that swill, anyway?"

It's nice to know that some things about you haven't changed.

Grimm offered this brief sentence and a smile. Wilhelm felt a twinge of guilt, realizing he'd done it again. He was so quick to spiteful speech and aggressive actions. It was a bad habit of his. Despite a desire and an effort to change, such a long-standing part of his personality could not be so easily transformed.

At length, he fell quiet, watching Grimm silently pour himself another drink. Wilhelm let himself be taken in by Grimm's gentleness. He realized, now, how he had been the beneficiary of so many kindnesses.

Unconsciously, Wilhelm touched the sword at his hip, drawing comfort from the familiar feeling. Suddenly, Grimm set the bottle of alcohol on the table, and with his free hand he pointed at Wilhelm's chest.

"—? Oh, the crest. I guess it's because I'm a knight now."

Grimm was looking at the dragon emblem on Wilhelm's left breast. It was a proof of status he had been granted upon promotion to knighthood; the crest bore upon it a Dragon Jewel.

"I guess it's pretty unusual for someone to rise from commoner to knight, but…well, when they found out about my background, it didn't take long for that talk to stop."

Wilhelm had once been seen as a symbol of something to aspire to, a commoner who had risen like a star to the highest ranks. But when it came out that his bloodline was related to Lugunican nobility, many people were even more surprised than when he had become known as the Sword Devil. One's birth has minimal impact on one's skills with the sword, but humans are simply happier if they think they see a reason for the way things are.

"It turns out not much changes when you become a knight. What about you? If you and Carol get together, you'll be part of a famous house. That's a quicker route to the top, if you ask me."

Tired of being interrogated, Wilhelm asked a pointed question of his own. Grimm turned so red that he didn't need to say anything to communicate his embarrassment. He put his glass to his lips as if to indicate that he would offer no comment. Wilhelm's ability to guess more or less what Grimm was thinking from his expressions and gestures was another recent difference.

Once he started paying more attention to what was going on around him, he was surprised to realize how much humans communicated without using words. That was what happened when one took observation skills honed on the battlefield and applied them to everyday life.

Have you told your family about becoming a knight?

"Contacted my family? No, not a word. Frankly, I don't even know how I'd face them. But it's also… Showing up the minute I get a promotion wouldn't look good. I want to at least wait until the civil war is mopped up."

Wilhelm's relationship with his birth family had come to light as a result of his promotion. Surely his family was aware of his rise through the ranks, but that was all the more reason to take care.

You mean like maybe once you're ready to bring home a girl to marry?

"Hrrrft!"

Wilhelm spat out his water at the words in front of him. He shot a glance at Grimm that said, *I never know what you're going to say next,* but Grimm was trying to suppress a smile. He had gotten Wilhelm back for earlier, and how. Wilhelm castigated himself for letting himself react.

Everyone's noticed how much you've changed. The whole squad is trying to figure out who's behind it.

"…Can't you find anything more productive to gab about?"

You probably know this better than anyone, but we were all surprised. Who managed to do this to you?

Grimm was completely convinced that the cause of Wilhelm's

change of heart was a girl. And he wasn't wrong, but if Wilhelm confirmed it here, he wouldn't be able to hide it from Theresia.

"Don't be dumb. I've had enough of this stupid—"

It would be really sweet if you became a knight for her sake... It's not Lady Mathers, is it?

"Like hell! I wouldn't have anything to do with that woman if Pristela sank into the sea!"

You don't have to get so upset.

Grimm was grinning, but Wilhelm had real goose bumps. He wished Grimm would quit joking around.

Incidentally, Pristela was a major city in the western part of Lugunica. It was at the conflux of several prominent rivers, a city of floodgates that had yet to suffer water damage in all the centuries since it had been built.

"Anyway, we haven't even seen her on the battlefield lately. We only run into her every once in a while."

I think that "every once in a while" is because she wants to see your face. It's cute.

After they had succeeded in eliminating the witch Sphinx, the Demi-human Alliance's magical offensives had become considerably less potent. That also meant far fewer occasions on which they encountered Roswaal, the special magical advisor. But she did, indeed, faithfully come to see Wilhelm, although rarely.

Carol stays with Lady Mathers, so we haven't seen too much of her on the battlefield, either. I'm glad about that. I know she's stronger than me, but I don't want her out there too much with the battles the way they are these days.

Wilhelm gave a short nod. "True enough." He couldn't stand it anymore and gave a great stretch of his back. Even though the Demi-human Alliance had lost Valga and its other pillars, its attacks hadn't ended. If anything, the alliance had gotten more violent than before, with little regard for the consequences. "I guess without a strategist to check them, there's no one to hold them back. I think taking death before surrender is stupid, but it's led to plenty of casualties."

They have no way to retreat, no matter how terrible the battle is.

The bloodbath at the castle had been the great last-ditch effort of the demi-human leaders. In its aftermath, it was unexpected that the flames of war should not only fail to subside but burn hotter. Or rather, one person had expected it—Valga. He had even hoped for it.

"Maybe he knew that his death would fan the flames of demi-human anger and turn this into a war of mutual destruction."

Even so, the demi-humans are at a disadvantage. They don't have the numbers. Valga must have known that.

Grimm seemed to feel it didn't make sense, but Wilhelm thought he understood. Valga Cromwell wanted to put an end to the world. The world was full of outrages and unjustified killing, and Valga wanted to do such damage to it that it turned on its head. If that was his goal, then the current situation was quite in line with it.

The flames of the demi-humans' anger aren't going out. I wonder if there's a way to end this fighting.

"I told him I would keep killing until there were no more enemies to kill. But…I'm not sure that's realistic anymore. If there's any chance, I think it has to be something more positive."

Positive?

"Something that will douse the flames of hatred and take away the fuel."

He felt like he was grasping at straws. If there had ever been such a possibility, the Demi-human War had changed things dramatically. What they truly needed was strength to match the rage.

Something even more imposing than Valga's ideals and the demi-humans' hatred.

"If we had someone or something like that…I wonder what it would even be called."

"—"

Wilhelm's whisper caused Grimm to fall into what appeared to be a thoughtful silence. Then he seemed to think of something and wrote slowly on his paper.

A hero.

He had written only those two words. Wilhelm nodded.

A hero, he thought. *Yes, a hero.*

Someone who was not just a hero in name only but a real one, like in the stories. Someone with more power than Wilhelm, the Sword Devil, or the renowned battlefield outfit Zergev Squadron, or the peerless royal guard.

Someone like the Sword Saint, who had once dispelled the terror that lay over the world…

If there was to be an end to this fighting, it lay in such impossible hopes.

4

"Myyy goodness. You're back sooo late."

"—"

When Wilhelm returned to his room, he found a woman lounging elegantly on his bed—Roswaal. Without a word, he stared at her. Her eyes were free of malice as she smiled at him; she seemed to be enjoying herself.

"You've been out on the training grounds, sweating up a storm, and now you want to turn all that heat on a member of the opposite sex… Is that how you're feeling?"

"I'm feeling awfully tired of seeing you just waltz into my room. What the hell is the barracks captain doing? Doesn't he realize he's supposed to keep suspicious people out of here?"

"He used to let me in because he was afraid of me. But now he does it as a favor to an old friend…or sooomething like that?"

"You need to mind your own business."

He recalled the salute the pudgy barracks captain had offered him as he entered the building. Wilhelm had dramatically improved his relationships with not just Zergev Squadron but also the other soldiers. Still, this was not going to help things any. If the captain let every visitor, well-wisher, and alleged buddy into his room, he might never get another chance to relax.

"So?" Wilhelm asked. "To what do I owe the displeasure?"

"Suuurely you know there's only one reason a woman abandons her shame at night to sneak into the room of the man she desires. A primal, instinctive—now, now, don't get so angry."

Wilhelm's glare had begun turning aggressive, and Roswaal immediately abandoned any flirtatiousness. She let out an annoyed breath, observing Wilhelm with her asymmetrically colored eyes. "I could haaardly make my affection more obvious, and yet you have all the reaction of a steel wall. I'm going to lose my confidence in myself as a woman at this rate."

"I'm happy to respond earnestly to people who have sincere affection for me. But if they don't, then I don't waste my time with them."

"Hmm." Roswaal closed one eye and lapsed into thought. Wilhelm ignored her and grabbed something to wipe himself down with. After he had parted ways with Grimm, Wilhelm had headed to the training grounds and was indeed very sweaty. He did at least possess enough discretion, though, not to start changing clothes in front of a woman.

"Then let's talk in a spirit of sincere affection. Not as a man and woman, unfortunately, but as friends," Roswaal said. The tone of her voice had suddenly changed, and Wilhelm looked at her. Roswaal was still sitting just as she had been before, but her behavior was completely different. It was a side of her he had seen only rarely, on the battlefield, when she had been displaying her full desire to catch Sphinx.

In other words, Roswaal was now well and truly serious.

"With the help of you and your friends," she said, "I was able to achieve my objective. Consider this my heartfelt expression of gratitude for your help."

"...Go on."

"The civil war is threatening to find its way into the territory of the House of Trias. Your family."

"Wha...?!"

Wilhelm's eyes went wide at this unexpected news. Roswaal folded her long legs and nodded gravely.

"Yes. I have some acquaintances around there. I'm sure this isn't easy for you to hear. I came here to tell you myself, fearing it might otherwise be too laaate."

"Why would you…? For that matter, why would they…?"

"Of course, there's nothing in the Trias lands worth attacking. The local lord and the royal army will both find it a bolt from the blue. Buuut the demi-humans aren't so logical these days. You understand?"

The demi-humans who burned with the remnants of Valga's hatred had nothing more to stop them, nor even anything to make them distinguish one target from another. Their actions might lead nowhere, yet the flames of this civil war could not be doused.

"Then again, I suppose it could be revenge against you for killing their leaders, my dear Wilhelm Trias."

"—" When one wounds another, it creates a reason for revenge. The beginning of this civil war, as well as its continuance, hinged on such reasons. And Wilhelm was in no position to condemn these actions.

"I think your best hope is to talk to your superiors. I believe our friend Bordeaux would not do wrooong by you. Although it might take some time."

Then Roswaal stood up from the bed as if to signal that their conversation was over. She walked right past Wilhelm, who stood ramrod straight, and headed for the door.

Before she could leave, however, Wilhelm demanded, "…Just what do you want here? What do you think you're going to get?"

Roswaal stopped. "I don't have any dark designs. It's unusual for me to feel such affection for someone. If I can help the few people I care about to be happy, so much the better. I promise my motives are nothing more sinister than that."

She didn't turn around as she spoke, and he couldn't see her face. Wilhelm swallowed heavily at the weight of her words. But then she shrugged and turned her head so she could see him out of the corner of her eye. She was smiling.

"What you do is your choice. Make sure you won't regret it."

And with that, Roswaal J. Mathers left the room.

Wilhelm stared after her. After a moment's silence, he came back to himself. He rushed to grab the overshirt he had just stripped off and nearly flew out of the room to go see Bordeaux.

When he got out into the hallway, Roswaal was already gone.

5

"First, let me confirm the situation. It'll depend what's going on, but I'll err on the side of deploying the squadron. Don't get ahead of yourself, Wilhelm."

When Wilhelm had told Bordeaux about the impending threat to the Trias lands, Bordeaux had nodded with unaccustomed seriousness and given this reply. He had then set off for headquarters.

Wilhelm watched him go. Reporting the problem was all he could do right now. He ground his teeth at his own helplessness, but he had enough self-control now to bear it. He had the emblem of knighthood on his chest; it was a sign of his awareness that he would no longer be permitted to act as rashly as he had before.

"Let me repeat that," Bordeaux had said. *"Don't get ahead of yourself. Knights are almost never stripped of their rank once promoted, but people know who you are now. You aren't just a nameless swordsman who can go anywhere he wants."*

Twilight was deepening as the curtain of night draped over the capital. As he walked along the main street, he replayed Bordeaux's words again and again in his mind.

He couldn't just wait quietly in his quarters. He had altogether too much time on his hands, and his feet seemed to drag him slowly but surely toward the plaza in the poor district. It was hours since he had seen Theresia, exchanged their usual words, and then parted ways. He had never before gone to that place twice in one day.

"Wilhelm?"

So he was surprised to find the red-haired girl standing in the darkened square.

Unlike the main street, this plaza opened onto the back alleys, and as such there were no artificial lights. It was a cloudy night, and he could barely see his hand in front of his face. Theresia couldn't possibly see her flowers in the darkness, yet she was waiting alone in that square.

Theresia looked at Wilhelm and blinked her blue eyes. "What's wrong…? You're making such a scary face."

"What's a girl doing out here at this time of night anyway?"

"Why, this almost sounds like… Ah!" Theresia clapped her hands as if she had figured something out. "Hmm…I'd sort of like to ask you the same question, but maybe it wouldn't be very polite. You don't look like you're much for jokes."

"……"

Wilhelm didn't reply, but something felt off to him about the way Theresia was talking, almost as though she was playing a part. As he thought about why this should be, he hit upon a possible reason—and what she was probably thinking.

This was almost the same conversation they'd had the first time they'd met.

"……"

Truth be told, Wilhelm didn't feel he had the time at this moment to indulge Theresia's little games, but she eyed him so innocently while awaiting his response that he couldn't help but play along.

He easily put on the grimace of annoyance that he had worn at their first meeting. Then he said, "There's a lot of dangerous people around here. It's not somewhere a woman should be walking alone."

"Goodness, are you worried about me?"

"I might be one of those dangerous people."

"You're not. I know that uniform—you're one of the castle's knights, aren't you? You wouldn't do anything wrong."

This last line took a turn as Theresia pointed to the emblem on his chest and smiled. Wilhelm smiled grimly at the words, then stepped up next to her. She was wearing the same clothes she had been that afternoon, and she was sitting in the same spot. So he assumed—

"You've been here all day?"

"…Yes. I guess I did hang around for a while." She stuck out her tongue as if to suggest this was something unusual, but Wilhelm suspected it probably wasn't.

Wilhelm had never tried to check on what Theresia did after they parted ways, but now he was sure she always sat here until it got dark.

"I'm not trying to be cute when I say that this really isn't somewhere a woman should be walking around on her own at this time of night."

"Thank you for worrying about me. But I really think it's a little late for that. And anyway, I won't be walking around alone, so it's fine. Someone is coming to get me."

"—"

"Don't worry, it's a girl."

"…I wasn't worrying about that."

It was just his imagination that he was relieved to hear it. And anyway, having another woman around wouldn't make things any safer.

"It's okay. She's a very strong swordswoman. Much stronger than me."

"Stronger than you? I think that would describe most swordspeople."

This girl didn't know the first thing about the fighting arts. She didn't make much of a comparison for anything. Still, though, it had been close to a year since Wilhelm and Theresia met. If this person had been acting as her bodyguard that entire time, maybe she had proven herself.

If Theresia had a bodyguard, did that mean she actually had a certain status in the world?

"So you don't go home. Is it because you don't want to be at your house?"

"Y-you certainly don't pull your punches, do you, Wilhelm?"

"It's a bad habit. My work has taught me never to hold back. So what's your answer?"

"…You could say yes, but…you could also say no. I'm sorry, I know that's complicated." Theresia's eyes seemed to gaze into the distance as she apologized. The feelings swirling in her eyes, how fragile she looked—Wilhelm cursed himself for his insensitivity. No young woman would spend the night wandering aimlessly around town instead of at home without a reason.

"What about you, Wilhelm?" It took him a moment to catch up with her question. Theresia was sitting on the step by the flower bed, hugging her knees and looking up at him. "Can I...ask about your home...? Your family?"

"My...family..."

"Right. I mean...I know maybe it's none of my business..." She smiled shyly. Normally, he might have been able to shoot something back at her. But at this moment, being asked about his family brought Wilhelm up short. After all, at that very moment his home, the House of Trias, might be in danger.

"...Did I say something wrong?" Theresia's expression clouded at his silence.

He cursed himself again for being immature. To tell Theresia about what was going on would only place an unnecessary burden on her. So why couldn't he summon up his usual indifferent look? He looked painfully at the ground.

Then Theresia stood in front of him and reached out her hands to Wilhelm.

"Stiffen that upper lip! Are you a man or aren't you?"

"—?!"

She gave him a hearty smack on both cheeks. Completely surprised, Wilhelm looked at her with wide eyes. Theresia put her hands on her hips and puffed out her chest.

"Whatever your relationship is to your family, it's obviously complicated, but it's not like you to let that make you all weepy. Do what you always do—you know, act haughty for no reason. You should swing your sword like a child, full of unfounded confidence. That's much better."

"—"

Her criticism was brutal. It stunned Wilhelm to realize that was how she thought of him.

Perhaps his silence made Theresia realize how sharp her words had been, for she quickly said, "Wait, that's not— Hrm."

Wilhelm's shoulders relaxed at this change in her. He exhaled, then smiled at her. Not one of his grimaces, but a smile from the heart.

"You really are a strange girl, aren't you?"

"H-huh? What makes you say that? I know I'm not quite normal, but I thought I said something pretty on the nose there." She sounded annoyed.

"Don't praise yourself. But...you're not wrong." He exhaled deeply again. It wasn't a sigh of longing, but a way of expelling all his emotions. "Swinging my sword like a child, huh...?"

A child with a sword would be a very dangerous thing. The image made him smile. But again, she wasn't wrong. Wilhelm was a child playing with a sword. He had remained a child even as time passed, as he grew up. He had just forgotten it somewhere along the line.

But now he remembered why he had taken up the sword, despite his immaturity.

"Let me walk you to the entrance of the poor district. Wait for your friend where there's some light."

"...Aren't you afraid she might miss me if I'm not in our usual spot?"

"Are you saying I should leave you here in the dark? Don't make me."

"That's true enough. I guess we don't have a choice, then. I'll let you help a young woman to her feet." Theresia sounded so confident as she held out her hand. Wilhelm took it and helped her up, and somehow the two of them never quite let go of each other's hands as they walked toward the entrance to the slum. In the heat from their intertwined fingers, Wilhelm could feel his own pulse.

They had threaded their way through several narrow streets when Theresia stopped on a side street near the main road. "I'll wait here," she said. "I think she'll be able to find me." Truthfully, Wilhelm wanted to see her all the way to the main street, but chances were she didn't want him and her bodyguard to meet.

"So now it's a girl by herself in a dark alleyway? You know, come to think of it, they do call prostitutes 'flower girls' around here..."

"Nobody's going to mistake me for one of those... Wait a second, surely that's not why you started calling me that?"

"No. It was because your head was full of flowers."

"Well, that's not very nice, either!" She turned red and batted him on the shoulder. Wilhelm let go of her hand and took a step away from her. His fingers still tingled with the sensation of her—but he set aside this moment of frailty and looked at her. Then, touching the emblem on his chest, he said good night.

"Be careful on these dark roads, Flower Girl."

"Be careful not to shirk your duty too much, good-for-nothing soldier."

These seemingly cruel words quickly gave way to smiles. Then he said, "Bye, Theresia."

"See you next time, Wilhelm."

This was how they always parted now. Wilhelm turned away from her and headed for the main road, feeling her eyes on his back. It was only after he was sure he could no longer sense her watching that he reached to his left breast and tore off the emblem.

· It was the sign that he was a knight, that the world had recognized him, that he could hold his head up when he met Theresia. Now, the nexus of all that meaning glimmered dully in his palm.

It was not brighter nor more beautiful than the sunlight glinting off his sword in the days of his youth.

"That giant, raging idiot!"

It was the next day, and Bordeaux was shouting his lungs out in Wilhelm's personal quarters. He vented his frustration on a desk, which broke in half, and a variety of awards lay scattered around the room. This was not exactly behavior becoming of a commanding officer, yet it was not enough to placate Bordeaux's anger.

"__"

Beside the enraged officer, Grimm silently set a hand on the devastated desk. From inside what was left of it, he picked up an emblem—the dragon crest of a knight. The disk also contained a note, on which was written just one word.

Sorry.

It was simple, unadorned—very much the sort of thing the rather boorish Sword Devil would come up with. Wilhelm Trias had removed the badge of his station and left the capital with only his sword in hand.

It may not have seemed very cultivated. But as the Sword Devil, it was his answer.

6

It had been no small choice for Wilhelm to abandon the sign of his knighthood. The emblem was the proof of acknowledgment by something as big and important as the kingdom itself. Once, he had been considered no more than a delinquent child, but the badge showed that he had been right all along.

From the day he had knocked on the door of the royal army until this moment, he had been focused single-mindedly on the sword. All that time, he had believed it was all he needed, yet he had been given so many things. There had been enemies. Allies. Rivals, comrades, superiors. Those against whom he swore revenge. And…

"Theresia…"

He whispered the name of the girl whom he now knew he cared deeply about. He put a hand on his sword as if to be sure it was still there.

To abandon his emblem was to leave behind everything he had gained in the capital. It wasn't that he believed they were without value. Rather, precisely because he knew they were valuable, he couldn't act freely if he continued carrying them. He had let go of them because they were priceless.

He did look back on them wistfully. He did feel guilt, regret, and anger. His emotions were like a muddy swamp. He had never managed a completely simple way of living. The days when he had merely wanted to be a sword felt as if they had never existed. And yet, neither did he hold that time against himself now.

"___"

He knew that even if he managed to deal with everything that was going on, he wouldn't simply be able to go back to the way things had been. His days had merely been so calm and complacent as to allow him to entertain such fantasies recently.

Like the one in which he extinguished the flames of war that raged around his homeland, was forgiven for throwing aside the honor of a knight, and then took Theresia's hand and brought her home to meet the Trias family. Just a fantasy.

Such thoughts had closed his eyes to reality, but the conflagration he found on returning home opened them with brutal force.

"Hrrraaahhhhh!!"

So the Sword Devil took his beloved sword in hand and, arriving at a home he found utterly changed, began his one-man war.

7

"What do you know about my feelings, Brother?!"

It was five years ago now that, after another one of their fights, Wilhelm had fled his home.

The House of Trias was a diminished noble family with a small territory in the northern part of the kingdom of Lugunica. Their former fame for feats of arms had already waned when Wilhelm arrived as the family's third son.

The two boys who preceded him were more than qualified to inherit the family headship, and Wilhelm spent his youth essentially unfettered by the demands of being part of the succession. There was one thing that caught the eye of this boy as he spent his days unconcerned with the running of the household: an heirloom sword hanging in the house's great hall. It was the one reminder of the days when the House of Trias had earned renown as disciples of the martial arts.

Wilhelm found himself drawn to swords, spending his days engaged in practice from morning till night. At first, his family had looked on in amusement, but after six years they were no longer smiling. The eldest son of the family began to take little swipes at his sword-crazed younger brother under the guise of friendly advice. Wilhelm's reaction to this quibbling led to a white-hot fight, and the younger boy's running away from home was in effect the final word.

He fled to the capital, where he joined the royal army and, eventually, became the Sword Devil.

These were his pitiful beginnings, which he was resolved not to reveal to Theresia or anyone.

The Trias lands he remembered were already wreathed in flames from a major demi-human attack. The vistas he thought he knew had been dyed red, and the mansion where he had lived until almost his teenage years had been burned to the ground. Perhaps the household had been totally unable to resist the attackers, because all that was left were signs of trampling here and there.

Of course. It only made sense. His brothers had been so soft and his family so complacent that the thought of resisting would not even have crossed their minds. His family had been bent on protecting themselves in any way other than combat. That was what had first drawn him to the blade. He would make up for what his brothers lacked.

And now, he should have had enough power to do so.

"Ruuahhhhh!"

His sword became like a whirlwind, and a mist of demi-human blood stained the Trias lands even redder. The demi-humans had successfully overpowered one meek human tribe, but now the Sword Devil slammed into their flank. The heads that looked up in surprise he sent flying; where hands and feet sought to oppose him he cut them off; cries of mockery and hatred could not be raised when he had pierced their throats.

He was covered in the blood of his enemies, his voice raw from shouting. He flashed his sword what seemed like a million times, and then a million more.

"It's the Sword Devil! The Sword Devil, the killer of Valga and Libre!"

As they realized who the rampaging human was, his foes began to press in upon him. They filled his vision to the right and left, breaking upon him like a wave along with their hatred. Still, he flew straight at them.

It was only at the start of the battle that things went well for him. The demi-humans had been caught off guard by the Sword Devil's appearance, but as they realized that Wilhelm was their only opponent, they began to let their numbers do the work.

It was many against one, and he was soon wounded. He might take ten lives with ten strokes of his sword, but the enemy would come back with a hundred blows from a hundred lives at once. It was naturally overwhelming, and Wilhelm, alone and without support, was pressed harder and harder.

"—"

He was surrounded by enemies. Right and left, behind and before, and all of them were focused only on killing him. He had no hulking ally to help him break through their ranks, no silent shield bearer to guard his back—no friends at all to form a battle line with him.

He was alone. He knew there had been a time when he had believed he could get by this way. But even then, he hadn't really been by himself. He could see that now, when it was too late.

"Grrahh!"

He took a wound to his back. He spun around and pierced his ambusher through the heart. As he did, more attackers closed in. He tried to jump out of reach, but his feet got tangled. He blocked from an unnatural position, feeling the impact in every bone in his body. He gritted his teeth; with a succession of silver flashes, the group of demi-humans went flying.

But his inelegant advance stopped there. The blood spatters covering him were not only from his opponents. The bleeding from his own wounds was too much. He fell to his knees, then collapsed where he was.

"H— Hhh— Hhhhhh!"

His breath was harsh and his fighting spirit was relentless, but his limbs no longer responded to his commands to do combat. There, among the piles of dead enemies, Wilhelm's beloved sword slipped from his hand. To let go of one's weapon while still on the battlefield was a pitiful thing. For the Sword Devil to drop his sword meant he was no longer even a demon, but just a man—no, something less than that. A shell.

Perhaps it was only fitting that a man should meet his end as an empty husk, having forgotten even the first wish that led to his being called Sword Devil and simply run ahead. In the end, why had he taken up the sword? What had he been able to leave to the world?

Nothing. Only a body, hollow and empty, a bit of airy nothing.

Could it really have been nothing...?

A massive demi-human stood beside him, looming over Wilhelm where he lingered between life and death.

"You were a fearsome opponent, Sword Devil," he said. "But your life ends here!" He raised his sword high, preparing to strike off Wilhelm's head.

The sight of his impending death stirred something in Wilhelm.

"—"

Countless shadows flitted through his mind—all the people he had encountered in his life. He saw his parents, his brothers, the people of the Trias lands, the other members of the royal army, Grimm, Bordeaux, Roswaal, Carol—and finally, Theresia, smiling, the field of flowers at her back.

Her face, her voice as she said "See you next time" were seared into his memory—into his very soul.

She had brought light into days when he had thought there was nothing, and in his mind's eye, her light mingled with the gleaming of the sword from his youth. He had believed he wanted to be a sword, but the many encounters he'd had and the interlocking bonds he shared with people were like heat and pressure to form him into a person.

He reminisced with fondness on both the days when he was steel and those when he was human. He still had so many memories of them.

"I don't want...to die..."

And so at this, his last moment, the desire to live was what slipped from Wilhelm's lips. He had taken so many lives, affected such nonchalance at the thought of death, yet when the end finally confronted him, his heart quaked with fear. He began to see the joy of being alive, his heart breaking with the terror that that joy was about to be stolen from him.

"___"

Surely that one desperate whisper would not be enough to buy clemency from the demi-human after he had killed so many of his companions.

The ruthless blade fell, speeding the Sword Devil toward the end of his life...

The stroke of the sword at that moment had a beauty that could last into eternity.

The head of the giant demi-human about to end Wilhelm's life went flying into the air.

The weapon that struck him was so sharp that the demi-human himself didn't realize what had happened. When his head landed on the ground, it showed no recognition of his own death.

Wilhelm was agog at what was going on above him. He was the one who was supposed to be facing his demise.

Then there was the rushing breath of a passing blade, a storm of silver streaks, and one demi-human after another was struck down. The shock of this fresh attack spread through the Demi-human Alliance. But it was scant trouble for the newcomer. No sooner had each enemy recognized the opponent's presence than they lay dead on the ground; in other words, it was the demi-humans' own deaths that alerted them to this new force.

"___"

This "someone" all but literally danced among the demi-humans, dispensing blow after blow and amassing piles of corpses. The strikes were so true and so sharp that Wilhelm thought perhaps some god of death was walking among them. A beautiful and kind reaper who took people's lives without letting them suffer the knowledge that they were dead.

This god of death had red hair that bobbed in a tail at the back of its head and wielded a flashing blade as if it were an extra limb.

"Red...hair..."

The reaper cut down all those around Wilhelm as if to protect him. Each time he saw this god of death land a strike, each time this person entered his vision, he felt a fresh tumult in his heart. For standing there was...

"Wilhelm! You great, dunderheaded idiot! We found you!"

He heard the bellowing voice at the same moment he felt someone violently grab him by the shoulders. Before his astonished eyes appeared Bordeaux and Grimm, and he could see the whole of Zergev Squadron with them, covered with gruesome spatters of blood.

"So even you can find yourself at death's door, eh? That's good medicine! You stupid, stupid, stupid idiot!"

"—!"

Wilhelm couldn't speak as Bordeaux berated him; even Grimm's mouth opened as if he wanted to say something. But none of them would actually be that hard on Wilhelm, whose body was covered in cuts, bruises, and wounds. Instead, Bordeaux made sure he had a good grip on the battered young man, then ordered the rest of the squadron to secure a way for them to retreat.

"S-stop," Wilhelm grunted. "Now's...not the time! I can't—! I can't rest now—!"

He shoved away the hand that held him and tried to drag himself toward the sword fighting ahead of him. But just before he reached it, he halted, grinding his teeth in frustration. He had enough self-awareness, enough pride as a swordsman, to stop himself there.

"—"

The flashing silver, the beautiful strokes of the blade, the utterly perfect attacks—these were the work of a god of death. Wilhelm had lived his life with the sword, given much to it, and he could tell.

Even if I work the rest of my life, I'll never reach that place. Only the one who deserves it can make it.

It was the summit, the place allowed only to the truly beloved of the sword and who had mastered this weapon of steel.

"Yaaaahh!"

This time, when Grimm lifted Wilhelm up, he didn't resist. He no longer had the strength. His endurance was at an end, and he felt he might faint away at any moment. And yet as long as he could, as long as he was allowed, as long as his heart could endure, he wanted to see this dance of the sword.

"Lady…!"

Now he found Carol was there, too, watching the god of death at work. She had a hand to her chest, almost as if she were anxious for that reaper, despite this display of unmatchable strength.

He stared stupidly. What was Carol seeing? How could she possibly watch this and look…worried?

Does she not understand how profound her skill with a blade is? Is she not enough of a swordswoman to know?

The technique he was seeing was so elevated that every swipe of steel made him despair for his own status as a swordsman.

"That… That god of death…"

"God of death? Don't be silly. That's the kingdom's ace in the hole—the true sword of the kingdom who puts us to shame. The Sword Saint."

The battlefield seemed far away now. His consciousness flickered. He caught just those two words as it faded away.

Sword Saint. The name given to living legends, carved into the history of the Kingdom of Lugunica.

But how could it be that she was the one to bear it…?

"__"

He had no way of asking her now. He couldn't even call out to her.

8

The battle for the Trias lands would loom large in the history of Lugunica. It was not that there was any special value to the territory in which the battle took place. The carnage wrought on the Trias lands was just another one of the tragedies that occurred throughout the Demi-human War. It differed from all the others in just one way: It would go down as the first stunning excursion of the era's Sword Saint.

Until that moment in the Trias lands, the Sword Saint of that generation had not once shown her abilities publicly. Some even doubted her existence or even the existence of the Sword Saint's blessing itself. But this battle abundantly proved the saint's true strength.

In her first battle, she single-handedly took the lives of nearly a thousand demi-humans, a feat that would have been impossible for anyone else. The event marked the appearance of a savior who could bring an end to the Demi-human War, which had become a confused morass. Everyone hailed her as such, and all praised the name of the Sword Saint.

As for the Sword Devil, who had abandoned his status as a knight and become an ordinary swordsman once more in order to protect the Trias lands, who had cut down three hundred demi-humans alone—his name was quietly forgotten.

The Sword Devil himself, however, couldn't have cared less. He had never cared much for records or awards. And any reason he might have had to be interested in them he had surely relinquished by then. What was important to Wilhelm Trias was in that field of flowers by that square.

It was weeks before his wounds had healed enough that he could go back to the plaza. He had been in one brutal battle after another, but now he walked down the familiar path with his battered but still beloved sword in his hand. Every time he walked this street, Wilhelm always felt a mix of emotions.

There was happiness and eagerness, depression and anxiety, frustration and even envy. But what he felt right now was not any of these. It was the sure intuition that she would be there. Wilhelm trusted his hunches. Especially when it came to whether or not she would be waiting to meet him in the square.

There was no need to put into words at this point what it was that made this intuition so certain.

"—"

When he reached the plaza, he sucked in his breath. He didn't have to look for her. Her presence was overwhelming. She was sitting on the steps right where she always was, her eyes playing over the flowers, which had now started to wither.

He didn't do anything as foolish as walking toward her. Instead he ran, drawing his sword soundlessly as he went. He brought the blade down with fearsome speed, striking like a thunderbolt to cleave her head in two...

"That's humiliating."

"...Oh?"

His earnest admission was met by only the briefest of replies. He had attacked with all his might, and she had simply caught the blade between two fingers. Without even turning around, she negated all the months and years he had spent honing his sword technique.

"Were you laughing at me?"

"—"

She didn't respond. The silence hurt Wilhelm more than anything else.

Even now, nothing about her willowy body suggested she was an exponent of the martial arts.

"Answer me, Theresia... Or should I say, Sword Saint Theresia van Astrea...!"

He wrenched his sword back from her with sheer force, then struck again. She dodged him without so much as a hair falling out of place. He found himself distracted by the sight of her flowing red locks, and before he knew it, his feet had been swept out from under him to send him toppling to the ground. Wilhelm, once feared as the Sword Devil, hit the pavement without even managing to catch himself.

"___"

He had met this girl so many times, bantered with her, grown closer to her without anybody knowing—and now she had knocked him down. Theresia looked at him where he lay. Her eyes were a piercing blue reflection of a sky that had never known clouds.

"Y-yaaaahhh!"

Wilhelm scrambled to his feet for another attack as if chasing after her retreating form. His strike was so strong and so true that one would never have believed it came from a convalescent. His battle aura was even stronger than it had been when he had earned the name of Sword Devil, when he had felled Valga and gone toe-to-toe with Libre.

His sword technique was so polished and pure that it seemed he had thrown away everything else he had once been. In this place, the secret plaza that only they knew, the Sword Devil brought to bear every ounce of his skill.

It was, without a doubt, the greatest and ultimate demonstration of Wilhelm's life as a swordsman.

"___"

And Theresia, without so much as a sword in her hand, avoided it as if Wilhelm were merely a little boy.

A light, dancing step revealed the size of the gulf between them. An impassable wall, an unbridgeable gap, an uncrossable chasm. They were utterly remote from one another. The divide was all too clear to both of them.

Theresia looked down at Wilhelm, who lay on the ground.

"I won't come here again," she said, her quiet good-bye.

She was holding Wilhelm's sword in her hand. When had she gotten it? The Sword Saint had stolen the Sword Devil's weapon, and he had been ignominiously sent to the ground not by the blade, but by a blow from the hilt.

She was so far ahead, and he was so weak. He would never reach her. He wasn't enough.

That was why she was looking at him that way.

"You shouldn't…be using a sword…with that expression," he said.

There was a limit to shamelessness. Whose fault was it? Whose powerlessness had led her to this? If he were stronger, if he had had an exceptional talent for the sword, she wouldn't have looked like this now.

"I'm the Sword Saint," she said. "I never knew why before. But now I do."

It was at once an answer and not an answer. It was Theresia's obscure signal that she wanted something from Wilhelm. When she really wanted him to listen, she never said so directly. She could be difficult that way.

"What you mean, why?!"

"Wielding the sword to protect someone. I think that's a good reason."

The exchange was like what they had once said every time they met, though there was no longer any need for those questions and answers.

The Sword Saint had preferred her flowers, unable to see the meaning in using the sword. Wilhelm's sin had been to give Theresia van Astrea a reason to wield her blade. He had given a reason to the woman who was stronger than any other, could take the sword further than anyone else.

"Wait…Theresia…"

She was already leaving; she felt there were no more words to speak.

Wilhelm couldn't move his limbs. He could hardly raise his head. Yet, driven by his frustration at Theresia and his anger at himself, Wilhelm managed to look up, his own blue eyes focused firmly on her back, since she refused to turn around.

"—"

She didn't stop walking, and retreated farther and farther. Soon his voice would not be able to reach her anymore. He had to speak before that happened.

"I'll steal that sword from you. What do I care about your blessing or your station...? Don't make light of wielding it...of the beauty of a steel blade, Sword Saint!"

She kept growing more distant, until he could no longer see her. Had his last words reached her? They must have. He must have made them reach her.

To speak of the beauty of steel to the one who was beloved of the sword-god was the Sword Devil's pathetic challenge to battle.

The two of them never met in that place again.

After that day Wilhelm Trias, the Sword Devil, was not to be seen in the royal army. Instead, the name of Theresia van Astrea appeared. She began single-handedly turning the tide of what had seemed to be an endless war.

Through sheer strength, she began to overwhelm the flames of Valga Cromwell's hatred and the unending battle. This was one way of rising to the old stories of heroism.

The name of the Sword Saint resounded throughout the land, bringing hope to the humans and despair to the demi-humans.

And so time went on, and as the flames of war began to wink out, so, too, the tale draws to its end.

But the love song of the Sword Devil yet speaks of the end of the Demi-human War, and the final meeting of the Sword Devil and the Sword Saint.

THE LOVE SONG OF THE SWORD DEVIL

Interlude

1

Carol Remendes had first met Theresia when she was fourteen. The House of Remendes had served the Astrea family, the house of the Sword Saints, for generations. Carol, too, had learned the blade for as long as she could remember, honing her abilities and being trained in her family's duties.

When the Sword Saint Freibel van Astrea passed on the blessing of the Sword Saint to the next generation, and a new Sword Saint was born, the responsibility of attending her fell to Carol.

Carol could still remember her first day of duty—she had been so nervous she thought she might faint clean away. It was only natural. Many of the great swordspeople of the Remendes family were present at that moment. Carol was, of course, quite a competent sword fighter compared to other members of her own generation, but if pure strength was the only condition for being an attendant of the Sword Saint, well, there were many other qualified candidates.

And yet it was Carol, young and immature, who had been chosen. She was confused.

"Are you the one who will be with me from today onward?"

She was actually rather thrown off her rhythm by the fact that the person she found herself attending was a girl younger than she was.

"Y-yes, ma'am! I'm Carol Remendes, of House of Remendes! I'm inexperienced as a swordswoman, but for you, Lady Theresia Astrea, I will spare no—"

"You don't have to be quite so nervous. Can I call you Carol?" Theresia smiled. Carol was somewhat calmed by this behavior, but she was also suspicious. It was hard for her to believe that this child was the Sword Saint, the one who had received the blessing spoken of in legend.

This girl is a sword fighter vastly more accomplished even than me?

Carol had spent no small amount of time diligently devoted to the art of the sword, and she had a certain conceit about her own abilities. It was unsurprising that such extensive training might cause her to doubt the true abilities of the "Sword Saint."

In truth, neither the way Theresia carried herself nor the way she acted gave the slightest hint that she knew anything of the sword, nor of the martial arts at all. It was not easy to simply accept the claim that she was the one who had inherited the most powerful of martial blessings.

"Lady Theresia, if it's all right with you, perhaps I could beg a lesson in swordsmanship from you?"

It was a very provocative way of speaking, but that, Carol reflected, was how she had been back then. She had believed then she was hiding her doubts, but she was sure now that Theresia had seen through her. The Sword Saint had put a finger to her lips, feigning thought, and looked back at Carol. Then she had said, "I'm sorry. It's not, so I'm afraid I can't entertain you with a lesson."

Bluntly, she had refused Carol's request.

This meeting did not give Carol a favorable impression of Theresia. Of course, that was no reason to abandon her duties. On that point, Carol was quite firm with herself, and Theresia never once complained about the way her bodyguard went about her work. It was another event that caused the distance between them to close—and changed how Carol thought about Theresia.

Theresia and Carol had been acting out the roles of a good master and a good servant for about two months. At the time, Theresia spent many of her days at home; she seemed to care little for her status as Sword Saint, and it bothered Carol tremendously. Now and again, Carol would request a lesson, but she was always turned down. This was one of the things that contributed to her annoyance as time went on.

"I'm going to find out if Lady Theresia really is qualified to be the Sword Saint."

Looking back on it now, she could only marvel at how foolish she had been. But at the time, it had seemed an excellent idea. If Theresia was not sufficiently capable, Carol would have to train her herself. This mistaken sense of duty played no small part in pushing her to act as she did.

Thus, Carol engineered an incident that would allow her to test Theresia's abilities with the sword. She had no intention of getting the girl hurt, but neither did she mean to be particularly gentle. Just a little test.

And as a result...

"Carol! Carol! Are you all right? You... You aren't hurt, are you?!"

Carol lay spread-eagle on the carpet, listening to Theresia's frantic voice. Her head was spinning too fast for her to tell what had happened. She had tried to set up an opportunity to test Theresia and snuck up behind her—and the rest was darkness.

"L-Lady...T-Theresia...?"

"Y-you're all right?! You're not hurt? Th-thank goodness..."

Theresia was looking down at the stunned Carol, all but choking. Her anxiousness had gone beyond words; she covered her face, and tears began to run from her eyes.

But the person who had caused the pain here, who had been in the wrong here—it was all Carol.

"I'm sorry! I'm sorry, Carol...!"

Watching the weeping Theresia, Carol understood with terrible clarity. Thanks to her own foolishness and insensitivity, she was the one who had hurt this girl so badly.

*   *   *

It was only later that Carol learned about Theresia's blessing. She was talking with Freibel, the previous Sword Saint and Theresia's uncle. He asked Carol to take good care of Theresia, and also spoke of the power she had been born with.

"She's had the blessing of the reaper since birth," he said.

This was an inborn blessing, something separate from the blessing of the Sword Saint she had been granted. It meant that injuries inflicted by Theresia's hand would never close and could not be healed, inevitably ending in death.

Carol shivered. These two abilities together showed Theresia to be truly the beloved of the battlefield. At the same time, she understood the meaning behind the tears Theresia had shed when she had hit Carol.

"___"

She stood, speechless to realize how foolish and hasty she had been, and then she was flooded with regret. Her feet were so heavy with self-recrimination that she could hardly return to Theresia's room. She had done something unbefitting a servant, and she was sure she would be released from duty.

"I apologize for what happened. I'll understand if you can't forgive me, but I'm truly sorry."

However, that certainty disappeared at the way Theresia lowered her head the moment she saw Carol. Carol knew it was she who needed to apologize, yet it was Theresia who looked defeated and apologetic. Trembling, she could hardly bring herself to look at her attendant.

Touched by the gentleness of Theresia's heart, Carol was wracked with shame. And it began to change her.

"Lady Theresia, your bath is ready. Will you allow me to accompany you?"

"Carol...you seem so kind suddenly."

"No, milady. Not nearly so kind as you."

After that, Carol came to sincerely respect Theresia as her master. This new Sword Saint, she found, was a gentle and thoughtful young woman despite the awesome powers she'd been given.

That was the reason Carol Remendes changed.

*   *   *

Once she knew the details of Theresia's situation, Carol became her confidante. Theresia had an extraordinary pair of blessings, which together made it seem her inevitable destiny was on the battlefield. Yet she hated to harm others and much preferred to admire flowers wherever she found them.

At the beginning, Carol had been frustrated that a Sword Saint would show no interest in using the sword. But once she had come to know Theresia, Carol realized that there was no problem with this at all. Though favored by the sword-god, she chose a life without the blade. Others might criticize her for this, but Carol was determined to take her master's part no matter what. It was a kind of penance for her former foolishness, but also her way of serving her cherished Theresia.

Carol would be just as happy if Theresia could go on in her placid, content ways, never having to pick up a weapon. But that wish was quietly being betrayed.

The Demi-human War, the civil conflict that threatened the kingdom, would not let Theresia escape.

2

"Elder Brother! I'm sorry! I'm so sorry…!"

"Lady Theresia…"

Carol held the weeping girl close, embracing her beloved master, trying desperately to comfort her. But she couldn't find the reassuring words she was looking for. Carol found herself pathetic; she hated herself.

Theresia's first battle as the Sword Saint was also the royal army's first defeat in the civil war. It was not that Theresia had not been powerful enough. The problem went deeper than that.

Theresia had been unable to fight or even pick up her sword. She had tied back her long red hair and clad herself in light armor, and taken up Reid, the Dragon Sword that only the Sword Saint could wield, along with her own blade. With the hopes of the kingdom on her shoulders, she had set out to battle.

And still she had been unable to fight. She could not bring herself to harm others. Instead her older brother, a guide for her to the last, had sacrificed himself. He had joined those fighting a desperate defense of the frozen Theresia and met his end in combat.

After Theresia's inability to bring herself to fight had gotten her brother killed, the sword became a curse to her.

"I'm sorry, Carol."

These had become the words with which an ashen-faced Theresia dismissed Carol each day.

Her failure to fight in her first battle had caused profound disappointment in the kingdom's upper echelons; she had continued to be unable to join the army in anything it did, and it seemed there was no hope left for the Sword Saint.

Requests for the dispatch of the defeated Saint were now filled by Carol, who went in her place. Of course, Carol did not esteem herself so highly as to believe she was really fulfilling Theresia's duty. But she continued to throw herself into the work in hopes of making things even a little easier on her master.

Carol knew full well that if Theresia were fighting, she would achieve ten times, a hundred times more. But Carol would also be happy if the opportunity never came. If her kindhearted young charge never had to use her sword...

Years passed, and the civil war dragged on. All the while, Theresia's ill luck continued. Her second-eldest brother and her younger brother both died in battle one after the other, and Freibel, too, lost his life in the war. The flames of this conflict seemed as if they would pursue Theresia everywhere, burn out every corner of her heart.

More than once, Carol had heard Theresia crying miserably in her room at night, "I'm sorry... I'm sorry...!"

Each time she heard the plaintive cries, Carol's heart filled with an unreasonable but irrepressible anger. Was it not enough? Would it not end? Why did destiny see fit to corner Theresia so?

"—"

How long would the attentions of the sword-god torment her?

Somebody, save her, Carol would pray from the bottom of her heart. *Anybody.*

Carol could not do it alone. She didn't have what it took. Let her be mocked as shameless; it didn't matter. *Somebody, help.*

She could only pray that the right person would find Theresia. She could only beg the heavens.

3

It was pure chance that Carol noticed the quiet change in Theresia.

Five years had already passed since the beginning of the civil war, four years since Theresia's ill-fated first battle. More and more often, Theresia spent her days outside rather than cooped up in her house. She was hardly out for pleasant walks, though. Carol had suggested to Theresia that it might be best for her not to be in the house. The reason was simple, and that made it all the more awful.

As the war worsened, various members of the House of Astrea, concerned that their status as Sword Saints would decline, were visiting on a daily basis to urge Theresia to rejoin the army. These encouragements came from people who had nothing to lose, and as the bearer of all their expectations, Theresia had to endure their "advice." Thus, Carol suggested that perhaps Theresia should get away from it all.

"Please, think of yourself first," she said. "You have to do what you think is right, Lady Theresia." She frequently saw off the depressed young woman with such counsel from her heart of hearts. She wasn't advocating simple escapism, but she felt unnecessary suffering should be avoided. Theresia might not be able to feel quite content, but she could at least find some harbor for a brief respite from the battering winds.

Theresia began to spend her time away from the house, some-where deep in the poor quarter. It was not an especially safe place, but it certainly afforded solitude. The flower seeds she planted came into bud, and when they bloomed, it would become a place where she could relax. Or so she had hoped.

"Lady Theresia…did something happen?"

One night, Carol came to the square to meet Theresia and found that her usual distracted air had given way to something else. Theresia had a rare smile pulling at her lips as she said, "I met a very rude sword today."

The words didn't sound promising, yet she seemed almost pleased. Carol was puzzled. It would be quite some time before Carol learned the true import of those words.

Not until she discovered that the person Theresia had met in the square that day was Wilhelm.

She had, it was true, prayed for someone to save Theresia, no mat-ter who it might be. So she wasn't technically in any position to complain. Yet she very much wanted to. Why, she wanted to know, did it have to be Wilhelm Trias?

It so happened that Carol had known Wilhelm before he and There-sia had met. Carol had often seen him on the battlefield when fulfilling Theresia's missions, and he could be a troublesome swordsman. There was no way, in Carol's mind, that a person with Wilhelm's particular qualities could ever mesh with Theresia's generosity of heart.

Wilhelm was like a blood-starved wild animal who had put on a human skin and learned to use a sword. That was Carol's opinion of the Sword Devil. He was the exact opposite of Theresia, who hated to hurt any living thing and was terrified by her own enormous power. It was inconceivable that they should see anything in each other, yet in that field of flowers, there was an unusual meeting of the minds.

Although she felt a little guilty about it, Carol had eavesdropped on their meetings more than once or twice. Each time, she had been prepared to leap out and cut Wilhelm down if there had been any trouble, but she had always been disappointed. Or, well, *disappointment* was not the right word. After all, she saw Theresia smile and laugh among her flowers.

It had been so long since Carol had seen a smile or heard laughter from Theresia. In the five years during which they had been master and servant, Theresia had spent only the first six months in anything like happiness. After that, the Demi-human War had erupted, Theresia had attempted her first battle, her heart had been broken, and her smile had disappeared.

But here, Carol saw the true Theresia van Astrea. And if Theresia was willing to acknowledge and trust this boy, then Carol begrudgingly admitted that she would do so, too.

It was at this time that Carol was also growing closer to Wilhelm's comrade Grimm. He, too, thought very highly of Wilhelm, and her impression of the Sword Devil began to change.

Ultimately, Wilhelm achieved great things in battle and was even granted a promotion to knighthood. He took the place that had once been reserved for the Sword Saint, Theresia, and now it was the Sword Devil people looked to as the one who would bring an end to the Demi-human War. Carol admitted with admiration that Theresia's judgment had been right.

After that, she saw a change in how Wilhelm thought and acted. The barely restrained, bestial intensity began to subside. He showed consideration for those around him and dedicated himself to living up to the hopes people had for him. He was attempting to be the very picture of knighthood.

The change was extraordinary. But everyone believed it, and even Carol found herself thinking more kindly of him. Though they still argued, she had no choice but to acknowledge who he was.

"Wilhelm..."

There was no need to describe the meetings between Wilhelm and Theresia. She waited for him by the field of flowers, greeted him with gentle visage and voice. Anyone in the world could have guessed what she felt for the Sword Devil. There was no question that the two of them cared for each other and that their hearts had forged a connection.

That pleased Carol, and she genuinely wished them happiness. It would be untrue to say she felt no jealousy toward Wilhelm, who had been the one who was able to tease out the true Theresia. This was part of the reason she would always continue to needle him publicly. But all the same, if Theresia was happy, that was enough for Carol.

Theresia had been hurt more than enough already. A girl who didn't deserve to be in pain had been wounded for pointless reasons by the unfitting destiny she had been given. So it was good if she could at last be happy. Carol wanted it for her.

She wanted everyone to know that Theresia van Astrea deserved to be loved, to see the smile that Theresia used only amid those flowers, to hear the laugh Theresia uttered only for Wilhelm. Carol was certain that the day would come soon.

But the curse that was the sword had not yet relinquished its hold on Theresia.

4

When the flames of war began to lick at Wilhelm Trias's home, he tried to contain them by himself. Grimm told Carol what was going on; she understood the gravity of the situation and couldn't decide what to do, torn between telling Theresia and not telling her. Carol didn't think much would come of letting Theresia know. But if she kept from her master the fact that the person she cared about had gone off to a hopeless battle, was that not itself a great betrayal?

Carol went back and forth, agonized over the choice, but in the end she told Theresia everything.

It was to be the moment when the current Sword Saint truly awakened.

"Lady Theresia...!"

Everything in the Trias lands seemed to be on fire. Amid everything, the sight of Theresia wielding her sword was terrible and beautiful. The flashes of her blade, the movement of her feet as she dodged the enemy's blows. All of it was like a dance that spoke to the absolute achievement of her technique. As a fellow swordswoman, Carol could only watch this display in astonishment and admiration.

But as Theresia's servant, Carol Remendes, she felt sadness and pain. Theresia stood guarding the blood-soaked Wilhelm, holding off the waves of demi-humans who attacked them. For the first time in her life, Theresia had overcome her reluctance, and on the other side of that hesitation was a sword technique like a tempest.

Carol understood how she had banished that hesitation, as well as what the result would be. There were no tears on Theresia's cheeks as she brought her sword to bear, yet it was clear that she was crying. Here, in front of the man she loved, she gave in to the destiny she had so long resisted, the fate that had cost her a member of her family.

"Lady Theresia…"

In the end, Carol had done nothing but make Theresia cry. Nothing had changed since that first time. Keenly aware that Theresia and Wilhelm were parting ways, Carol was wracked with the sense of her own guilt.

5

Wilhelm quietly disappeared from the royal army, Theresia's name and renown replacing his own. That first battle in which she had failed to fight was covered up, and the battle for the House of Trias was presented as the Sword Saint's first combat. Afterward, Theresia rose to achieve all that was expected and hoped of her.

She gave the kingdom her selfless loyalty. All and sundry praised the beautiful Sword Saint and her exceptional prowess, the kingdom stirred with the second coming of a legend, and Theresia van Astrea became a hero.

And in the wings was Carol, supporting her mistress as she had always done.

"Thank you again, Carol," Theresia said with a small smile. But it was fleeting, not her true smile. That expression, the one more beautiful than any of the flowers she surrounded herself with, was not something Carol or anyone in the kingdom could evoke. There was only one person who could do that.

And that one person—that man, the Sword Devil—was gone. No one knew where.

Eventually, an end came to the fighting, though it left a great unease behind. It was Theresia herself who put a finish to the kingdom's long civil war. Beloved of the sword god, spending herself for the kingdom, she ended the conflict and became a hero.

Her name would go down in legend, and her fame would be eternal; she would be spoken of for generations to come. And eventually, no one would care about the life of one young girl named Theresia. Her love of flowers, the smile she revealed to one particular man, would be cut away by her life with the blade. It was a source of endless frustration to Carol to see Theresia dragged along by the path of the Sword Saint.

She had once prayed for Theresia to be saved by someone, anyone. Now she prayed for the same thing, but not at the hands of "anyone." If Theresia was to be saved, there would be only one man who could do it. And so Carol prayed desperately for him.

But her wishing was fruitless; her prayers went unanswered.

Nothing changed. Theresia became a hero, and the day of the ceremony arrived.

THE LOVE SONG OF THE SWORD DEVIL

Final Stanza

1

Days passed. Then months. Then two years.

Many people counted those two years as beginning from the day of the Sword Saint's first battle. Only a very few who had been involved knew that the actual beginning dated to several weeks prior to that.

The Sword Devil had disappeared and, as if in his place, the star of the Sword Saint began to rise. One girl, beloved of the sword god, accomplished what an entire army had not been able to: She ended the Demi-human War that the royal forces had wasted themselves on for close to ten years, and brought peace to the kingdom.

The Demi-human Alliance had continued a grassroots resistance, but the blade of the Sword Saint was able to uproot even the desire to avenge Valga Cromwell. In the end, perhaps the demi-humans found that they had raised their fist but no longer had anywhere to bring it down.

The Demi-human Alliance had lost those who had led it at the beginning of the war; they had continued to resist through the inertia of those leaders' ideas. The Sword Saint simply removed any reason they had to continue with that inertia.

Talks between Jionis Lugunica, the present king, and Cragrel, the representative of the demi-human faction, ensued. Thus, the Demi-human War, which had afflicted the kingdom for nine long years, ended shockingly peacefully.

"You look stunning, Lady Theresia."

Theresia van Astrea had changed into a formal outfit, and Carol could not help exclaiming. Theresia's red hair now reached down to her hips. Her eyes were still blue as a cloudless sky, and her skin was almost translucently pale. She was the picture of irresistible beauty, which was only fitting for Carol's master.

"Thank you, Carol. Your dress suits you perfectly, as well." There was that thin smile again. Carol was dressed up much the way Theresia was, and as grateful as she was for the younger woman's words of praise, there was a loneliness in her heart that separated her from her master.

Today there was to be a ceremony to mark the end of the war, with Theresia as the guest of honor. She had ended the endless conflict between humans and demi-humans. The whole world would be introduced to Theresia, the Sword Saint, the embodiment of humanity's hope.

It was a day that left Carol with a flurry of emotions. She was also proud, of course—there could have been no greater honor than to serve at Theresia's side as her attendant.

The common people were immensely enamored of Theresia. It seemed as if everyone who could get to the capital had packed into the castle to try to get a glance at her. It was unmistakable proof that Carol's master had truly been acknowledged and embraced by the world.

"—"

And yet in profile, Theresia's face, so beautifully made up, suggested only how fragile that world was. Carol knew the reason, and that was why her emotions were so confused. She knew why, and for whom, Theresia had really fought. She knew how long her master had been tormented by her gift and how she had pushed aside all that pain to take up her weapon and fight as the Sword Saint before the man she had loved. And Carol knew how Theresia's heart had broken after that, when they parted.

How wonderful it had been to see Theresia relax among those flowers and fall in love. Carol was aware of all this. And it only increased her pain.

"I envy you, Trias."

He had a place deep in the hearts of both her precious master and the man she herself cared for. The fact that he wasn't here today made her immeasurably sad.

2

Perhaps Theresia stopped in her tracks because the woman's sheer presence was so strong. They had been going from the changing room to the ceremony hall, and a woman with indigo hair and mismatched eyes had been waiting.

The woman smiled and walked easily toward Theresia. "So this is the hero everyone's talking about, the one who brought an end to the civil war... I see. You are indeeeed the very picture of a flowering beauty. But I'm quite afraid you seeeem to be missing something."

"__"

"The wooorld is about to meet the Sword Saint. Surely she should be carrying a blade?" She almost sounded like she was teasing, but she held out a sword—a ceremonial blade in a white scabbard.

"You're..."

"One who need not be introduced at this time. Although I confess, I do know a greeeat deal about you. And on that basis, I advise you to take this."

"__"

"Don't worry about whether it will go well with your dress. There are more important things in the world. And anyway...I should think you of all people will always look best carrying a sword."

One of the two differently colored eyes winked. Theresia hesitated for a moment, then took the proffered weapon.

"That's good," the woman said. "Come now. I'm just a biiit of a busybody."

As if to announce that her work was done, she said no more and walked off, away from the ceremony hall. Theresia thought about calling after her, but at length she only watched her depart. The hall was packed with people who had flocked from all over the country to get a glimpse of the Sword Saint. She could hardly disappoint all those people on a mere personal whim.

"That's quite virtuous but also a bad habit. Every once in a while, it wouldn't hurt to do something selfish like he did."

Theresia thought she heard the woman's voice, even though that was impossible. Then she started walking. She came to the end of the corridor, where the hall came into view. A great heat pressed upon her.

"So I gave my romantic rival a bit of help. I can practically see him frowning about it riiight now."

Theresia thought she heard the woman's voice again, sounding somehow both amused and sad at the same time.

3

The ceremony went as smoothly as anyone could have hoped. At first, there was a murmur in the crowd when the Sword Saint appeared bearing her ceremonial blade. But as Theresia strode through the hall, the surprise vanished, replaced by complete adoration for the twin presence of the girl and her sword. Even the king himself was taken by the lithe girl concealing exceptional power, so much so that he practically forgot he was there to give an award, and only stood transfixed.

As the evening went on, everyone reflected that every move she made held the beauty and elegance of a flower. They saw how precious she was and how the base and martial steel was unsuited to her. This girl shouldn't be made to wield it. Her face in profile seemed to suggest her soft and gentle nature, and that all she wanted was to admire beautiful flowers.

"—"

Then Theresia looked up. She had knelt to receive her commendation from the king, but now she rose and turned around.

A dark figure walked slowly into the hall, slicing through the fevered enthusiasm of the crowd. Others in the room followed Theresia's gaze and were struck mute when they saw him. He was dressed from head to toe in a muddy brown overgarment, a pathetic sight to behold. The dirt and blood clinging to his skin made it seem he had not so much as bathed recently. His appearance was practically calculated to provoke the contempt of those who saw him.

But this was not what drove the people to silence. Rather, it was the bare steel in his hand, and the overpowering aura of battle he exuded.

"___"

The guards stationed in the hall began to move, but Theresia herself stopped them. As the shrouded figure walked toward her, Theresia began to close the distance herself. Finally, she was watching him from the dais permitted only to the ceremony's participants, and he was staring at her from the foot of the platform.

"___"

A beautiful, white sacred blade came up. In parallel, a rusted and blunt sword rose. And then, as if on a signal and without a sound, they leaped at each other.

Many in the audience felt that both of the fighters turned invisible at that moment. But the ringing of steel on steel held their attention.

This sword dance was being played out at a speed the average person's eye could never follow. The flashes of the blades became indistinguishable, their clash-like music, and eventually people began to weep. They could not see the fight and could barely hear it; they were simply overwhelmed.

Thereupon, each of those in attendance renounced what they had felt before, that the sword was unsuited to Theresia van Astrea. In that battle, they saw the beauty of steel, that it was fit to be reverenced, how devotion to it made a person shine. Who could have known that the sword could teach others about beauty?

"___"

As for those few who could follow what was going on, what they saw astonished them. Thrust and parry, swords locked together, stances switching—both Theresia and her assailant were at the peak of swordsmanship.

It made sense that the Sword Saint should be thus. Many of them had participated in the civil war and seen her abilities with their own eyes. But who was this who attacked her on nearly equal terms?

The Sword Saint had ordered the soldiers to stay back, and the king likewise instructed them not to intervene. They obeyed, watching silently, but wondered if they should not be doing more. Who was this enemy? Some demi-human extremist who opposed the end of the war? Then again, the humans were not monolithic. Perhaps this was someone dissatisfied with the conclusion of hostilities.

If so, they had to stop this. But was it even possible? None of the soldiers could have involved themselves in such profoundly high-level combat.

"___"

They could see the Sword Saint's face as she worked her ceremonial blade ceaselessly, her attacks falling like a storm. Let us be completely clear: No one could stop this girl in love. Her eyes were wet, her cheeks red, and each exchange brought the Sword Saint happiness as she fought.

Her hair was like a flickering flame, her eyes like a cloudless sky; the beautiful and gentle beloved of the sword god was shimmering with joy. This battle with the demonic swordsman before her shone as nothing else had in this world. It was the most dangerous meeting in history, and she was enjoying it to the full.

"___"

Among those who were close to the Sword Saint, the ones who also knew the Sword Devil felt their souls tremble. All that they had wanted to see, all that they had wanted to know, was here in this moment. The man who had struggled to be a sword, who had been called a devil—what had he found at the end of his path? What had he now resolved himself to?

"___"

Their swords flashed until the flashes ran together; many strikes became a single strike, creating a sound that left the world behind. It was almost like music—a song of swords created when the utmost technique met the most polished steel, a song that produced limitless emotions. Everyone was held captive as the love song of this shy boy and girl played out without shame before them.

"—"

But even the most beautiful voice must eventually take a breath, and an end came. The battle was over, even though one might have wished for it to go on forever.

"—"

The sound of shattering steel, no longer able to withstand the intense blows, cracked like thunder in the hall. The reddish-brown blade snapped in half, the tip spiraling through the air. Here at the end of their battle, the end of the two sword fighters' meeting, the Sword Saint's sacred blade—

"I—"

"—"

"I win."

The Sword Saint came quickly down from the dais, her footsteps audible. The only remaining sword was the superb, half-broken dull blade in the demon's hand. Its shattered edge was at the Sword Saint's pale throat, and everyone in attendance understood.

The Sword Saint had lost.

She had been irrefutably pulled down from the summit of the sword.

It took them a moment to notice something else. The girl who was still standing there, having dropped her sword. She was nothing more and nothing less than a beautiful young woman in love.

"You're weaker than me. There's no more reason for you to wield the sword."

Who could say such a thing to the Sword Saint, the girl who had scaled the highest heights of the sword?

Only someone who could show her a greater love than the sword god.

How diligently must he have worked to reach that point?

"If I am not to wield the sword…then who?"

"I will inherit your reason for bearing the sword. You will become why I do so."

How many hundreds, how many thousands or ten thousands, how many countless setbacks and failures must that swordsman have endured? How many battles must he have fought to earn that claim?

This most awkward speaker let his hood fall back. The young man who appeared had a serious countenance, but his hair was unkempt, his face covered in mud, and his eyes were stern.

"You're terrible. Putting a person's decisions and resolution all to waste…"

"All these things that you think I'm putting to waste, I will take up from you. As for you, forget that you ever held the sword, and live a life of peace. You could… Ah, yes. Perhaps you could grow some flowers. But only in peace, under my protection."

"Protected by your sword?"

"That's right."

"And you would be so kind as to protect me?"

"I would."

His declaration was without compromise or hesitation. He would not be moved, even if the sword god himself stood against him. His resolution had pulled this lovely young woman from the throne of the Sword Saint through nothing but his own strength.

"—"

Wordlessly, Theresia placed a hand on the flat of the outstretched blade and took a step forward. They were close enough to touch, to feel each other's breath. Theresia's eyes welled from emotion, and she began to smile and cry at the same time. And then, through her smile and her tears, she said what she always did at their meetings.

"Do you like flowers?"

"I've learned I don't hate them."

*   *   *

Because you're there with them. Because that field of flowers is where I met you.
Because they are the world you love, the beauty you wish for.

"Why do you wield your sword?"
"To protect you."

And because you are the seed of my world.

Slowly, they drew closer to each other, the distance between them shrinking until it was nothing at all.

They could feel the fire of each other, and the heat of their kiss was enough to melt solid steel.

The first question she asked him when their lips parted made him so intensely shy that he could barely answer.

"Do you love me?"
"Can't you tell?"

4

The dance, the meeting, and finally the kiss, ended.

Carol, absorbed by the dance, seeing the meeting, and watching the kiss, wept openly. Before her she saw Theresia's true face, the one she had given up hope of ever seeing again.

Look, she wanted to exclaim. *Look at that*, she wanted to shout. She wanted the world to know how kind this person was, to know that when she took up the sword she was stronger than anyone, and yet she was kind. Carol wanted everyone to see that in the presence of the man she loved, Theresia was only a sweet and caring girl.

"—"

Grimm had found his way to her side. He, too, was watching the embrace, squinting as if staring at a bright light.

Suddenly, a memory came to Carol. A conversation the two of them had back before Grimm had lost his voice. Somehow the subject of *that man* had come up, and Carol had been criticizing him fiercely.

"Hmph. A nickname like 'the Sword Devil' is dishonorable for a swordsman. If he can be confused for a demon, it means there's something twisted about the way he lives!"

Grimm laughed. "You're certainly merciless, Carol. I guess I can't deny what you're saying. But…"

"But what?"

He had looked rather weak-willed as he laughed, but he was contradicting her. She looked at Grimm questioningly. His reply came with a pained smile but with real confidence.

"It's possible that the first person to call Wilhelm the Sword Devil was me. When I saw how he fought the demi-humans at Castour Field, I was so terrified by it that that was what I called him."

"What's wrong with that? It certainly describes the way he acts on the battlefield…"

"True, he does look like a devil when he fights. I agree that fits. But…" He scratched his cheek. "He's a swordsman who fight like a demon, so we call him the Sword Devil. But I think we may just be stating the obvious."

"What do you mean by that?"

"Maybe when you've really committed yourself to something, there are times when you have to become a demon… Maybe Wilhelm looks like one to us just because he's so single-minded. I don't know anyone else who looks so terrible when they fight. I don't know anyone else who's so serious about the way he lives."

His voice was quiet but impassioned. Carol found herself feeling jealous. Could this be it? Could this be why she resented that man?

"Maybe 'Sword Devil' really is the right name for him," Grimm said. "Wilhelm is absolutely dedicated to the sword, completely serious about how he lives, and that's why we call him that. And I'm sure it's because—"

5

"Sword Devil!! Sword Devil Wilhelm Trias!!"

Even as Theresia asked for his heart, even as he looked away from her, someone called his name, a name he hadn't heard in what seemed like a very long time. Wilhelm turned around.

In that instant, the spell that had been cast over the hall broke, and all the soldiers and military men in attendance came back to themselves.

"Wilhelm, you great, raging idiot!"

"—*rrr!*"

Among the soldiers who came rushing toward him, he saw a familiar hulking shape and young man, and his shoulders relaxed. He wasn't going to resist. But the thought of what would come next made him profoundly tired. So much so that he considered simply absconding with Theresia and disappearing into the distance.

"Listen, you!" As he was considering the possibility, Theresia had puffed out her cheeks, still holding on to him. She was a woman who threw herself into whatever she did, be it laughing, or shouting, or pouting, and still very much the same person who had charmed him in that field of flowers. "There are some things a person wants to hear you say out loud!"

"Ahh," Wilhelm groaned, realizing that she was still trying to continue the conversation from earlier. He was profoundly embarrassed to have to put his true feelings into words. Even if one might question how he could remain so reticent after having just shared a kiss in front of the entire audience hall.

"—"

After a second, he shook his head. He couldn't refuse her direct request.

Wilhelm took a deep breath and turned back to Theresia, leaning in toward her ear. Her face turned red, her eyes expectant. He caught his breath at her loveliness, and the words stuck in his throat.

Finally he said, "I'll tell you sometime, when the mood takes me."

It was the first time in his life the Sword Devil had ever been taken by cowardice.

6

And so the tale comes to an end.

A tale of bonds forged in the midst of the nation's civil conflict, the Demi-human War.

A tale of the days when one boy, enraptured by the beauty of the sword, dedicated himself to the nobility of steel.

Of how this boy became a young man, how he met a young woman, and found a love he could never have attained with the sword.

Of a Sword Devil, a man who found himself standing before one woman, who once wished to be a sword, who lived with such dedication as to be called a demon, and who, through the heat of living, became human.

Of a girl, too, the Sword Saint beloved of the sword god, who had surpassed all others, and whom the young man returned to what she once was—a young woman in love.

Relating all these things is this humble song of the Sword Devil's love.

A love story enough to make one dizzy with passion, a romance that blazes in the heart.

People call it "The Love Song of the Sword Devil."
It is nothing more than this, and nothing less.

AFTERWORD

Hello and thank you, Tappei Nagatsuki here. Yes, that is my name, and it's a pleasure to have you here, whether you're one of the people who knows me as a gray cat or not.

Thank you to everyone who's followed me all the way through *Re:ZERO Ex 2*. I really doubt there are many people reading these "side stories" who haven't read the main story, and I'm thrilled to have fans so dedicated to my series.

I've now published ten books in almost exactly two years, give or take a month. It's your collective encouragement and support that have allowed me to manage this. Thank you so much, and I hope you'll continue reading.

Now, as for this volume specifically, it's a sort of spin-off using characters who have appeared in the main series. Just like with the previous Ex book, none of the actual main characters of the regular series show up here.

This story takes place about forty years before the events of the main series. As a writer who adores prequel material, I really enjoyed doing this. Our protagonist, Wilhelm, along with some of the supporting cast, may yet make appearances or be name-checked in the main series, so have fun looking out for those cameos.

✻   ✻   ✻

They say people are their histories.

Perhaps you could consider who Wilhelm will become in forty years, i.e., at the time of the main series, and how he will have gotten that way. By taking what an author has written and imagining subsequent events, I think you can come to enjoy the story even more.

Thanks to all the readers who have supported me as I create this story, a TV anime of the series is going to be released.

The creation of an anime requires the dedication and cooperation of a great many people, and production is proceeding well. As the original creator, I'm trying to help out where I can, and of course the entire production team wants to make the series something that longtime fans will recognize and enjoy.

It's a fact that you can get more detailed information about the anime on the official homepage—but you could also consult the belt around this book. I hope you didn't throw it away!

Okay, I'm running out of pages, so it's time for the traditional offers of gratitude.

To my editor, I-sama, thank you for being so quick to give me the green light on all kinds of outrageous requests. It wasn't enough that I got a geezer on the cover of the last book; you actually let me have one as a main character for this spin-off, and for that I'm very grateful. It gave me a chance to tell a good story.

To my illustrator, Otsuka-sensei, thank you for another volume of beautiful illustrations. There was a large cast, and the fact that this story was set in the past means there were a lot of characters who will only appear in this novel, making your task very difficult. Yet you were as quick and accurate as ever in your character designs—truly impressive. I look forward to continuing to work with you.

To my designer, Kusano-sensei, you've done wonderful work as always. When I see the cover illustrations from Otsuka-sensei, I always find myself wondering eagerly what you're going to do with them. After ten volumes together, I've come to trust your work, and this was no exception.

To Daichi Matsuse-sensei and Makoto Fugetsu-sensei, who do the *Re:ZERO* manga, thank you for creating such an enjoyable version of this story that takes my world and gives it colors and shapes. I apologize for asking you guys to help publish, including your comic, three books at once. Thank you again!

In addition to all of the above, I want to thank the MF Bunko J editorial division, the sales staff, and the proofreaders, along with all the bookstores. These books wouldn't exist without all of you.

And finally, I want to extend my deepest thanks to my readers for all your heartfelt messages and letters of encouragement. It's thanks to all of you that I've managed to publish ten books to date. I hope we'll go on together for a long time.

I hope I'll see you again in Volume 8 of the main series.

November 2015
Tappei Nagatsuki
(Writing with fingerless gloves,
hands shaking with the cold.)

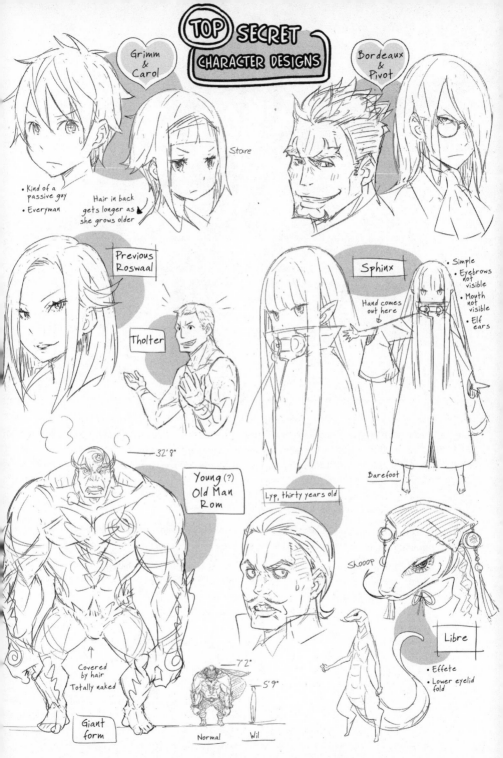

Wilhelm

"Right, now that this blood-soaked and altogether too manly main story is over, it's time for everyone's favorite, the Notes Corner! Hey, Wilhelm, don't look so serious. Come on, give the people a smile."

"…We don't have time for banter. I don't want to get my butt kicked by your attendant for not doing what I came here to do. I'm going to start now."

"Gosh, you get so embarrassed when you have to be out in public…"

"Hey…!"

"Okay, here come the notes. First of all, the anime that's got everyone's attention. There was some information on the belt running around this book, but maybe some careless people threw it away without looking at it, so let's make sure we fill everyone in."

"It'll start broadcasting in April 2016. Some new key visuals have been released. They've also talked a bit about the story, and it's sounding pretty good."